POSTAGE DUE

POSTAGE DUE

9.95

*To Jerry, who is our
treasured friend!*

Jon and Lois Foyt

Jon Foyt

Lois Foyt

The Book Guild Ltd.
Sussex, England

The Book Guild Ltd.
25 High Street,
Lewes, Sussex

First published 1995
© Jon and Lois Foyt 1995

Set in Bembo

Typesetting by Wordset
Hassocks, West Sussex

Printed in Great Britain by
Antony Rowe Ltd.
Chippenham, Wiltshire.

A catalogue record for this book is
available from the British Library

ISBN 1 85776 021 2

PREFACE

Every country looks to its citizens, hoping those individuals who are motivated to become leaders will act for the good of the people. Yet some countries racked by oppression may come up short on human resources and have to reach out to those countries overflowing with talent.

We adventurous people who are responding to the call and exporting ourselves afar will be following the footsteps of Fulbright scholars, Peace Corps volunteers and Crusaders of all time. We will be called upon in today's free market world to enhance the process of enterprise. But we will do more. To quell the ill winds of The Country's history and to weave a fabric of mutual respect with dialogue between the generations, we will draw upon The Country's heritage, whether fantasy or reality, and the riches of national gold, whether legend or fact.

—Toledo Squires, rallying his governmental team
at the Sangre de Cristo Ski Lodge high above
Santa Fe, New Mexico, in August 1991, for their
mission to The Country in Eastern Europe.

1

'Our programme is *American Achievers*. And as my millions of viewers know, we focus on discovering "The Gold of Entrepreneurship". I'm your hostess, Hortense Alger. My guest this evening is rapidly becoming one of our neoteric folk heroes. He is Toledo Squires – an outstanding archetype of free enterprise in America.'

The camera moved right, zooming in on an athletic-looking man with ruddy complexion seated in a red leather wing-chair. He was likely in his late thirties, or perhaps, camouflaged by trim physical condition, slightly older. He wore a light blue shirt with a silver and turquoise bolo tie, a Western jacket and a white stetson. Obviously not a conformist in dress, he broadcast an appearance of being independent in both thought and motivation. Seeing the camera focus on him, Toledo tipped his hat before removing it, revealing curly brown hair. The set of his jaw made him appear taut as a sprinter at the starting-block.

Ms Alger swiveled the lofty stool on which she had placed herself, looked into the camera and continued with her introduction, 'Mr Squires recently sold his mutual fund analysis business where, with an unrivalled approach and unique software, he and a staff of experts scrutinized invest-ment funds and reported often surprising conclusions to brokerage houses and individual clients. His firm's buyer was none other than Merrill Lynch itself, who paid ten million dollars and also awarded him a seat on their prestigious board of directors.'

Shifting her gaze from the camera down to her interviewee, she smiled. Quickly she returned her attention to the camera and into the living-rooms of America – and a few cocktail lounges as well – commenting, 'Not bad for one of our young American entrepreneurs, especially as he started his company only a few years ago in the spare bedroom of his rented California bungalow.'

Her pearl necklace, red fingernails and dark blue silk dress filled everyone's screen with the colours of a waving American flag. She wore a bejewelled crown upon her head, a patriotic halo of sorts meant to emulate the gift from France in New York harbour, signalling to those who sought financial freedom the idea they, watching her show, were sailing into its lucrative port of entry.

Ms Alger rounded out her introduction with, 'Mr Squires earned an MBA from the University of Southern California to add to his undergraduate degree in computer science from San Jose State University. After five years in positions of increasing responsibilities at Microsoft, he started his own enterprise. Now, attention girls! Mr Squires is a bachelor!' She paused for the fact to sink in before resuming. 'To begin, Mr Squires, perhaps you will tell our viewers how you have managed to remain single?'

An out-of-bounds question, Toledo felt, yet confrontation accounted for Ms Alger's popularity with her audience. He knew she held a psychology degree and an MBA from an Ivy League school where rumour put her in the same class as the television network president.

Her question made him want to escape from this talk-show studio. What was he doing here anyway? He suspected she would ask him to set forth a one-two-three-step process on making big money for the how-to generation, but he was anxious to be on with his next project. Yet having been billed by Ms Alger as a role model among entrepreneurs, couldn't he take advantage of this opportunity of appearing before millions of viewers to announce his impending crusade? Didn't he really have a seminal message to convey to other business adventurers? Yes, of course he did.

But he realized he must first address her question. He smiled at one of the cameras, the one with the red light blinking, looked up at her and laughed nervously. He said, 'There are so many attractive women these days – physically and intellectually – as great as the number of mutual funds, and there is so little time to do the necessary research. . . .'

'All work and no play?' Ms Alger teased. She shifted her inquiry and said, 'But your work has paid off, Mr Squires.

You identified a trend that few others recognized at the time – the increasing flow of capital into mutual funds. And so you formed a company that took advantage of this imminent boom rising on the horizon of American financial markets.' In a tone of voice pitched to penetrate any person's façade, Ms Alger said, 'Now tell us, Mr Squires, how is it you were so sanguine? Who gave you the original hot tip?'

'I suppose how ideas are conceived is a conundrum,' Toledo replied. 'Perhaps the concept was triggered by an article I read or a thought that came to me one day while running. Mutual funds were springing up like wild flowers after an April rain. And there was a need to separate the professionals from the amateurs among the thousands of investment managers and research analysts who were flocking to set up and direct them. I wanted to know each of their personal backgrounds, their motivations, their education, their prejudices and their biases.'

Ms Alger interjected, 'There are almost five thousand of these US funds today, pooling their shareholders' money and investing in a broad range of stocks and bonds. In all, they control more than two trillion dollars.'

Toledo nodded. 'Yes, so I asked myself: could there be sufficient talent on Wall Street to address such diversity properly at a time when managers are trained to specialize?'

'Were you trying to predict their performances?'

'Yes, that was my objective,' Toledo said. 'Tabulating the published track records of the funds was relatively easy, it simply required voluminous computer input and output. Our big hurdle was sorting out hidden gems, such as the temperament and motivation of the fund managers.'

'You drew up a long menu for yourself,' Ms Alger commented. 'But how could you possibly analyse each of their manager's objectives? By using a New Age crystal?' she added with disbelief. 'I've always thought everyone was motivated to make enough money so they could own an apartment on the Upper East Side of Manhattan or buy a house in Malibu and drive a flashy sports car with a cellular telephone.'

Toledo smiled. 'Our American system of rewards offers a multitude of prizes, more than just houses and cars. But to answer the first part of your question, I can tell you that in addition to our staff reading the *Wall Street Journal* and other business publications, we keyed in on the names of fund managers, followed published birth announcements, engagements and weddings, real estate transfers, police blotters, court house recordings, social and gossip columnists and obituaries.'

'Very interesting. You mean, each of these events may affect a person's performance?'

'Yes. For example, if a fund manager is going to have a baby, he or she becomes very concerned about job security.'

Ms Alger said, 'I know the feeling. So you mean, he won't take risks?'

'It is a judgment call. If we read that a parent has died, we anticipate a period of mourning, which we find translates to inactivity.'

'Missed opportunities?'

'Exactly.'

'Really sounds like a lot of work.'

Toledo shrugged. 'Not so much with computers.'

'Is there no privacy any more?'

'Privacy went out with the advent of PC networks, electronic bulletin boards and E-mail. We plugged into as much of this type of data as we could ferret out. But I believed – and I guess I was right – these so-called off-balance sheet items determine the performance of people and therefore the performance of the funds they manage.'

'Ten million dollars right, I would say. You were offering a service no one else had available.'

Toledo thought now he could talk about his next undertaking, and he leaned forward in his chair, ready to begin.

Instead Ms Alger said, 'So, what does your success mean for individual investors, our cable viewers? The purpose of our television talk show, you know, is to provide practical knowledge.' Her gaze moved from Toledo to engage her viewers as she added, 'Let me remind everyone we will be opening our telephone lines in a few moments. We're flashing the numbers on your screen now. One for Southern California and one for the rest of the country. Overseas callers use the third number.'

Behind Toledo and Ms Alger the stage set displayed a replica of a bank vault, its thick circular door ajar, allowing viewers to see stacks of glittering gold bullion stowed inside.

Ms Alger's voice rose as, continuing to look into the camera, she said, 'We'll be right back after this commercial break.'

The red light on the camera went out. Promptly a young woman rushed onto the set carrying what appeared to be a bundle wrapped in a blanket. With surprise Toledo watched Ms Alger unbutton the top two buttons of her dress and snuggle the bundle up to her breast. She undid a window in her bra and began right before his eyes to work her left nipple into the grasp of a pair of tiny, eager lips.

'Thank God for commercials,' she said, adding, 'would you like something to drink, too? Coffee? Water?'

'Pouilly Fuissé?'

'Really! I do believe you're nervous.'

'A bit. Natural, I suppose.'

'But after your success I should think nothing would fluster you.'

'You mean, money is the answer to everything?' Toledo replied.

Ms Alger adjusted her baby's position ever so slightly, ever so tenderly. 'I used to think so, but then I had him.' She looked down at the baby face and its engaged lips. 'The experience was exhilarating. Immediately afterwards, literally for days, I saw everything around me in a revitalized perspective – society, people – and I suddenly knew how television worked, saw the electrons zipping along. I saw the stars above and the people on them.'

Toledo smiled.

Adeptly Ms Alger switched nipples and asked, 'Ever see how vivid the New England fall colours are on a bright sunny day?'

'We don't have the season changes in Southern California like back East.'

'Then you don't understand my experience?'

Toledo said, 'Oh, but I think I do – the sudden enlightenment of being in touch with the whole world. When I conceived the idea for my business and received my grandmother's loan, I knew my venture would come alive. And again I felt the same elevated sensations when I sold my company to Merrill Lynch.'

'And made all that money,' she said in a statement, not a question. 'But you didn't advance beyond money. You see, I did. You rich people look at things through currency-coloured glasses, unlike the rest of us, don't you?'

A fragrance of resentment seemed to join the aroma of her sweet perfume. Too sweet, he thought. He would have preferred a less saccharine measurement to life.

'Just asking,' she said, 'so don't take offence. All part of the show.'

'Show business?'

'Business is business, show or tell, Mr Squires. But before we resume I must ask you. . . . I want to set up an investment programme for Joshua here. I'm not raising him simply to receive recognition and God's love. I want the little guy to grow up rich – like you. I brought him into this world, so I owe him that much.'

'Yes, I know the feeling of responsibility. I was committed to my business, and now I am dedicated to my next idea. Ideas are the same as babies. Once you have them, the duty to them is just beginning.'

'That's why I'm putting aside money each month from my pay-cheque. So will you recommend a mutual fund for him?'

'Does he like stocks or bonds?' Toledo asked, watching the child's lips suckle.

'He likes a college education eighteen or so years from now and a car and loud stereo to study by.'

'Fifteen seconds, Ms Alger,' came the producer's voice.

The young woman promptly returned and gently retrieved Joshua.

Ms Alger covered herself. A second before the red light on the camera flashed at her, she fixed a smile. On cue she said, 'We're back with Toledo Squires and his personal success story on how to win a quick windfall by playing the American game of free enterprise.'

Toledo thought now he would have a chance to unfurl the blueprint for his next endeavour.

But turning to him, Ms Alger said, 'So, tell our viewers, what was your game plan?'

Toledo fidgeted, but resigned himself to carrying out her how-to assignment. 'Let me begin by suggesting there are two types of free enterprise.'

Ms Alger looked doubtful. 'Sounds pretty academic.'

Toledo smiled.

'What are these two types?'

'Well, in the first type of enterprise, you work hard according to your business plan, which, like college, has a defined period of time. The freshman start-up is pretty mechanical. In the sophomore year you're building the team, and as a junior you're expanding your markets. As a senior, you receive your rewards, as I did when I sold the company. You have a sense of tremendous accomplishment.'

'And in the second type?' Ms Alger asked.

'It's a lifelong commitment to a single company. With your saved-up or borrowed capital you work at building up a business that you hope will grow into a blue-chip company. The first approach has a completion date, and the other garners its reward in the process. I intend to follow the first approach in my next enterprise.'

'Small business is what made America great. Now that you've made your million – or millions, I should say – tell us about what you are going to do next?'

Toledo began without hesitation. 'It's pay-back time, and I – '

'Funds you borrowed initially to get your company going?' Ms Alger interrupted.

'More than that,' he explained, 'because early on I repaid my maternal grandmother the five thousand dollars she loaned me to start the business. Of course, I'll always be indebted to her for her moral support.'

'Not everyone has a rich grandmother.'

'But she's not rich. The money she loaned me was her proceeds from my grandfather's life insurance policy. I'll never forget the day. It was our birthdays. She and I share the same day and the same hour – as a matter of fact it's tomorrow. She told me to think of the money not as a loan, but rather as a royal grant.'

'Why royal?'

Toledo smiled a little. 'She believed her Southern lineage can be traced back to what she refers to as American aristocracy – James Oglethorpe.'

'You act as if you don't buy her belief.'

'Well, we should each be allowed the freedom of our own imaginations,' Toledo replied. Nervous, he felt he should explain further. 'Oglethorpe was the Englishman who founded Savannah, carved its unique street pattern out of the virgin Georgia forests back in 1733.'

'I'd forgotten.'

Worrying some might think he was demeaning his grandmother, Toledo quickly added, 'She believed in me, much the same way Queen Isabella trusted her financial explorer. I've always loved playing these roles with her.'

'We have our first caller,' Ms Alger announced. 'Go ahead St Thomas, Virgin Islands. . . .'

'Yes, thank you,' a male voice said. 'I enjoy your programme, Hortense.'

Ms Alger smiled. 'Thank you. Your question please.'

'Mr Squires, you mentioned trying to determine the motivation of investment managers. . . . Is there a difference between how men and women approach their tasks?'

'Well, I've always thought most men want to direct others,' Toledo said.

'And women?' Ms Alger asked.

'To me, women seek to influence life around them, whether it's a spouse, an employer, a child or a market-place.'

'Next caller,' Ms Alger said, letting his observations alone. 'Kokomo, Indiana, go ahead. . .'

Another man's voice. 'I'm a banker here. So I'd like to know how you financed your business – after the initial loan from your grandmother was exhausted.'

'Did you sell stock to the public?' Ms Alger asked.

'Good question,' Toledo said. 'No, I had backing from the Bank of America. An interested loan officer supported my company right from the beginning, and he stands ready to back my new – '

'A caller from Spokane,' Ms Alger interrupted.

'A man's voice said, 'I'm a stockbroker here – one of your subscribers. My clients and I want to thank you for your excellent analysis of mutual funds. You've certainly made the right calls. We've made a lot of money and been saved from making the wrong investments, too. Quite uncanny how you could pick the winners, really.'

'Glad for your success,' Toledo said.

The caller added, 'I hope your investment advice is not going to be replaced by the Merrill Lynch bull.'

'Do you have a question for Mr Squires?' Ms Alger wanted to know, her voice sharp.

'Yes, Mr Squires, is it luck or do you have a secret formula for attaining your business goals?'

Toledo smiled. 'There's no secret. Success is an individual accomplishment and can't be tied to luck, any more than failure can be blamed on another person. My philosophy is we each make our own wake as we sail through life's waters.'

'Easy for a man to say,' Ms Alger said. 'You men can chart your own courses.'

Toledo held up an index finger. 'Women have maps these days, too.'

'Our next caller is from Sacramento,' Ms Alger announced. 'You're on the air. . . .'

A young woman's voice, sceptical but curious, asked, 'Tell me, Mr Squires, is ten million dollars enough money for you? For your lifetime, I mean? Or do you hope to accumulate more wealth?'

Ms Alger looked questioningly at Toledo. 'Aren't you going to retire, live the life of luxury, buy a flashy sports car, build a big house and cruise in your sixty-foot yacht? That's what most of us would do once we hit our jackpot.'

'No, as I've been trying to tell you,' Toledo quickly replied, 'I'm not ready to retire. I have another task to undertake. This next endeavour requires tens of millions of dollars. And I am prepared to invest my current winnings as seed money toward realizing it.'

'That remark should trigger another question,' Ms Alger said. 'Next caller. Fort Worth, Texas, you're on. . . .'

'Yes, thank you, Hortense. Mr Squires, do you personally hope to influence the policies of a company as big as Merrill Lynch?'

'Yes, I do. Actually my next undertaking dovetails with what I want Merrill Lynch to do. I want them to promote free enterprise in new market economies, and in the process generate business for themselves in Eastern Europe – in each of those former Communist countries. Getting back to my own plan, I'm putting together a team of very qualified individuals who are dedicated to spreading our Yankee know-how to one particular country. You know, we lived with this pervasive Cold War thing – for how many years?'

'Some say fifty,' Ms Alger suggested, cringing at the thought of all those years having passed by.

'And now we've won,' Toledo said, looking intently into the camera. 'So what are we going to do about it?'

'What do you mean?' Ms Alger asked.

'Well, for example, we must inspire people in the Eastern bloc to own and run their own businesses, as well as invest in businesses of other entrepreneurs by buying the stocks and bonds of their companies. That's what I mean.'

'Do you expect Merrill Lynch will join with you in your outreach?' Ms Alger asked.

'I'm hoping they will, and at our forthcoming board meeting I'll be urging them to set up branches there. Look at the potential. All those people yearning for consumer goods. And consider the sheer size of those markets. The opportunities awaiting us in Eastern Europe are greater than opening the American West a century and a half ago. Besides, we've made promises.'

'Promises?'

'Yes, we – our government – the West, propagandized them, told them to throw off the Communist yoke. We promised them a better life. They did, and so far we've wasted a lot of time jawboning aid programmes.'

'Another call,' Ms Alger said. 'San Francisco, you're on the air.'

A woman's voice came through his earpiece. 'Mr Squires, why is it you are permitted to make so much money on one transaction while the rest of us struggle to pay the rent and feed our children? Don't you think it's unjust for one man to come away from a day's work with so much money?'

'How do you answer her, Mr Squires?' Ms Alger asked.

For a moment Toledo wished he could defer the tough question to one of his business school professors for an academic reply. He was suddenly conscious of the camera staring at him. And the camera represented millions of eyes across America and around the world. He must not be flippant or in any way demeaning in his reply. He sensed the entire capitalistic system was on trial and he was suddenly being shoved in front of the jury and told to speak as its defender.

'Money is not an end. It is really a means to achieve goals. If you are at this time in a survival mode, as are many of the former Communist countries of Eastern Europe, I suggest you ask other people for assistance. . . .'

Ms Alger helped out with, 'Social programmes, classes at your local community college, for example. . .'

'Exactly,' Toldeo said. 'Keeping in mind your actions should be goal-oriented so that when you advance yourself past the survival stage, you too can assist those others who have been less fortunate.'

'You're saying, money should be regarded as a tool and not just an end-all?' Ms Alger asked.

Toledo smiled, releasing the last of his nervousness. He was beginning to enjoy this talk show, and he wondered who was watching. Surely his dear grandmother from her home in Savannah. Maybe even her fellow Georgian, former President Jimmy Carter, whom he knew through their joint efforts for the charity Habitat for Humanity. Or possibly the head of his business school, his former professors, perhaps the chairman of the board at Merrill Lynch, and even the top people at Microsoft. People who might join his new team. And hopefully the attractive investment analyst who had been on the speakers' panel with him at the recent private Merrill Lynch seminar.

His thoughts were abruptly interrupted. The woman caller said she was from Santa Fe. A sensual voice. A familiar voice? Katherine Mondragon's voice?

'My first question is in reference to a recent seminar I attended. I'd like to ask Mr Squires if he agrees with the premise stated there that it's virtually impossible to examine the facts about companies apart from the spin put on them by their image builders. I mean, were you able to separate reality from fantasy?'

Katherine's lilting feminine laugh tantalized Toledo, for now he was certain of her identity. 'It's easy,' he said. 'Look at it this way – I'm sure you don't have any problem separating love from lust.'

There was a pause before she asked, 'And second, do you have in mind any particular Eastern European country where you plan to launch your programme of exporting Anglo know-how?'

17

The voice was indeed Katherine's. Katherine Mondragon, the tall Hispanic woman he'd met at the seminar. She'd asked him a lot of questions about Microsoft and other software companies, both large and emerging smaller ones. Good questions, too. She'd said she was with the State of New Mexico and managed their investment portfolio.

Toledo turned to face the camera as he tried to formulate his answer. He asked himself if he should reveal specifics of his plan. Wasn't that where politicians always lost – getting into the precise patterns of the flag they were ready to run up the pole? If he named the country he ran the risk people might laugh. He could lose credibility. He visualized people snickering at him, shaking their heads in disbelief and switching off their television sets. He imagined bartenders using their remote-control devices to switch to *ESPN* and bring up some basketball game on the screen. Or was it football season? They interlaced so much these days.

Yet he reminded himself there might be others who, hearing and seeing him on television, would come forth to help in his plan. Mentioning the specific country would introduce them to real people needing assistance.

So Toledo looked into the camera and imagined he was addressing each viewer as they sat with him around a kitchen table. He forgot about his signal having to travel the miles linking the studio to the satellite orbiting the Earth and zipping back down to receiving dishes, there to fan out along a nexus of cables – or in some places delicate strands of fibre-optics – leading through towns and across the vast American countryside to a receiving television set.

His imagination carried him to yet a further point where he fancied himself looking into the dark brown eyes of Katherine Mondragon as he replied to the second part of her question. 'Yes, as a matter of fact I do have a specific country in mind.'

'Well?' Ms Alger pressed, leaning over him.

Into the camera he said simply and intimately, 'It is a little country – a kingdom by the sea – and in the very near future I'd like to personally share with you my vision of what I hope we can accomplish there.'

2

Athens, Georgia, 1933

'We have a young visitor coming all the way from Hungary, Grace Dear, and you are to be her official guide for the day,' the headmistress announced to the young woman attired in the finishing-school uniform of pleated grey skirt and starched white blouse with black ribbon tie.

Sitting at her desk, her books neatly stacked according to size, Grace promptly stood up and replied with respect, 'Yes, Miss Crawford.'

'She is a member of European royalty, so here's your chance to demonstrate the social graces in which you have been instructed.'

'She's really royalty?'

'Yes, and I understand she speaks several languages, so you will have an opportunity to test your French.'

Grace toyed with a lock of her hair. 'And my history of Europe, as well?'

'If you like, but don't go off on one of your tangents of imagination with her. You must pay attention to your assignment. Her mother is visiting relatives in North Carolina and has dispatched her daughter down here on the ten forty train from Raleigh. She has only a few hours to spend with us. Jefferson will drive you to the station, and I want you to be kind to him, especially in front of our guest. None of your teasing.'

'But Miss Crawford, we girls really do like him. . . .'

'Then treat him fairly. He's like family. He's our Negro.'

'Yes, Miss Crawford.'

As the strict disciplinarian continued to deliver the details of the day's instructions, Grace tried to concentrate, for she knew if she didn't remember the schedule exactly, Miss

Crawford would be visibly displeased and a reprimand would surely follow. She hated being reproached by anyone. She couldn't understand why having imagination was deemed a fault. What was so wrong with her mind wandering, taking her on exploratory flights of fancy? Why must life be so mechanical, so precise, so exact? Why must behaviour be either right or wrong? And why was she obliged to pay attention to everyone else when the only times people paid attention to her was when she didn't follow their instructions and remember their rules? With her father she was given no opportunity to ask questions. He would take on that horrible countenance, his rage surging up before he struck her with the back of his hand or his black belt, which he could somehow whip from his trousers in one swift motion.

Miss Crawford's voice grew louder, startling Grace, and she heard the prim headmistress say, 'Walk her through the campus of the big university, point out to her the details of its ante-bellum architecture. Remember to show her the splendid white columns and large Doric capitals of the Greek Revival chapel.'

Grace wished for just once Miss Crawford would ignore the heritage of the town's old buildings. But in her mission of enhancing their education she made certain her students were conversant with Southern architecture – in addition, of course, to demeanour, etiquette, the French language and sufficient history to be able to carry on an intelligent conversation with any Eastern or Virginia-educated man they might meet during a social function or at a church conference. In stressing why a proper and supportive Southern wife must be knowledgeable about matters in addition to gardening and the social graces, Miss Crawford would gesture vigorously at her calendar and remind everyone these were modern times – the 1930s. The world, she would say, was shrinking, and the need for knowledge, even among wives, was expanding.

'Take her on a tour through the magnificent library,' Miss Crawford went on. 'Today's the one day of the year the original of the Constitution of the Confederacy is on public display, so remember to draw her attention to it. Afterwards, you and Jefferson will bring her back up here.'

Imagining the figure of a young girl with a crown in her hair and a fine white organdie dress, Grace was eager to meet the royal visitor and said enthusiastically, 'Yes, Miss Craw-ford.'

Grace noticed how the headmistress's black hair was drawn so tautly into a bun that the skin around her temples was pulled back, narrowing her eyes into focusing slits.

'Introduce her to your sister students,' Miss Crawford continued. 'Have her accompany you to your afternoon class devoted to the Nature and Use of Textiles. Afterwards escort her to my office. In private and before you and Jefferson drive her back to the railway station, I shall discuss her possible enrollment with us.' Looking sternly, Miss Crawford demanded to know, 'Are you listening to me, Grace Dear?'

Grace nodded and stumbled out with, 'Yes, Ma'am, I sure am.' With more enthusiasm she asked, 'What is the princess's name?'

'Geraldine. She is younger than you. So don't forget you are responsible for her while she is with us here in Athens. Do you understand?'

'Yes, Miss Crawford.'

'Good, now repeat my instructions back to me.'

★ ★ ★

Jefferson drove the black Ford right up to the track-side and opened the rear door for Grace. Stepping from the car, she looked him over from head to toe and saw his chauffeur's cap was askew – her chance to taunt him. She pointed and said, 'Straighten your cap, Jefferson, we are meeting a member of European royalty. And button your coat, too,' she added. 'We don't want Princess Geraldine to think you're a field-hand.'

'Yes, Miss Grace.'

In the valley around her she saw the dogwood trees in bloom. Thousands of white four-petal clusters surrounded her with visual luck; a country's hope for its new president. A new hope for herself, Grace thought, with the prospect that one day marriage might save her from her father's punishment. Yes, new hope all around amidst the black clouds of the Depression that were proving as pervasive as the grey steam of the train now filling the air of the little canyon, the hollow where for some reason the railroad had built its depot. This soot-covered brick station was hardly a fitting place in which to welcome royalty. She should have snipped a branch of dogwood blossoms to present to Geraldine.

Grace watched the detraining businessmen in their spring suits and flat straw hats. She wanted to reach up and snatch one of the hats, fling it into the air like a little aeroplane – watch it sail through the dark steam still belching from the engine's smoke-stack, and see it come out the other side, its light colour now blackened to the shade of Jefferson's skin.

Adjusting his cap, Jefferson said, 'Maybe she missed da train.'

'Don't be a silly goose, Jefferson!' Grace looked along the platform and exclaimed, 'There she is.' To Grace, her charge was a beautiful young princess who exhibited a munificent manner as she waited, ready and willing to grant an audience to whichever of her subjects might formally approach.

Walking up to her, Grace said without doubt, without hesitation, 'Welcome to Athens, Georgia.'

The younger girl nodded and smiled. 'You must be Grace, my official guide for this bright day.' She gestured at Jefferson and said, 'And you must be Grace's African slave.'

Grace's jaw dropped.

Jefferson said, 'Ah, no, Miss Princess, ah's free now.'

From Geraldine's lilting laugh, Grace recognized her guest's tease, and she instantly warmed to her. 'I asked Jefferson to cut down a dogwood tree with all its blossoms to present to you as our welcoming gift, but he wouldn't do it.' Grace turned to him. 'Would you, Jefferson?'

'I'm disappointed, Jefferson,' Geraldine said. And she laughed again, a laugh not constrained by rules, free as the Georgia whippoorwills. 'I would have pressed the blossoms into one of my books and taken them back to Budapest.'

'Off with his head,' Grace proclaimed.

Jefferson rubbed his neck as he opened the Ford's rear door and the two laughing girls clambered into the back seat.

'Are you actually a member of royalty?' Grace asked as Jefferson drove up the hill into town.

Geraldine grew serious. 'Yes, my father, rest his soul, was an Hungarian count.'

'But your mother is not Hungarian?' Grace asked.

'No, she's from North Carolina, and she's about to remarry

22

– a French army officer, very handsome too.'

'What happened to your father?'

'He died. Actually killed in the Budapest food riots after the war – some say by the Communists. But I have a friend who is a Bolshevik, and he's not someone who would kill a member of royalty.'

'And so you retain your father's titles?'

Geraldine nodded. 'Yes, my mother and I, and my sister too. But my father lost our money in the Great War. He bought Austro-Hungarian government bonds, trying to be patriotic and support the war effort. Of course, Austria-Hungary lost, the country was split and shrunk, and the bonds became worthless.'

'We've read in our history books about the Great War – started in Sarajevo with the assassination of your archduke – but you know, I've never related wartime to actual people until now.'

'Oh, let's get to know each other better, Grace, instead of talking about war.'

'Yes,' Grace replied at once. 'We'll do something fun to remember this day.' Veering from her assigned mission, she said, 'Jefferson, drive us out along the Oconee River to the Old Mill. The caretaker there will fix us a tall glass of ice tea.'

'But Miss Grace, Miss Crawford's instructions were to carry yawl to the university campus and then back to your school.'

'Never you mind, it's only a short detour,' Grace said, and giggled. 'If Miss Crawford doesn't know, she'll take no reprisals.' She turned to Geraldine. 'Besides, I'm supposed to show you the high spots of Athens.'

'Well, all right, Miss Grace, but it be your idea, not mine, if Miss Crawford do find out,' Jefferson said, shaking his head.

Grace smiled at Geraldine. 'We'll talk by the rapids while we tingle our toes in the water. What fun to get away from school for a bit. The spring wild flowers are coming out, and the cool air is stimulating during these weeks before the weather turns so summery hot and humid. And I want to show you our famous covered bridge.'

Geraldine squealed with delight as the car entered the cavernous interior of the wooden bridge with its hand-hewn timbers. 'We're wrapped up in a present,' she exclaimed, and laughed that contagious laugh again. 'Do not open until Christmas.'

At the Old Mill, as Jefferson left for their ice tea, the two girls walked down to the water's edge. Removing their shoes and hosiery, they pulled up their skirts and waded into the rapids, the rushing water bathing their legs. 'Ooh, the water's cold,' Geraldine squealed, 'but refreshing after my long train ride.'

'Let's sit a while,' Grace suggested.

They sat together on her favourite boulder. Grace watched the sun glinting the water cascading around them. She thought if she were to toss in the air the contents of the pouches of all the diamond-cutters in the city of Amsterdam, the brilliance of the display couldn't match her Oconee – here at this special spot in the midday sun. Those times she sat here before, Grace envisioned jewels shining in a crown upon her head and imagined a king sitting beside her in his robes, tall, dark and handsome.

Now she observed the younger girl beside her. The sunlight defined the silhouette of Geraldine's royal posture. In the freshness of the Georgia spring this majestic creature's beautiful white dress seemed whiter than snow, whiter even than the dogwood blossoms, whiter, Grace thought, than feminine purity personified.

Jefferson arrived with two tall glasses of tea, a wedge of lemon perching on the rim of each, and they drank.

'Sweetened,' Geraldine said, surprised.

'Could you serve ice tea otherwise?' Grace asked.

'Well, yes, usually without sugar, and then if you want to add it, you do so yourself.'

'Not here in the South,' Grace replied, thinking the Southern way was the only way.

A spring breeze blew, ruffling their hair and billowing their skirts.

Grace gestured down at the water racing past their rock. 'I wish my life had a purpose as serious as this river. The Oconee has a destination, knows where it is going and moves steadily toward its ocean.'

'Well, I know where I am headed,' Geraldine said.

'You do?' Grace asked with surprise.

'Yes, I know someday I shall become a real queen.'

Grace hesitated only momentarily before blurting, 'Yes, me, too. I often daydream about it. Especially when I read books by Mrs L.T. Meade. I'm reading her latest, *The Queen of Joy*.'

'I know her books. But they're fantasies, and I plan to accomplish the real thing,' Geraldine went on. 'Someday I'll marry a handsome king who rules one of our little kingdoms somewhere in Europe and I will be his queen.'

'I know a lot about Europe,' Grace said. 'Miss Crawford has us study Pinkerton's nineteenth-century travel guides to countries around the world. She is constantly reminding us, "These works make it possible for students to be at home in all lands and all ages".'

Geraldine giggled. 'Those guides are a little out of date.'

'But until I met you, they were all I had to tell me about Europe.'

'I'll tell you about my Europe,' Geraldine offered. 'It's full of castles, handsome kings and beautiful queens, romance, parties and music, music, music. . . .'

Grace sighed. 'Oh, I wish I could be you. All my life I've wanted to be royal. But in America all we have to look up to are our ancestors. I've imagined them to be royal.'

'Who are they?'

'Well, my grand-daddy Thatcher – he was a Civil War general, you know – said our family actually goes back to the aristocracy of James Oglethorpe.'

'That's wonderful,' Geraldine said. 'Why doesn't your father make a royal match for you with an English duke?'

'Because my father hates me.'

'That's terrible.'

'He calls me Grace Dear, and then he beats me – tells me it's for my own good, that it's going to hurt him more than me. Why can't he love me?' she fretted.

'Do you have a beau?' Geraldine asked.

'Yes I do – Elmer Templeton. He's a banker in Savannah. Actually, he's just getting started with a bank that was able to reopen after President Roosevelt's Bank Holiday.'

'Has he proposed to you yet?'

'Maybe he will after I graduate this spring,' Grace answered.

'Do you want him to?'

'Yes, I guess so.'

'Cigarette?' Geraldine asked, pulling a silver case from her little purse.

'You smoke?' Grace replied, drawing back. 'You're only how old? Sixteen?'

'Actually fifteen.'

'You look eighteen,' Grace said in admiration.

Geraldine smiled. 'My mother doesn't know about my smoking yet. But all the women in Europe do it now. It's quite the fashion. Very sophisticated, too. Here, have one.'

'But I've never. . . . My father and Miss Crawford won't allow. . . .'

'Come on, you're older than I. You should be up to date. Smoking one cigarette won't kill you. These are Turkish, too, not the bland American kind.'

'How do you do it?'

Geraldine lit her own and demonstrated the technique. She handed the cigarette to Grace. 'Here, take a puff.'

Grace did and began to cough uncontrollably.

Geraldine laughed.

Watching from a shady rock at a respectable distance, Jefferson shook his head.

Recovering, Grace blurted, 'If my father saw me smoking a cigarette, he would lash me with his belt.'

Geraldine looked at the older girl in alarm. 'You don't mean it?'

'Yes, but I'll tell you a secret. I turn to one of the books written by Mrs Meade and escape into a world of joy. Reading her books gives me strength, and some day, you mark my words, I'll be a real queen and no one'll dare beat me. My king will see to that.'

'My mother says we girls are responsible for our own lives, and we can't rely on others to shape them or make things happen.'

'I've always been told my life was predetermined in heaven,' Grace said. 'Miss Crawford says God has a plan for each of us. My father says that, too. He beats me when I deviate from his plan – get off course, as he calls it. Trouble is, I'm never quite sure where the course is supposed to lead.'

Geraldine finished her cigarette, flipping it into the rapids. She swung her legs back and forth, splashing water on Grace and herself. She laughed at the fun. 'Yes, my king will be my companion in life,' she said. 'He'll be taller than me. But I'll choose him. Yes, I'll make our romance happen. And he'll love me.' She laughed again as she stood up.

And Grace vowed she too would someday match the royal stature of this beautiful young Hungarian–American girl who now towered above her on the bank of the Oconee River in rural Georgia.

3

Given the three-hour time difference between California and
Georgia, Toledo didn't call his grandmother until the morning after the talk show. Disguising his voice, he said, 'Western
Union with a singing telegram for your birthday . . . but we
weren't told how many candles to fire up. . . .'

Her laugh danced across the continent and she exclaimed,
'How wonderful to hear from you! Happy Birthday yourself,
my favourite knight. Toledo, you tell Western Union to stop
at seven, one for each of my decades, and we won't worry
about the sum of all the years.'

'Bambi Deer,' he began, loving to address her by the
nickname he had made up when he was a little boy. The rest
of the family called her Mother Dear, but since he thought
of her as a free-spirited creature, he had christened her Bambi
Deer Bounding Through The Forest, or Bambi Deer for
short. 'It was after midnight your time when I left the
Hollywood studio, so I waited until now to call.'

'That's all right, Toledo, you may call me anytime, day
or night. How wonderful to see you on television!' she added.
'My stars, all those callers – and that woman emcee – why,
today's young women ask the most embarrassing sorts of
questions. I can understand her inquiring about your business,
but I think she stepped over the line with those personal
questions about family.'

'You should host a talk show, Bambi Deer. Invite all the
seniors to call in. Be with the times. Think of the many older
people who love to watch television today.'

'No, it would never work. Most people my age are too
reticent to call long distance. I would simply sit there talking
to myself,' she said with a quiet laugh. 'Even if I had a guest,
I could never delve into such private matters. In my day
hostesses were gracious, polite; intelligent, of course, and

28

perceptive, but not so direct with their questions. Miss Crawford made certain her students were versed in the social graces.'

'Being on the show gave me a chance to lobby my idea of expanding Yankee know-how into Eastern Europe.'

'Toledo, I have always advised you not to use "Yankee" when you really mean "American". And what was it you said to all those listeners about my royal lineage? I believe you referred to it as "my little fantasy"?'

'Give me a break, Bambi Deer. You're not really royalty. You simply enjoy the idea of it.'

'Some day I will be,' she answered indignantly. 'You just wait and see. Like my friend Geraldine,' she went on. 'She became a queen, you know.'

'Did you like your grandson's appearance on the talk show?' Toledo asked.

'You don't want to hear about my royal friend?' The disappointment in her voice was obvious. 'We met years ago at Miss Crawford's. . . .'

'I really have to go,' Toledo said impatiently. 'Another call to make.'

'Toledo,' she began, and then choked up.

'What is it, Bambi Deer?' he asked, concern in his voice.

'They are making me move.'

'Yes, at our family meeting in Georgia we talked about your moving – all of us sat down and discussed the reasons, remember? You agreed with Lorraine and Horatio and me. You said you were willing. You even quoted this royal friend of yours – words of wisdom she passed along to you sixty years ago about not being afraid to venture forth. You do remember?'

'Of course. Why, I can even recollect your great-great grandfather and the story he told me about the Confederate gold. But his secret was meant for my ears only.'

'Infamous Grand-daddy Thatcher. I would love for you to tell me some of his stories when I visit you in your new home next week. And together we'll tour the Glorieta Battlefield site outside Santa Fe.'

'The Gettysburg of the West,' she said. 'Yes, Grand-daddy told me about the clever Union officer who really won that battle.'

'By destroying the Confederate supply train. Grand-daddy told you a lot about the Civil War, didn't he?'

'The War Between the States? Yes, and the generals, the Confederate generals. Declarations of theirs never put into print.' Her voice dropped so low Toledo could barely hear her words. 'But I'm having second thoughts about leaving my native Georgia.'

'Now, Bambi Deer, you have decided. The South-West is to be your new realm. Look at it this way, dear heart: coming to Santa Fe is your next conquest. During this semester of your life you need family nearby. Lorraine and Horatio are right there in Santa Fe, and I'm much closer, too.'

'But there will be strange people.'

'The other residents of the retirement home are very friendly, and Lorraine assures me the staff is quite capable of meeting your every need. . . .'

She was unconvinced. 'In case I get lost trying to find my way back to my apartment. . . .'

'You won't get lost.'

'But can you imagine living in an apartment? Proper families live in houses. Apartments are for military and transients, people without roots.'

'Nonsense, you're fifty years out of date on that one.'

'But what about my house here in Savannah?'

'You signed the papers, Bambi Deer. It's been sold. The house is far too big for you to keep up on your own. You wouldn't want the home place to fall down around you, now would you? That's no way to care for an old friend. From here on, gracious loving people will take care of it for you.'

'But the buyers are Japanese and they will be at a real disadvantage.'

'How's that?'

'They won't be able to talk to my house.'

Toledo laughed. 'What do you mean?'

'My house does not speak Japanese. And it has to be spoken to from time to time, or else it gets very upset.'

Toledo thought for a moment. 'Well, I'm certain they speak English too.'

'Yes, but with a foreign accent, not true Southern. I have tried to converse with them. I had trouble, so I am afraid my house will not understand them either.'

'Your house will learn to speak Japanese – a rewarding accomplishment,' Toledo tried.

'Well, maybe so,' she said, sounding only partly reconciled.

'You are moving to New Mexico, and you're a-twitter about it. I know you too well. Lorraine and Horatio will meet you at the Albuquerque airport and introduce you to Santa Fe.'

'When will I see you?'

'In a week or so. I'll come and visit you. We'll speak of our good fortunes. Yours and mine.'

4

Toledo immediately placed another call. With the anticipation of unveiling a magnificent statue, his voice proclaimed, 'Katherine Mondragon.' A pause ensued. He waited. She came on. 'I'm returning your call from last night,' he announced.

'But you didn't answer my question as to which country.'

'I thought I'd reply in person.'

'Are you in Santa Fe?'

'Not yet. First, I must make a presentation before the Merrill Lynch board of directors meeting here in LA.'

'And they will know the name of the country before I do?' Her voice was lilting, its rich feminine sound arousing. 'Don't you want to rehearse your presentation before a good critic?'

'I want to be spontaneous with all my experiences.'

'And you're planning an experience in Santa Fe?'

'If I have an invitation.'

'You have. Do you want to know my schedule?'

'Yes.'

'The La Fonda Hotel. Friday evening.'

He said, 'I'll call you from my plane on the way into town.'

5

Once each year the board of directors of Merrill Lynch, the world's largest stockbrokerage and investment banking house, fled the familiar flumes of Wall Street and convened somewhere out there in the hinterland, north of the borough of the Bronx or west of the Hudson River. At these meetings long-term policies were avidly discussed, voted upon and set. Fresh surroundings allowed the board members an opportunity to view how other people elsewhere lived – that is, those in America who had been assigned to a location of lesser significance. New York, there was no doubt in the minds of many, was the charismatic centre of the world, financially, culturally, medically, educationally, legally, ethnically, gastronomically, and about any other way one sliced the fruit of life – the reason Manhattan was known to those who yearned for the ultimate living experience as the Big Apple.

This year's site was in downtown Los Angeles at the Bonaventure Hotel. High atop, in fact. There, in a large conference room adorned with a vertical rock fountain wall, these wise men of American business gathered, hoping to enjoy views of the Pasadena Rose Bowl, Rodeo Drive in Beverly Hills, the Bel Air golf-course, Santa Monica and the yachts at Marina del Rey.

Except this day the smog was so thick the board members, looking out of the wraparound windows in the all-male private club, saw only an enshrouding cloud of automobile exhaust and death-carrying carcinogens. Thousands of their stockbrokers, on behalf of clients, bought and sold the stocks of those companies making and selling the products that produced the cloud.

With no view to linger over, the Chairman called the meeting to order, and the board members got down to the business at hand – planning their corporate future.

The first member to advance his particular plan was met with a guffaw from another, who said, 'Charley, we called that play last year and lost yardage.'

'But if we'd had support from the entire team, we'd have made a big gain,' Charley retorted.

The next director, also using sports imagery, portrayed his scheme for the future as 'a Hail Mary for big bucks'.

But the Chairman admonished him. 'Too risky a play, George. You're betting the game on one pass.' Appraising the other directors, he added, 'So far, gentlemen, all I've heard are warmed-over versions of old and familiar game plans.'

Nodding at Toledo, the Chairman said to the group, 'Had you watched the *American Achievers* programme with Hortense Alger last night, you'd be aware our next speaker has a new idea he wants us to consider. And how about that TV woman? You know, she just might be a politically correct addition to our board,' he suggested off-handedly.

'Every team can use a cheer-leader,' one member said, and laughed.

The Chairman smiled. 'Hopefully Mr Squire's chalkboard will signal something different for us, a new play to run.'

As he rose, Toledo realized his presentation would most likely gain their support if he, too, spoke in sports metaphors. A player on their own team was presenting the plan. Not some Slovak or Croat or Hungarian or Romanian or Pole or Ukrainian or Albanian or Serb or Bosnian or Moldavian or another unnamed immigrant fresh off a boat from Lower Slabovia. But one of their own. A member of their own board of directors. Their own in-group. He wore the same uniform – well, almost. The members would likely make allowance for his bolo tie and stetson hat, attributing his nonconformity of dress to his rookie status.

Looking about, Toledo saw mostly grey heads and full jowls. He said, 'Gentlemen, World War Two is over and the final whistle has blown on its Cold War post-season.'

One grey-hair's face grew red as he said, arm upraised, index finger pointed towards heaven, 'We must not forget World War Two, the one time in America we were united – all of us on the same team, working toward a common goal. But those Communists are still around. Mark my words, they'll regroup, like the devil's army, and return to attack us any day. . . .'

'No, they've departed, gone like yesterday's trains from Grand Central Station,' Toledo said. 'Today we've a revised schedule of arrivals and departures. The update includes connections to and from Eastern Europe.' Oops, he warned himself, stick to sports examples, not trains. He rushed on with, 'And we have new stadiums in which to play our game.'

The director who now spoke up was the well-known General George S. Goforth, US Army, Retired. 'Yes, I see your point, Mr Squires,' he said. 'As a board we have an international responsibility to look to expansion; to set up new forts on the frontiers of finance, so to speak.'

Smiling, Toledo thought to himself, my God, now we've got military metaphors. But it did appear he could count on one supporter among those sitting around the conference table, water glasses, Cross fountain-pens and yellow legal-size pads at their beck and call.

Toledo pressed a button and a large oil-painting of the Spanish Mission at Santa Barbara slid aside, revealing a pair of video monitors with high-fidelity speakers. On the screens his computer projected a map and a chart. Simultaneously his state-of-the-art computer produced the sounds of Eastern European folk music. He now wished he had programmed a military band instead. Yet he steadfastly went on.

Calling their attention to the left screen, he said, 'Gentlemen, look at the profit potential. Populations of the many European teams currently excluded from our American investment league are shown on the map.' Toledo directed his pointing beam so that it highlighted each country's figures. Pointing the beam to the right screen, he said, 'Shown here are the potential commissions from the multitude of underwriting possibilities of stocks and bonds – both initial public offerings and private placements for their capital-short industries – as well as financings of governmental debt, all of which await us in these newly freed and newly formed countries behind what was the Iron Curtain.'

'But sometimes those countries default on their debts,' one said. 'I'll stick to US Treasury bonds, thank you.'

Another said, 'And foreign countries have Greek alphabets.

35

I'm not sure I'd want to learn any new languages.'

'Let's keep in mind Mr Squire's plan means raising lots of capital – clearly a lot of profits for us if we can get ourselves into position,' another said.

The Chairman stood, signifying it was decision time. He looked around the room, confirming he had the attention of each member. 'Profits are our first priority, gentlemen. Mr Squires, why don't you select one little country somewhere on your multicoloured map, pop over there and help the locals set up a market economy, assess the potential for us and run the place for a year. You could entice a few of our politicians, generals and economists to go along with you – maybe one or two from our Wall Street offices, perhaps even someone from this august board of directors. See if you can turn the country into a model for capitalism. Pre-season scrimmage, you might say,' and he guffawed.

Several men chuckled.

'Then come back to our next year's planning session and describe to us all that you've accomplished. If we're enamoured with your performance, and the programme you present is creative and makes sense to us, we'll support your plan for our expansion into Eastern Europe. We'll remake the whole nine yards over there into our own gridiron.'

Around the big table several men appeared sceptical, while others applauded, some with more enthusiasm.

'Yes, give the boy a chance,' General Goforth said loudly as he rose. He slapped Toledo hard on the back. The strength of his endorsement sent Toledo's torso forward.

The general leaned down and whispered to the bent-over Toledo, 'Count me in, I've some definite ideas on what we should do over there in those places to straighten things out.'

His upper body slowly returning to upright, Toledo watched the general raise his swagger stick, signalling the moment was upon them. He thought if the military man were to shout out an appropriate command, the charge of the financial brigade, armed to the teeth with high-tech American know-how, would be underway.

Coughing, Toledo said, 'Thanks very much for your support, General Goforth.'

His body rigidly at attention, the general replied, 'Simply doing my duty.'

Buoyed by the Chairman's blessing, a vision of success blazed across Toledo's mind. He was ready to lead a capitalist crusade as holy as any dispatched centuries earlier by the Church in Rome.

Yes, he had selected the right country from among those former Communist puppet states. Following a well-conceived master plan, his team would turn the little state into a model for American ingenuity. But he did prefer the expression 'Yankee know-how' in spite of Bambi Deer's remonstrance.

6

Mother Dear resolved there would be no tears. For months she had anticipated her move from Savannah to Santa Fe with tenacious apprehension. Now, on the dawn of the actual day, she was determined to get on with it, taking the attitude her relocation would expand her outlook and allow her to reach higher plateaux with magnificent vistas.

As a young girl she had enjoyed flights of mind. Imagination played a vital role in her life. Hadn't it allowed her to face her father's rage and his subsequent beatings? And later, hadn't she also survived a marriage to a domineering Southern banker? Through it all, fantasy was an escape from her father and Mr Templeton. So, addressing her imminent departure, she concluded her ample imagination would accompany her on this journey.

She had lived through years as an abused daughter, and then as the battered wife of Mr Templeton. In those days such treatment was a private matter, Mother Dear reflected. Oh, for present-day mores to have been applied back then, for she could have found sympathy, help and perhaps even escape. She had seen television talk shows with women and children describing abuse. They thought such behaviour was a modern-day malady. She wasn't surprised at the escalating number of cases being reported to police and social workers today. 'Abuse has always been with us,' she said out loud to herself. 'Except now people are talking about it.'

Back then, she reflected, women were treated as property They were subject to male discipline, whether from a father trying to instil behavioural rules or a husband asserting domain over his castle and everything and everybody within. Mr Templeton would allow his rage, contained during his business day, to explode at night with a violence directed at her. Through those painful and unhappy episodes she could read her books and enter her private imaginary world.

But this day – today – was going to be different. The change of venue, moving from her home in Georgia to a little apartment two thousand miles away, required a special spark in her imagination. These winds of change were of unknown velocity, direction and temperament. She hoped for benevolent pilots during the ups and downs of the immediate trip ahead, with a change of planes in Atlanta and another in Dallas.

Adding to her concerns was the difficulty of packing her treasures of the past into two travel bags.

Pastor Waters arrived to collect her concurrently with the new owners and their moving van bringing their belongings from Tokyo. The husband and wife bowed politely. Mother Dear tried a smile. She regretted it was so weak. She gave her favourite old teddy bear, ancient and worn, to the little girl with the straight black hair down to her shoulders, and then thought how silly the act must appear. Nevertheless the little girl hugged the stuffed cub with one arm while clinging to her father's trouser leg with the other.

With tears in her eyes Mother Dear implored the couple to care tenderly for her house. Affectionately her hand lingered on the mahogany banister. Wishing them a happy life in her home to match her half-century there, she bid the couple farewell. They smiled and bowed again. As she drove off with the minister, she waved, more at the house than at them.

Knowing that to some people, especially men of the faith, there are only three plateaux in life: birth, marriage and death, Mother Dear was not too surprised when Paster Waters drove to the cemetery on their way to the airport. He must be assuming she would want to pay her respects in one last visit to the graves of her beloved parents and her devoted husband.

Instead all she saw as Pastor Waters' car moved slowly past the Georgia marble tombstones was the vacant plot next to Mr Templeton's grave. It was meant for her. Well, she thought as she removed her wedding ring and dropped it into her purse, her silent prayer had been answered; her spirit would not toss and turn in torment by his side for eternity.

Once inside the terminal building, Pastor Waters helped her along the jetway onto the commuter plane, where he gently clasped her little hand in his, bidding her goodbye.

Soon the craft sped down the runway and rose into the sky. Mother Dear looked down and saw Tybee Island and the surf of her Atlantic Ocean. The plane banked, scaring her a bit. As she left Savannah behind her, Mother Dear saw the *Waving Woman*, a bronze sculpture placed on a pedestal beside the harbour. The local legend told the story of how, after her husband was lost at sea, for the rest of her life the woman greeted every ship, apparently hoping her man would be on one of them. Out of her mind, they said, but was she? For in the human equation, Mother Dear thought, hope must serve as the lighthouse showing the course to sanity.

Mother Dear was somehow good with maps, and being in the plane looking down was almost the same as studying an atlas. As they passed over Athens, Mother Dear identified the covered bridge on the Oconee River where she and Geraldine had talked those many years ago. She was thrilled with the fact Geraldine had realized her destiny. Far away in some little country in Eastern Europe, before the war.

She recalled Toledo's conversation on their joint birthday. He had encouraged her, saying she was actually moving to a new realm. The thought of seeing her dear grandson carried her through the bustling Hartsfield International Airport and onto the much larger jet.

On the long flight from Atlanta the plane flew too high to see the land so, seated on the aisle, Mother Dear fell asleep. Before making the approach to Dallas–Fort Worth, the copilot and one of the flight attendants came to her seat, smiling.

The pilot announced over the loudspeaker, 'Ladies and gentlemen, we are privileged to welcome Mrs Grace Templeton to the friendly skies. Not only is she the oldest person on the aircraft, but this is her first flight, so we are giving her a special award.' The stewardess pinned a pair of flight wings on her blouse as the copilot saluted. Mother Dear thanked them each with a kiss, feeling she couldn't be more jubilant if she were the queen of Flight 482.

She noticed the attendant wore a name badge, *Daisy*. She visualized her own name in crewelwork on a velvet ribbon affixed to her blouse above her newly awarded wings. Yes, badges were a good idea. Even the copilot wore one, *Captain Rogers*. She resolved in her queenship to sign a decree ordering each of her subjects to display their names so she could address them properly.

Leaving Dallas, she remained wide awake for the short flight to Albuquerque, her mind in a heightened state of alert over the impending change in her life.

Inside the Albuquerque terminal, she was greeted by her daughter. Lorraine's perfunctory hug was followed by a self-conscious 'hello' from her son-in-law, Horatio. Did she really know these people?

Mother Dear was enraptured with the geometric Indian motifs on the terminal's overhead beams. They seemed to punctuate her arrival. Bigger-than-life sculptures of Native American men and women welcomed her as she passed by their pedestals. What were their legends? Perhaps their stories were written on the colourful hand-crafted pots.

Leaving the terminal, the landscape she saw was a panorama of wide-open spaces with far-off mountains. She felt herself entering an enchanting reality.

A little more than an hour later, trying to sound upbeat, Lorraine announced, 'Here we are, Mother Dear, at the Methuselah Retirement Home. You've arrived.'

Lorraine's voice came across to Mother Dear as anxious, actually on edge. Lorraine added, more with hope than conviction, 'I know you'll enjoy yourself.'

'Time will tell,' Mother Dear replied, her voice faltering. Trying to gather her wits, she said, 'And please do not talk to me as if I were a child.' She reached up into the sleeve of her hand-knitted sweater and extracted a Kleenex, which she quickly applied to her eyes, dabbing at the forming tears.

Was her freedom to be taken away? Liberty – a luxury reserved for younger people who could drive their cars, move freely about, do their own shopping and their own housework. She tried to define the fear of this frontier, but couldn't. Once across this border, would she be leaving her domain of independence and entering a forbidding totalitarian state?

Confronting this threshold of her life, Mother Dear recalled Miss Crawford's words. Often when she counselled her students, the headmistress would reiterate the doctrine of self-determination to which she implored her girls to subscribe: 'Regardless of the situation in which you find yourself, you have free choice of your own acts.'

7

'Isn't this nice?' Lorraine remarked.

'Stucco applied over a double wall of adobe bricks,' Horatio said in his deep voice. 'Made out of mud, Mother Dear.' He laughed. 'Keeps the interiors cool in the summer and warm in winter.'

Mother Dear glanced up to see him look away sheepishly. In Lorraine's mind her husband was here to help settle her in, not to make observations.

'Here there are real people for you to talk to,' Lorraine said. 'You won't have to talk to yourself any more.'

Horatio opened the car door for Mother Dear and smiled broadly. 'Your permanent wave is lovely,' he offered.

Though she knew Lorraine had required him to rehearse his words, Mother Dear smiled.

Stiff from her ride, Mother Dear climbed out and stretched as straight as she could. At the airport she had overheard Lorraine whisper to Horatio that she had shrunk six inches in as many years. But at the jet ramp when a wheelchair was offered, Mother Dear surprised them. She told Lorraine to ride and wheeled her daughter to the baggage claim.

'They have a fine routine here,' Lorraine said. 'You won't have to lift a finger, even to change the sheets on your bed – once a week the cleaning girls will do your apartment.'

Mother Dear looked again at the South-West-style building in front of her. The late afternoon sun turned its earthen colour into a golden glow, beckoning her. More to herself, she said, 'The Methuselah is a pleasant surprise.' She turned to Horatio, 'And you say it's made out of mud? My stars!'

'Yes, it's not at all like one of those nursing homes.'

'How many times do I have to tell you, the Methuselah is not a nursing home – it is retirement living,' Lorraine told him sharply. 'Fitting for her since she's still up and around.'

'Yes, but there is always a nurse on duty for all of the old folks,' Horatio answered.

'That's covered in the monthly rent.'

'And should you ever need them,' Horatio said to Mother Dear, 'doctors are on call.'

Lorraine glared at him.

Rows of large open windows looked down on Mother Dear, three floors of them, in fact, each housing a potential friend for her to meet. Yet she knew not one of them at this moment, any more than she really knew her daughter and this large oaf-like man. She breathed deeply and said, 'The cloudless sky can only be described as azure. Quite a different sky than we have in Georgia. The sunshine here is brilliant.'

'Almost every day is like this,' Lorraine said quickly, as if the weather was one item she had forgotten to mention. 'They say the clear light is why there are so many artists in New Mexico.'

Mother Dear scanned the parapet of the retirement residence. 'I thought so. Look, there is a Savannah sparrow. It must be migrating to Mexico. They fly, you know, guided by a special streak in the sky only they can see . . . some say the stars direct them at night . . . marvellous, isn't it?' Speaking to the sparrow, Mother Dear asked, 'Or are you on your way back to Savannah?'

Ignoring the bird, Lorraine went on, 'Just think of the things you'll be able to do. The Methuselah is like a fountain of youth where you will meet . . . ah . . . people of your age. They'll be in the apartment next door, walking down the corridor or riding in the elevator. You'll compare notes with fellow residents at dinner in the Great Hall, at the piano concert in the lobby, or during van tours through the mountains to the Indian dances. They don't have Indians in Georgia, do they?'

'Of course we do – the Cherokees. Why, Chief Van was one of their leaders. He lived in a house like mine. That is, until the awful federal government forced him and most of his tribe to march all the way across the country to Oklahoma. The only difference between Chief Van and me is that I flew. And see the wings my pilot gave to me.' She pointed proudly at her pin, but her eyes filled with tears.

'Look at it this way,' Horatio said, 'you'll be free from all those strict Southern social conventions.'

'Seniors at the Methuselah have shed constraints like butterflies bursting from their cocoons – it's a second childhood, but without teachers, parents or chaperones watching over,' Lorraine added.

'Why, I bet they even have poker games in the "rec" room,' Horatio whispered to Mother Dear.

Mother Dear beamed, her imagination at work. She had always been good at poker, played secretly with the girls at Miss Crawford's and later in Savannah with a clique of friends in the garden club, hoping no one would find out.

By her side Horatio said quietly, 'Personally, I'd enjoy having such an opportunity.'

Poor Horatio, Mother Dear thought, so much under her daughter's dominance. He was probably pondering what life would be like starting afresh: rid of his boring state government job, employed instead in a more gratifying enterprise, supported by a more compassionate wife.

Growing impatient, Lorraine rushed on, her voice rising, 'You see, Mother Dear, almost everyone at the Methuselah is from somewhere else – their sons and daughters were attracted to Santa Fe, moved here and later brought their parents, or parent, so they could be close by in their . . . ah . . . final years.'

'Parent?' Mother Dear exclaimed. 'You mean there may be single men living here?' Delicately she touched her white curls, appraised her face in a little pocket mirror and applied fresh lipstick.

Lorraine nodded, smiling the indulgent smile of someone humouring another's quaintness. She hugged her mother awkwardly and hurried forth with the rest of her litany of reasons that in her mind – and she was sure, society's – justified the removal of her aging parent from Georgia, concluding with, 'And here you can attend regular Sunday services.'

Horatio's big hand gently guided Mother Dear's elbow, ready to apply a firmer grip in case she might start to fall. Together they followed Lorraine towards the entrance.

Mother Dear's attention was diverted to a man in white overalls. As she watched, he applied paint to the door jamb. His hand trembled until his brush engaged the wood, then it steadied. With precision he instructed his brush downwards along the line that delineated the jamb's cobalt blue from the golden hue of the stucco.

'Wonderful, they employ old men here,' she announced.

The tip of his painter's white-billed cap pointed in her direction, and his hand resumed its vibrations.

'Hi, cutie, I love your hairdo and your outfit. You're not from around here, though, I can tell. Are you coming here to live with me?'

'You live here?' Mother Dear asked. 'Are there any more like you inside? I may enjoy this place after all.'

'I'm Tom. I've been here two years. I love to paint. The activity steadies my hand.' His hands shook as he aimed the brush towards the open can. 'They let me paint what I want when I want. It's my recreation. You see, painting allows my mind to work, to wander, to fantasize, to explore. I enjoy painting. These wrinkles, though,' he said, pointing at his face, 'I can't paint them over, nor smooth them out with spackle. Not even painters' putty will disguise them away.'

He extended a quivering hand towards her. She required both hands to capture his larger one. She treasured his hand for a while, her frail body vibrating in sync. 'My name is Grace. They,' and she tilted her head towards Lorraine and Horatio, 'always call me Mother Dear, but now that I have arrived here, I am going to call myself Grace again.'

'Grace it shall be, my dear,' Tom said.

'Let's get you introduced inside, Mother Dear,' Lorraine said.

'I'm in steady hands here with Tom. We shall chat,' she said as she released his hand, her own trembling subsiding. 'Are you married?' she asked.

'Was.'

'I was, too – to a banker.'

'Mine ran off, couldn't stand me continually painting the house. But, I ask you, why is that so bad? Lots of men sit in front of the TV and watch football. I painted, stayed sober, enjoyed my house.'

'Did you change colours?'

'Oh, no, couldn't. I'm colour-blind, you see, so someone has to supply me with the proper paint can.'

'I think it was your wife's lack of a palette, not yours,'

Grace concluded as she moved through the door which Horatio had opened for her.

In the lobby of the Methuselah, Lorraine was obsequiously greeted by a woman who was introduced to Grace as the Activities Director. Her face was fixed in a set smile. She appeared preoccupied with logistical matters, being quick to excuse the empty vase waiting on the piano by saying the florist was late delivering freshly cut flowers. Grace wished at that moment she could select a dozen roses from her Georgia garden and present the bouquet to the woman.

'Welcome to the Methuselah Retirement Home.' Turning to Lorraine, her hand gesturing towards Grace, she said, 'My, she's a sweet one. Here for our comfy Assisted Living Wing?'

'No, I don't need any assistance,' Grace replied, striving to gain the woman's attention.

Unbelieving, the Activities Director's eyes rolled upward. Continuing to speak to Lorraine, she rushed on as if she were reciting her part in a grade school play. 'That is where we look after the resident twenty-four hours a day. Three meals delivered to their room, regular sponge baths by the nurse, therapy as prescribed, their medication, a doctor on call at all times. They're quite happy there.'

'I am perfectly able to take care of myself,' Grace retorted.

'That's what they all say, at first,' the Activities Director said as she winked at Lorraine, the two of them sharing, of course, the truth about aging parents.

'She's in Independent Living,' Horatio hastily explained. 'No need for those additional expenses yet.'

'Quite independent,' Grace said, trying again to engage the woman's eyes. 'I shall take my meals in the dining-room along with everyone else, thank you. Bathe myself. And I do not do drugs.'

'She's not on medication?' the woman asked, surprised, continuing to address Lorraine with an occasional glance at Horatio.

'I am in good health,' Grace said, her voice rising. 'In Savannah I walk a half-mile every morning.'

'There's a landscaped patio here with a little path for you to walk on,' Lorraine quickly advised her mother. 'Six times around equals a half-mile – they've measured the course. If you are still trying to be active when the snows come, you can loop around the interior hallway. And there are no stairs to climb,' she added.

Grace tugged at Horatio's sleeve. 'I shall have to sit a moment, catch my breath.'

Her son-in-law nodded and said reassuringly, 'It's the altitude – seven thousand feet. Takes a while to adjust. It's OK to rest for a minute.'

She sat on a high-back South-West-style wooden chair which, it seemed, had been waiting expressly for her. 'Do you have my spirits of peppermint?' she whispered to Lorraine.

Reaching into her bag, Lorraine retrieved a small bottle. 'I looked all over town and finally found it at a little neighbourhood drugstore – the last bottle on their shelf.'

Grace tried unsuccessfully to unscrew the top. 'My fingers are not so nimble any more,' she said.

'Let me do that,' Horatio said, and the bottle disappeared inside his hand.

Grace took a sip. 'That will revive me.' She smiled.

The Activities Director caught Lorraine's eye and said softly, 'But spirits of peppermint is eighty proof. . . .'

Lorraine stopped her with a quick negative head-shake.

The Activities Director began to narrate her schedule of forthcoming events: 'Tomorrow we offer a van tour to the Indian corn dances at Santo Domingo Pueblo. The next day is our trip to the supermarket – some residents like to store food in their apartment though we provide three meals a day. This weekend we have a lunch in Lamy and watch the east and west Amtrak trains make their Santa Fe stops. Passengers detrain to buy Indian jewelry, and then—'

'My grandson will be visiting me soon,' Grace interrupted, her breath coming easier. 'And I so look forward to his visit – he is such a dear little boy. Why, it seems only yesterday he came to see me in Savannah. Rode the train – all the way from El Paso. Had to change in New Orleans, of course. And all by himself. He was dressed in his little blue suit – matched his eyes – with a red bow tie, and his hair so curly. Yes, it seems only yesterday.'

'He was nine then,' Horatio said with pride. He held out his hand, chest high, and added, 'Up to here on me. But now – ' his hand went above his head – 'he's this tall.'

48

Grace looked worried. 'But how will Toledo find me?'

'What did you say your grandson's name was?' the Activities Director asked.

'Toledo,' Grace announced.

'No, his name, not where he's from.' The Activities Director's eyes again rolled towards the ceiling.

'Toledo,' Grace repeated.

The woman's eyes sought out Lorraine.

'Toledo,' Horatio said emphatically.

'Toledo?'

'Yes, Toledo,' Lorraine said. 'That's his name.'

'But that's the name of a town . . . in Michigan, no, Ohio, I believe.'

'Spain,' Lorraine said.

'He is named after the town where he was conceived,' Grace explained.

Aghast, the woman's hand, fingers outstretched, flew to her chest as she exclaimed, 'You are a most extraordinary old woman!'

8

They stood before each other, Toledo and Katherine, nude human figures.

'Do you wear your stetson all the time?' she asked. 'You're attractive with it on, and I'm sure even more so with it off.'

Toledo seemed surprised. He reached up and touched the greyish felt of his hat's high crown, then smiled. 'I'd forgotten I still had it on.'

'I like a man who wears a hat – but who also remembers to take it off.'

'How'd we get this way, anyway?'

'It all began as we entered this hotel room. I removed your bolo tie as you were saying, "Why shouldn't I be named after a town?" You went on to say to me, as if I didn't already know, "Toledo is an important place – historically and architecturally." And then as you started undoing my blouse, you said with a determined look in your eye, "The next undertaking I've assigned myself is to match its mettle in history." "Very clever," I said.'

He was tall, muscular.

She was tall, curvaceous.

'Then, kicking off my shoes, I told you I could trace my Mondragon family back to your ancient town in Spain.'

'Yes, I recall your saying, "A Mondragon rode with Cortez in 1540."'

'I think that was when I took off your shirt.' Katherine admired his torso and said, 'And now that I've had the opportunity to contemplate the curls all over your body, I'm willing to wager those under your hat are captivating, too.'

Toledo took off his stetson and received a purring 'ooh' from Katherine. 'Now we can pretend we're two nude models in the studio of the Renaissance sculptor Cellini,' he said. 'Or, better still, the more modern Rodin – you know,

50

he was the first to take photographs of his models to study their body contours and shadows in another perspective.'

'What sort of stance do you think one of those famous men would have us pose today? *The Kiss?*'

'Certainly not me as *The Thinker.*'

'Nor me as Venus. . . .'

Toledo chuckled. 'She gave her right arm for a man. . . .'

'No, not for a man, but for good investment advice. Shh, models aren't supposed to move, let alone talk, especially to each other,' she whispered.

'How do you expect me to be quiet in the presence of your voluptuous body. Don't you understand? Statuesque females stimulate red-blooded American males.'

'Yes, I know that. I mean, I've been told that. But you see it's different for women, for me.'

'How so, Katie?'

'I asked you to please call me Katherine. I don't like short cuts. They don't work in investment analysis, and they don't work in life.'

'OK, Katherine, let's talk about these differences.'

'Well, in this role of woman, I sometimes think I'm obliged to conceive, to develop an embryo and nine months later to deliver a baby into this world.'

'But I don't see this procreation role as a sexual turn-on, especially for you,' Toledo said.

Katherine shrugged. 'It's the mission of a woman.'

'Who made such an assignment? The missions I've been assigned to undertake don't include fathering a baby. An offspring is a responsibility and could even be an impediment, don't you think?'

'But consider how bringing a child into the world offers an opportunity to develop the little guy into an imaginative adolescent and later an adult person. A chance to instil creativity and see the results of your caring labours. At times I think being a mother would be a fun experience for me, and for my baby.'

Toledo looked at her questioningly. 'And at other times?'

'I think I don't have to. The truth of the matter is I really don't know what my real mission in life is, if I have one, other than to care for my family, revere my Church and do my job well.'

'Go on.'

'Well, you see,' she began and blushed, lowering her eyes while reconciling the idea of revealing intimate thoughts. Determinedly she looked up into his eyes again. 'I produce one fertile egg a month; meanwhile, you manufacture hundreds of thousands of sperm. As should all women, I must be selective. Performing at life's maximum, I might bring forth a dozen – God save me – babies. Whereas you could father, if you are so inclined – and most American males feel their mission is just that – several thousand offspring, fertilizing half of womanhood. The record is, as I recall, five thousand – set by some Turkish sheik with a receptive, fertile harem.'

She paused, appraising his body. 'It's more than simple birth control. We women desire a deeper feeling for our partner in case, even with protection, our ready, waiting fertile egg chemically announces to an eager, virile sperm that's wiggled outside your condom, "Come here, let's get engaged." I mean, if I am going to endure nine months of gestation followed by delivery, I want the baby to be a product of affection.'

'Naturally.'

'I haven't experienced some vision in which I make a mark on society, or even influence it. I am simply a 32-year-old woman who grew up in the typical Hispanic family and, by the grace of God, after college won a scholarship to the MBA programme at Stanford.'

Reaching onto the dresser for her handbag, she extracted a leather photograph case. 'Here is my family outside our old adobe farmhouse in Chimayo.' She pointed. 'These are my seven younger brothers and sisters.'

Examining the snapshot, Toledo commented, 'You are the tallest. You said your father died?'

Lowering her eyes, she said slowly, 'Yes. He cut and sold firewood for a living. It was one of those icy days in January when the sun didn't come out and the roads stayed slippery all day. His pick-up skidded – the tyres were bald, he didn't have the money for new ones. That's when I began to get interested in the abstract process of finance.' She covered her face. 'His truck went off the road – the High Road from Taos – on his way to delivering a load of firewood to Santa Fe. . . .'

Toledo put his hand gently on her shoulder.

'You see, if he'd just understood he could have gotten a loan for tyres – based on his income – he'd still be alive today. But back-country people don't savvy the money resources available to them. They believe you must save, have enough cash in the cookie jar in order to make a purchase.' She allowed his hand to remain on her shoulder.

'So you're supporting the family?'

Katherine nodded. 'But it costs. . . .' She pointed to a heraldic shield in the photograph. It showed a pheon, a quarrel-like instrument, engrailed into a globe as if thrown from a crossbow. 'Our Mondragon family crest,' she said proudly. 'An ensign signifying dominion. Goes way back to the Spanish Colonials in Nuevo Mexico.'

'Several hundred years?'

'Yes, that's my heritage. So you see, Mr Toledo Town, I'm a normal, native South-West woman. But you believe in some higher pursuit. You have this airship you've coloured with ambition, and you cling to it – sailing toward the sunrise, pulling you ever upward in your search for self-realization. How did you become so attached to it? Tell me – to me your male motives may be as sexy as your beautiful body.'

His fingers reached a responsive destination.

She squirmed away. 'No, Toledo. Talk to me first!' Pulling the white sheet from the bed, she draped herself. 'I don't want our relationship to be like two drifting clouds, momentarily clinging to each other in orgasmic delight.'

Toledo laughed. A deep laugh. An embarrassed laugh. He moved away. He seemed to be ill at ease with so much light in the hotel room. His voice weak, he asked, 'Are you seeking a more permanent relationship?'

'Formalizing a living arrangement might be a comfort, especially financially. But coupling connotes mutual duties, so I have mixed feelings. I think I need a drink,' she added.

'A rough week in the state's investment department?'

'As a matter of fact, yes,' Katherine replied. 'Programme trading of stocks defies prediction – these damned computers act as if they're running the markets and we're their high-tech servants. Our investment advisory firms are pushing us in another direction. And I have my own view of which stocks and bonds to buy and sell. Also, that watchdog assistant the governor hired is breathing down my neck. She's got some hot-shot degree in international monetary management – thinks she's smarter than Queen Elizabeth.'

'Whoa! Time out. The office is closed. This is Friday evening – our time.'

Katherine laughed, untucked the sheet and jumped up on top of the bed. Gaining her balance, she stood towering above him, her head almost touching the ceiling. From her vantage point she looked down and admired the ribbons of muscles on his torso.

Looking up, Toledo admired how the light from the crystal chandelier highlighted Katherine. Radiant strands of her hair dancing across her face hinted at her free spirit. 'You know, my grandmother's going to like you,' he said.

'Better clothed, I should think.'

'She's an open-minded woman. In fact, I've been closer to her over the years than to my own mother.'

'Why is that? Little boys are supposed to cling to their mother's skirts.'

'Lorraine's were always starched and ironed. But Grandmother's a romantic – sees past the daily routine to the fun of life. I suspect Grandmother experienced her fill of drudgery with Mr Templeton, being housewife and available lover. I believe she secretly coveted a loftier life.'

'Mr Templeton?'

'Her husband of some forty years. Always called him mister. I guess familiarity was reserved for under the covers, but only when he rang.'

Katherine frowned. 'With such insensitive treatment from a husband, I can't understand why she didn't get a divorce.'

'In her generation, divorce wasn't a popular option. I'm sure it never occurred to her. Instead she escaped into a dream world in which she was born to royalty,' Toledo explained.

'Then it was really your grandmother's fantasies that inspired you to undertake this special mission you're talking about?'

'Well, I suppose her stories have influenced me.'

'And who else gave you these command assignments? Your first-grade teacher or your high-school football coach? Who inspires people such as you? Your motives mystify me. Where is this drive of yours leading you?'

'Do you want to know about my sexual desires or my national designs?'

'Start with the country, because I can recognize the state of your sexual resources with my visual ruler.' With delight she recorded his look of embarrassment and thought she would always remember his ensuing sheepish little laugh.

Looking at her seriously, Toledo began, 'I have this insatiable desire to run a country.'

'But which country? And why, for heaven's sake? Are you some sort of closet czar?'

'Maybe.' He reflected a moment. 'But I do believe every man must have a plan, and when achieved, he must devise another, and so on.'

'Score after score,' she suggested.

'You do have a lively imagination. But seriously, I believe the measurement of a man's accomplishments should be more than money and material possessions.'

'Of course, for unselfish people in this world like priests and nurses on the battlefield and starving authors who write for the sake of literature, fulfilment doesn't have a dollar sign.'

'But I'm not averse to viewing money as a tool. It'll take a lot of dollars to do what I want to do. Of course, the money's not for me personally.'

Katherine's tongue clicked in disbelief.

'You see,' Toledo went on, 'in my current plan I yearn to manage a nation by structuring its economy so its people enjoy life, while at the same time preserving its past and building its future. I want personally to be part of history.'

'There are less complex ways to spend your time, like, for example, being employed or running a little business somewhere,' she argued.

'I've done the business thing, had a business plan that worked – in spades! Made a lot of money for myself, too. So why should I do a similar thing again? At this juncture in my life I yearn for real adventure and at the same time give a little back to society.'

'Your grandmother's done a real job on you – instilling social obligations, I mean. With a track record like you're building, you're sure to go to heaven.'

'There's too much I must do before I advance to those Elysian Fields. Besides, who ever heard of accomplishing anything up there. Challenges lie here, on Earth! Here's where we are obliged to perform to our fullest!'

He appeared, she marvelled, imbued with duty to self and country, some country, somewhere. 'Promise me you'll at least consider some alternative ways to spend your time.'

'I've already discarded alternatives.'

Her look gauged him. 'I believe you really are serious!' She thought to herself, if he achieves this bizarre goal and I am there by his side I'll be his queen and he my king. 'I've never met anybody who wanted to do that!' Her fantasies were in full motion. 'You want to be. . .' she tried not to say king, because royalty was no longer accepted in America; in Canada, maybe, but not here in the good old egalitarian USA. But she said anyway, 'You want to be king? Is that what you were thinking?' She laughed. 'You *would* make a model king.'

'And you a tall, statuesque queen.'

'Since childhood I've dreamed of becoming a royal investment manager.' She winked at him. 'Does your queen manage her country's portfolio?'

'I would decree it.'

Smiling, she delicately lowered herself onto Toledo, awaiting his biological response, which was prompt.

9

Katherine brushed aside strands of her long sable hair. 'Let's continue,' she said.

'I'll try to summon my reserves.'

'No, that's not what I mean. You still have to tell me the name of the country, how you're going to accomplish the task, and why.'

'Let's do that over some food,' Toledo suggested. 'I'll phone for beef enchiladas and wild rice.'

'Chicken fajitas for me.'

'I'll ask them to use buffalo meat. . . .'

'I prefer *el pollo*. Blue corn posole, too,' he said, 'from Cochiti Pueblo. I'm famished.'

'Wine?'

'You bet. From that winery on the Rio Grande where they've grown wine grapes since the 1500s.'

'And sopapillas?'

'Definitely, with honey from Taos, raw, unfiltered.'

Katherine ordered in New Mexican Spanish interwoven with American slang, concluding with, '*Bueno*, pal.'

She turned to Toledo and said, 'Now start at the beginning.'

'It all began in southern New Mexico –'

'Wait till I put that stupid crown on my head and announce: "Welcome to *American Achievers*. Our cameraman is ready to record your first-hand oral history".' She laughed, holding an imaginary microphone. 'Those who do spectacular things should be part of the cultural archives, don't you think? Look into the camera. Be frank, explicit. Which town? Why did you live there? Name it! Don't feign being bashful. Tell the videotape and me about yourself. I'm serious.'

Toledo tilted his head, crossed his eyes, pulled his earlobes out straight and said, 'Name of the town is La Mesilla.'

Katherine dissolved in laughter.

'My father, Horatio, had begun working for the state. My mother was a railroad telegrapher, the last before microwave relay. Her messages were dominant and strong – even then.' Toledo's thumb and index finger simulated sending code. 'Neither she nor the Morse – which she can still tap out – have changed.'

'You weren't rich?' Katherine seemed surprised.

'No, not with Horatio's salary and Lorraine earning a pittance.'

'Go on. Your mother is assertive?'

'So much so that Horatio thinks he can't express himself.'

'You don't like strong women?'

'Strong is OK, but domineering is, well, domineering.'

'Which am I?'

'Triple "S".'

Her eyebrows rose.

'Strong, sexy and sweet,' he explained.

'OK, you are free to continue.'

'Well, I'd watch the tourists in their big motor cars visiting our historic Butterfield Stage town. I'd read in the El Paso newspapers about the powerful and wealthy. I began to visualize affluence.'

'Go on, tell about the town.'

'La Mesilla had the prestige of being the capital, albeit briefly, of the Confederate state of Arizona which included New Mexico.'

'Can you image what life would be like today if we were part of Arizona?'

Toledo laughed. 'You see, the Confederacy coveted California's blockade-free ports and its gold. Colorado's mineral wealth, too. When war came, Texas volunteers marched up the Rio Grande. They thought they'd won the battle of Glorieta Pass east of Santa Fe, but their supplies were burned by Yankee troops. They had to pull down the Confederate flag from the plaza in Santa Fe and trickle back to Texas. Glorieta was the Gettysburg of the West.'

'Go on.'

'My father's ancestors settled in La Mesilla in 1854, after the area was purchased by the United States from Mexico, a deal negotiated by James Gadsden – he was a Southern railroad man seeking a rail route to California. When the

Confederacy was formed, people in La Mesilla supported it.'

'Didn't want to give up their slaves?'

Toledo shook his head. 'No, they didn't have any. It had little to do with slavery. They believed a Confederate railroad would bring them a better economic deal.'

'But this land was empty.'

'Except for Indians, minerals and water. My high-school teacher explained the Confederacy objectively.'

'That's rare. Who was he?'

'A woman, from England. She gave us their perspective on the War Between the States.'

'So, you became a champion of the Confederate cause?' Katherine asked.

'No, I was caught up in how emerging nations should be governed if they are going to endure beyond their initial revolution.'

'After the euphoria of the revolution has worn off?'

'Exactly. I was critical of those Southern leaders who were convinced their cause was holy and took their ultimate success for granted. Revolutionary leaders need time and help. The Confederate leaders had too much to do and too little time. Moreover, they couldn't agree among themselves on a course of action.'

There was a knock at the door.

'Clothes!' she yipped, and they each grabbed robes.

The waiter, his coat a bright New Mexico yellow with red braid, his brass name badge announcing *Emiliano*, delivered the food and decanted the red wine.

Toledo scooped the chicken and vegetables into the tortilla and spread green chilli sauce. 'We don't get the good New Mexico chilli in California,' he said.

'Want a teeny bite of the buffalo meat?'

'Only a taste, please. I feel I shouldn't eat a native American animal – it's part of our natural environment.'

'Lower in cholesterol,' Katherine explained, 'but do continue with your plans to start a revolution.'

'No, you don't understand, it's the challenge of what comes after that attracts me. Let somebody else rise up and throw the rascals out. Act Two – when I arrive – demands planning, adept management and solid financing for the nascent republic to survive.'

Katherine nodded. 'Do you fancy a great big country, or

a little itsy-bitsy one? By yourself or with the help of tough cowboys recruited from that bar on Upper Canyon Road? And tell me, will you finance this cash-draining effort with the change in your pocket or will you sell bonds on street corners?'

'Let me explain.'

'You do understand that any explanation of how you would finance a plan of this magnitude will be pretty unbelievable.' She hesitated. 'Have you been pulling my leg?' She attacked her enchilada. 'Your quest is so unbelievable, I'm curious.'

'I'll try to explain.'

'Bottoms up.' She emptied her glass and took her vitamins with a sip of mineral water.

Toledo watched her. 'You're healthy,' he commented.

'Yes. In case one of your exhilarated sperm cleverly swims out of the restraint of your condom and responds to my fertility, I'd like, at that precious, that creative moment of life, to be in top physical condition.'

'That's sexy!'

'OK, commercial break over. Tell us, Mr Squires, how and where are you going to carry out your contrivance?'

'Where was I?'

'Let me review: your idea is to manage the aftermath of revolution as a business. With competent people, I presume, instead of guerilla warriors with loaded rifles and big fat ammunition belts strapped around their necks. Rebuild the economy, create jobs, afford women equal opportunity. . .'

'You made up that last part.'

'While desperately trying to keep control during the aftermath amid the divergent political emotions' – she frowned – 'in that vulnerable period when those thrown out try to restore their prerevolutionary status. Counter-revolutions, you know, are an axiom of history.'

'That will be the tough time,' Toledo agreed. 'But if we are properly organized, our team suited up, our plays memorized, our goals fixed firmly in our vision. . . .'

She threw a pillow at him and ducked as his throw boomeranged back.

'Seriously, there are a number of us who want to make a difference. Our management skills, to put it immodestly, from good education and top-level experience in government and business, must be utilized. We have a responsibility to ourselves and to society to do more than simply advance selfish careers and fill our pockets with money. We envision broader vistas to see, new prizes to win, higher mountains to climb.'

She laughed a mocking laugh, relegating him to the bone-yard of absurdity.

'Did they teach you cynicism in business school?'

'The opposite: realistic goals are obtainable.'

'And mine are not, you are implying?'

'I mean only to be practical,' she said. 'But tell me, in this resurrected Confederacy, are you planning to own slaves? I can read your classified advertisement placed in the local weekly: *Equal opportunity slaves wanted; no experience necessary. Modern housing and health insurance provided. Lifetime commitment required.*'

'I can assuage your fears. We're certainly not going to march in and enslave the people. They're going to be major players on our team.'

'Uh huh.'

'I am talking about the approaching twenty-first century.'

'Utopia lies over the rainbow,' Katherine said, 'a place to pine for, a Disneyland dream world where all is well, like a heaven you perceive up there in the sky. A place where you lure your team onward with promises of unending touchdowns with splendid extra points, all coming like multiple orgasms.'

'You've got to have idealism for inspiration at the beginning of any undertaking. I'll rely on the members of my team for creative checks and balances. But now you're asking me to get down to the nuts and bolts?'

'I couldn't have said it better.'

'To be practical, the down-to-earth paradigm is money.'

'Oh, is that all? And now, viewers, since our hero, Toledo Squires, has made several millions of dollars in a ruthless business endeavour, the windfall profits only partially filling his pockets, let's ask him how he plans to pay for this billion-dollar lark? Will he print sheets of million-dollar bills or choose to sell bogus bearer bonds in international airport washrooms?'

His face was red, its colour defending his past career. 'To set up a business takes guts. To run it, imagination and hard work. To finance it, creativity, not to mention placing my borrowed capital at risk. Few people dare take those kinds of chances!'

'Tell how you will pay off powerful folks such as tribal chiefs and union leaders, as well as those obstructionist bureaucrats who erect hurdles in every path you pursue. What currency will you use to massage their egos? Beads, trinkets, blankets, mirrors?'

'Gold,' he said firmly.

'Oh, you're going to lift the national cache from Fort Knox and zip off into some satellite country's sunset. Clever.'

'Gold is the universal currency,' he said. 'Like sex, everyone understands its function.'

'Thank you for an interesting, albeit fanciful, discussion. I wonder what else is on television.'

'I will get the gold,' he assured her. 'That is, I intend to find where it is while I'm here in Santa Fe. That's why I flew in from California.'

'Oh, I thought you came to see me.'

Trying to recover, his face attempting a smile, he said, 'Uh, of course, you were the primary reason I gave up my bowling date.'

She nodded her head vigorously up and down, her long hair flouncing, making it apparent she didn't believe him. 'OK, out of curiosity I'll allow you the heist of the gold, but only to hear you out, watch you reach your peak. Which country have you selected for your little romp? And where is the gold?'

'Are we off camera?' Toledo asked. 'Grandmother knows where the gold is hidden. It's been her secret ever since she was a little girl.'

'Will she share her secret with you after all these years?'

'I'm counting on her doing so,' Toledo said. 'And if you come with me to visit her tomorrow, perhaps you and I together can come up with a way to entice her to tell us.'

'To the Methuselah Retirement Home?'

'Yes, for dinner, along with Horatio and Lorraine.'

'That reminds me,' Katherine said. 'There's a handsome, elderly investor named Carter Calhoun who lives there. We introduced ourselves at a seminar we were both attending. We've talked a couple of times since then. I had lunch with him once in the Methuselah Great Hall. He has a remarkably broad knowledge of the field of finance. His outlook is like a painter confronting an unspoiled canvas – fresh and without the bias you get from a lot of these stock-market pundits who are trying to get you to buy a certain stock so they can unload their overvalued inventory.'

'I hope you'll have a chance to say hello.'

'Oh, I do, too. You know, he would have been quite a catch in his day. I was born sixty years too late.'

'I'm glad you and I are together in our generation,' Toledo told her. 'But tomorrow, you and I are going to visit the world of this older generation.'

'To pry the location of the Confederate gold out of your grandmother.'

'I want you to help me find out about her secret, diplomatically. It's been a long time since her grand-daddy Thatcher –'

'What did he do?' Katherine interrupted.

'Buried it, or hid it somewhere in the South in 1865. Grand-daddy Thatcher was a soldier-politician entrusted with the Confederate gold by Jefferson Davis after General Lee's surrender at Appomattox. Thatcher and Davis were together on a special train on their way to Georgia for what was to be the last meeting of the Confederate cabinet.'

'Really? The whole train was full of gold?'

'Yes. But the story goes blank from there,' Toledo said. 'Grand-daddy Thatcher is supposed to have hidden it or something.'

'You mean they never found the gold?' Katherine's eyes sparkled. 'And your grandmother knows where it is?'

'Yes, but he apparently swore her to secrecy. Anyway, her memory may be fading in the sunset of her life. Maybe it has already set.'

'And you think I might be able to help her recall his story? Maybe someone already has.' Katherine thought for a moment. 'Lorraine or Horatio, or her gentle podiatrist, or her minister, or. . . .'

'If we do find the spot and there's a gaping hole in the ground, we've lost. But we would be remiss not to try, wouldn't we?'

'OK, I'll help, and if I'm successful my reward will be a

seat at the round table.'

'Joining the other knights I'm recruiting?'

'Only if they include, say, a former US President – Jimmy Carter, for example,' she chuckled. 'And an astute banker, an eminent economist, a former chairman of the Joint Chiefs of Staff. Plus assorted mercenaries who will maintain order during the turmoil of the counter-revolution.'

Toledo nodded. 'All of the above.'

'You're kidding?'

'There's no reason why someone who has been president of one nation shouldn't go on to help run another. As you know, corporate executives move from one company to another all the time. So why not utilize the skills of political leaders the same way?'

'Good point.'

'All my knights are worldly,' Toledo went on. 'In fact, John Axminster at Bank of America has arranged for an international credit accommodation based on my recovering the gold. Do you know him?'

'The Rhodes Scholar? Yes, I researched his papers on monetary systems for Third World countries for Mr Calhoun.'

'Yeah? John is a bright guy.'

'But tell me, what's the line of credit for? To pay you a salary?'

'None of us needs a salary. The money will provide working capital, ready cash so we can bring the country up to a competitive and modern industrial speed.'

'Assuming your plan is viable,' she said, 'and that is iffy, what country are you going to . . . ah . . . take over?'

'Are you ready for the proper introduction?'

She nodded.

'Now remember, countries are much like people. They have feelings, emotions and pride, as well.' After a dramatic pause, he said, 'Katherine Mondragon, may I present to you The Country of Albania?'

Politely Katherine extended her hand in greeting, pretending to shake. 'Do you live somewhere near Yugoslavia, next to Macedonia?' she asked The Country.

Feigning a different voice, Toledo answered, 'Yes, near the Macedonia of Alexander the Great.'

'What language do your people speak?'

'My people can't decide between that of the Ghegs, north of my Seman River, or the very different dialect spoken by the Tosks in the rugged mountains of my southland.'

'I'll bet the folk music of the Ghegs is groovy.'

In his own voice, Toledo said, 'And that of the Tosks is torrid.' He laughed. 'A truly national language is one of the items on our agenda.'

'Way down on your priority list, I should hope,' Katherine said. 'Actually, you may be better off fragmenting the language further, encouraging a dialect for each valley in the folds of their mountains, making it difficult for the tribes to communicate with one another, so they stew around and stay off your neck. But why,' she asked, 'did you choose Albania?'

'It's to be a surprise for my grandmother. I hope to accomplish my task of remaking The Country by the time her eightieth birthday comes around.'

'You mean, give her The Country as a birthday present?' Katherine said with surprise.

'Only symbolically, of course. At her gala birthday party I plan to present her with a framed certificate reporting the results of a plebiscite in The Country confirming her as the Queen Grandmother.' Toledo smiled as he recalled the eccentricities of his grandmother. 'She's always wanted to be royalty, it's been her fantasy. At that moment her dream will become a reality.'

10

Wide awake, Katherine stared into the dark silence of their Santa Fe hotel room. Insomnia, she had supposed, was a condition limited to old people. But in this never-time she was indeed experiencing it. Good, she thought, the midnight consciousness would afford her an empathy that might help her speak effectively with Toledo's grandmother.

The gold's location was her secret, and shouldn't her privacy be respected? In any case, what would entice the grandmother to volunteer the information to her grandson? Old people gave their treasured heirlooms to favoured family members, didn't they? The older they got, the more they might feel compelled to reveal secrets, burdening someone else with the responsibility. So she could point out to the grandmother that Toledo's strong shoulders should now carry the weight of this more than 100-year-old secret.

Toledo, by her side, deeply breathing, was having no difficulty sleeping. Katherine thought about the strange workings of the male, his mind and his body, and asked herself if his scheme might be attainable. Did he actually see himself running a country? Surely such an idea was possible only in fantasy, certainly not in a real place with real people immersed in their own unique culture with subtleties foreign to him.

Until a few years ago no one had thought an individual could gain control of a major corporation. But one day a clever person sold high-interest-rate junk bonds to finance the purchase of a large corporation, accomplishing a leveraged buy-out by pledging that corporation's assets. Soon corporate raiders began repainting the business canvas across America.

So why couldn't a person pledge a country's assets and do a similar sort of take-over? It was logical, she admitted. Could this lover by her side become a philanthropic raider of emerging countries? Not a raider, but a princely ruler?

If she remained by Toledo's side, she could design the investment strategy for the country's portfolio. After all, she was now in charge of investing the general fund of an entire state – skills transferable to a country.

She imagined a strange new land with unbridled opportunities. At Stanford, several professors said a person should devote a span in their business career to public service. In her new altruistic role, perhaps she could convince the women of Albania there was more to life than babies and washing clothes in the local stream. As queen, she could work towards improving literacy among children and adults, too. And by enticing a few of her medical friends to hop across the Atlantic and join with her, they could create an Albanian health care system which would serve as a model for other Eastern European countries. Yes, perhaps she, too, could make a difference, in a far-away and strange land. In Albania.

As her mind worked, she realized she knew little about The Country. Maybe everybody already read and wrote and was healthy. No, for a half-century the former Communist countries were run by tyrannical dictators. The Country was overdue to make up for these nightmare years.

Toledo turned, snuggled, and was quiet again.

Katherine drifted off to sleep. In a dream, she floated aloft inside the wicker basket of a giant hot-air balloon. Illustrated on its billowing silk panels was a helmeted knight waving a royal banner depicting a double-headed eagle with entwining necks.

The balloon sailed gently and serenely above the green and fertile coastal plain. She looked down upon her subjects and their little farms. Leaning over, she gave a queenly wave, perfunctory and continual. Below, men looked up and doffed their country caps. The women, dressed in native costumes, responded by waving their aprons. Little children pointed towards the drifting lighter-than-air device and yelped with delight.

Her balloon drifted on, rising over fertile valleys sandwiched between tree-studded mountains. She saw the elongated map of Albania drawn in relief. Its rugged mountains and valleys began to resonate with the sound of folk music.

A chorus of deep male voices sang lustfully of liberation.

On musical cue each singer thrust two fingers upward in a 'V' sign for the people's victory in the revolution against Communism. They were singing, *Albania, my Albania, land of the sons of eagles.*

The balloon soared, catching an upward air current, ascending higher and higher. She felt exhilarated and knew how eagles must feel. She sensed an erect and pulsating Albania ready to thrust into the twenty-first century.

Suddenly out of the blue a pointed spear found its mark on the unprotected chest of the helmeted knight. Reacting to the force of the hit, the gondola spun wildly, its centrifugal force propelling a weeping Katherine into the sky. She tried to cry for help but was unable to utter a sound.

Toledo was there, concerned. She might be awake. Yes, she was. His lips kissed hers, ever so tenderly. How could a man be so gentle?

She basked in his attention, savouring his fragrant body. Her dream, now indelibly imprinted on her mind, played over and over, a dream whose rhythms she knew she would later find herself humming while hiking or at her desk in the state capitol. On those occasions she would recall the landscape and the gallant people of this far-away land. But she would simply ignore the dream's ending.

11

Grace opened the door to the Methuselah's landscaped patio and greeted Carter Calhoun. 'Bless my heart, never in all my life have I so eagerly looked forward to my morning constitutional.'

'You and I, Mrs Templeton, are opening our minds to another day even before most people are up.' Signalling that the moment to begin their walk was at hand, Carter raised his polished ebony cane, pointing its ivory tip towards the brightening cobalt-blue New Mexico sky. 'Let's see if we can make our way around twice today – I know the air is thin and you've just moved up from sea level.'

'That's very thoughtful of you. Everything is an adjustment, but with your encouragement I think I can today – that is, if we don't go so fast.'

He looked anxious. 'Yesterday's pace was too quick for you?'

'I was totally tuckered out.'

'Oh, I'm sorry. Let's set reasonable goals we'll be able to achieve.'

Here was a man, Grace thought, who might chart a course of action for her that, unlike her father or Mr Templeton, she could understand and subscribe to. The smile in his eyes suggested a compassionate attitude. A curly lock of his white hair fell quizzically across his forehead. To Grace, this punctuation conveyed his curiosity – an open-mindedness – and she looked forward to exploring the fields of inquiry they might walk across.

She marvelled at his ability to take long strides without having to look down – he had no fear of tripping and falling. Instead he looked straight ahead, his pace in cadence with a forward tune. And there was the warmth of his hand supporting her arm. But to her surprise she noticed a day's growth of beard on his face. Her impulse was to touch her fingertips to the stubble, but, of course, she didn't.

They were approaching the centrepiece of the courtyard, a small pond, and she said, 'Oh, see the little goldfish.'

'They're Japanese golden cyprinidae.'

'Good. Now I feel better. The buyers of my Savannah home are Japanese. Listen, their little fishes are telling me everything is all right in Georgia.'

'Do you miss your Savannah home?'

'No, not any more. It's better to look forward rather than back.'

'I quite agree with you, Mrs Templeton, but we are new friends, and perhaps we should introduce ourselves in terms of our personal histories.'

Grace paused by the pond to observe a fountain cast in the form of a Franciscan priest. Water flowed forth from his outstretched hand. She gestured towards the statue and said, 'Yes, but first introduce me to your bubbling padre.'

Carter laughed. 'You continually surprise me, Mrs Templeton, with your witticisms. This holy man standing before you is Father Marcos, the Spanish priest who claimed to have found the Seven Cities of Gold. He went back and told everyone in Mexico City. His story induced Coronado to launch his 1540 expedition into what is today New Mexico.'

'But why would the priest tell anyone about his seven cities of gold? Could he not keep a secret? Surely he would know that whomever he told – especially a conquistador like Coronado – would invade the cities and probably plunder them.'

'Perhaps that was a mistake,' Carter admitted, 'but maybe he so believed in the Word and so wanted the Word to go forth that he told his story in order to inspire the explorer to blaze a trail for others to follow.'

'Bringing the Spanish way of life – their religion, their advanced civilization, their know-how – to the northern frontier?'

'Yes, I should think that was his motivation.'

'But secrets are for keeping,' Grace said.

'For a while, perhaps, but there comes a time when they must be shared.'

70

Grace walked on and soon stopped to admire a tall sugaro cactus.

'Out of place here,' Carter said. 'This one's been transplanted from the Sonoran, the vast desert Father Marcos and Coronado had to cross. The journey was treacherous and long, took them weeks, even on horseback.'

'They were indeed dedicated,' Grace said in admiration. 'I've never thought of myself as being quite so committed.' She laughed, 'Except to my dreams.'

As they moved on, Carter said, 'I was blindly enthralled in my earlier years – wedded to my job more than to my marriage. But that's no excuse.'

'But, Mr Calhoun, you must not apologize for what our generation believed was important. Those were the days when men ruled their public and larger world, and women were more cerebral and enclosed in their private world. Today's generation is different – men and women want to share the elements of their respective spheres.'

As they completed their first lap, Grace said, 'Tell me about your early career.'

'I was an investment banker,' Carter answered. 'As I look back, I guess I was also an explorer. Difficult for people to understand today, perhaps, but back then what I did was quite imaginative.'

Grace was enjoying his mellow tones. Walking was easier. 'Please go on, tell me your story while we continue our walk. You know, today people are much more open about their feelings and their desires than in our day. But this *is* our day, so tell me about yourself and your dreams.'

'My tale may require several morning walks. But you and I do have time on our hands . . . don't we?' he added.

Grace smiled.

'Well, it was 1924,' Carter began. 'I was living in Greenwich Village – a student at NYU, where I'd enrolled after completing prep school in Virginia.'

'Were you one of those provocative Bohemians whom we girls at Miss Crawford's school pined about?'

'No,' he chuckled, 'but I rubbed elbows with many of them. They were interesting people, imaginative and fun. I'd often go to a coffee-house called the Waverly Inn. There one day I met this young poet, Edna St Vincent Millay.'

'My stars,' Grace exclaimed, 'her beautiful poetry still touches me. We memorized *Renascene* at Miss Crawford's. The young poetess expressed herself eloquently. And you actually talked with her?'

'Indeed. Vincent, as we knew her, had just returned from her travels abroad. Many of her friends spent their time in Paris, but she ventured farther east.'

'How did her story inspire you?'

'Well, I was looking for a career after graduation. Her descriptions of those little Eastern European countries, their people and their needs gave me ideas for economic opportunities.' He winked at Grace. 'And she also told me about her two weeks of horseback riding in Albania with one of her Italian lovers.'

'My friend became queen of Albania!' Grace exclaimed.

Carter looked surprised. 'You knew Queen Geraldine?'

'I met her once. I was given the privilege of escorting this very important visitor around my school.'

'She had quite a whirlwind romance with King Zog.'

'Yes, I treasure the letter she wrote me.'

'What a coincidence! You must tell me about your meeting with her.'

Grace smiled at the memory. 'We were just schoolgirls with big dreams. She realized hers, and I am still dreaming.'

'Sometimes dreams are frustrated by reality. That's what happened to me. This new world which we thought the Great War had made safe for democracy soon turned into chaos. Ignorant diplomats in their smoke-filled men's clubs in London, downing their Scotch, brought about this disorder by arbitrarily redrawing the map of Europe.'

'All those bewhiskered men,' Grace commented.

'Beards were the style then – as was smoking big cigars.' Carter laughed. As they circled the pond again, he continued his story. 'Well, after NYU I went to Wall Street, where I was employed by a large investment banking house. I was educated and well connected. That's what business was all about – connections.'

'Need I remind you, Mr Calhoun, connections between European royal families led to that war – the war to end all wars.'

'*Touché.*'

'You must have been swimming upstream against the isolationism of the 1920s,' Grace observed.

'Well, I tried to convince my firm to allow me to explore investment banking with the new governments and industries in the new Europe. I pointed out we could earn handsome underwriting commissions. They finally agreed, dispatching me on my first trip to Europe.'

'How exciting.'

'So I went. But with my appearance – clean shaven, a non-smoker, and drinking only the occasional cognac – I felt out of step.'

'You were so young.'

'Yes, of course.' Carter made a circling motion with his cane, taking in the patio. 'But since I've been at the Methuselah I've freed myself from the popular social conformities.'

'Is not shaving first thing in the morning one of your statements of freedom?' Grace asked.

He laughed. 'Ah, you've caught me up again, Mrs Templeton.' He deliberated for a moment. 'As that young man, I saw my mission perhaps in the same light as our Father Marcos. I wanted to get the word out to government officials of these new European countries that my company's investment underwritings could provide the capital for the social and economic programmes that would benefit their people.'

'What happened?'

'I learned the hard way about road blocks – the prejudices of the men running the countries, jealousies and hatreds between ethnic groups, the misconceptions the leaders laboured under. I tried to cope with the different cultures while convincing their leaders of the merits of my financing plans.'

'Wasn't there at least one visionary in all of Europe who held the same fresh outlook as yours?'

'Yes, the tall, charismatic king of Albania, your friend's royal husband, King Zog. He believed my approach was right, and he eventually entrusted his country's finances to me. Taking on these responsibilities was a pretty heady experience for a young man right out of college.'

Tom, the avocational house-painter, approached on the path, unopened paint can in one hand, his other, shaking, holding a clean brush. His billed cap and smock were both spotted with splashes of various colours, together creating an abstract painting, Grace observed to herself.

'Good morning, Tom,' she said. 'Another door today?'

He smiled and waved a shaking hand and brush. 'Yes, and a beautiful morning for it, too.'

'Tommy, we've been talking about Albania,' Carter said.

'Never been to Africa,' he said.

'No, no, Tommy. It's in the Balkans. Here, let me show you.' Carter stopped by a sandy patch of soil. With the tip of his cane he drew the boot of Italy. 'From here you sail, as I often did, across the mouth of the Adriatic Sea to Durrës, a port on the coastal plain of Albania. To the south is Greece and to the north is what used to be Yugoslavia. . . .' His cane sketched the boundaries of both countries.

Tom watched. 'You do a worthy sand painting. A different colour for each of your countries would liven up your map, but I wouldn't know which colours to suggest,' he said. 'Right now I'm headed for breakfast – toast and orange marmalade. Can't paint on an empty stomach, I always say.' He chuckled. As he left he said, 'Thanks for the geography lesson.'

The interruption seemed to have made Carter impatient, for he promptly thrust the tip of his cane into the remaining country he had outlined in the sand. He looked at Grace, smiled and said proudly, 'And this area here – smaller than Belgium – is my Albania.'

'And did you find a lover to ride horseback with across the landscape of your Albania?' Grace was quick to ask.

Carter choked. 'As a matter of fact I did. Am I an open book to you?' Slowly he added, 'In those days divorce could ruin an investment-banking career, otherwise. . . .'

She didn't hear the rest of his sentence for she suddenly realized her jest had actually made him share a secret that, without a doubt, he had never told to another living soul. He had had an affair with a woman in a far-off land.

'The game of finance is more fun played in the open,' she heard him continue. 'But if I were to do so now, would I be taken seriously or would I be regarded as simply another retired investment banker over the hill?'

'Most of my strait-laced friends in Savannah are over the hill, but, Mr Calhoun, I am certain you are not. They feel they have lived such exemplary lives they're now entitled to sit back and receive laurels.'

'There is a certain attitude retired people adopt toward life,' Carter said. 'But I find myself wanting to become directly involved once more.' He looked wistfully into the blue sky. 'Oh, to be young again.'

'We are what we imagine ourselves, Mr Calhoun,' Grace said and smiled. 'If you feel free, you can do anything you want, regardless of age. No one here is stopping any of us from doing anything, even leaving.' She didn't want to leave, not now, and go back among those boring friends in Savannah. That first day she had. But not after she met Carter. Back home she never met anyone new.

They walked on, completing their second lap. 'But age is against me – it's against us all,' Carter said. 'If not physically, it's mental. If not in our minds, then in the attitude of those with whom we come in contact.'

'Yes, but you and I do not have to worry about such prejudice here at the Methuselah, do we? Our community is very supportive, and I'll bet in favour of any new ideas we might hatch.'

12

The call was from the Methuselah Activities Director, who wasted no time expressing her concern to Lorraine. 'Your mother – '

'Is she all right?' Lorraine interrupted urgently.

'Oh yes, she's physically well. Takes long walks every morning with that handsome and prosperous Mr Calhoun. He's an early riser, too.'

Relieved, but annoyed at being bothered, Lorraine asked, 'What's the problem then?'

'She's not participating in our scheduled activities.'

'Is that a problem?'

'Well, we have so many fun things going on, you know. But after her walk she sits in her apartment. We here at the Methuselah are anxious about her well-being. I mean, when one is able, one must participate. Until, until. . . .'

'It's too late, you mean?'

'Or until we can no longer take care of ourselves and must be moved into the Assisted Living Wing.'

'What should I . . . we do?' Lorraine asked.

'Well, yesterday when we talked, she showed me a picture of her grandson, Toledo. My, he's a handsome man. Your mother thinks he's coming to visit her sometime soon.' The Activities Director hesitated. 'But we're accustomed to older people making unfounded predictions.'

'A geriatric trait?'

'Yes, but if he is coming, I'm sure her seeing him will perk her up. And if I know when he's coming, I'll personally escort him up to your mother's apartment.'

'Yes, I am sure you would enjoy doing that,' Lorraine replied. 'I am expecting him – he's supposed to be flying in any day now on his jet from California. I'll call you as soon as I hear from him.'

Hanging up, she said to Horatio, who was at his computer keyboard, 'Why hasn't that son of yours called?'

'What'll happen when the money from the sale of her house runs out?' he blurted. 'See here, look at these figures on my screen. If she lives many more years, the cost of her support: rent, clothes, hairdresser – really much more than her social security cheque – why, it'll break us.'

'But I've invested the proceeds from the house sale in a high-yield mutual fund,' Lorraine said.

'The one Toledo advised you not to buy into?' Horatio asked. 'The one where they caught the adviser taking kickbacks from some stock promoter?'

'The income we do get from that fund plus her monthly social security will at least go part of the way toward paying her rent. Thank heaven she's enrolled in Medicare B.' She sighed with relief.

'But her expenses are due to increase,' Horatio said. 'And if she lives too long we'll be talking about the added costs of putting her into a nursing home.'

Lorraine shuddered. With resentment in her voice, she said, 'If Mr Templeton had lived another decade, the bank's insurance might have provided extended health care.' She added sarcastically, 'If your piddly government job paid a decent salary . . . as it is, it barely pays enough for us to live on.'

Horatio's eyes looked vacantly into his computer screen.

'Yes, as humans we're supposed to cherish life,' Lorraine said softly, 'but when it comes to dependent parents, one can't help but consider their death as financial relief.'

Horatio turned away from his keyboard. 'I'd never admit it publicly, but you're right, dear.'

Lorraine waited a moment before she added, her voice lowered, 'And there is the cost of a funeral. It'll come sooner or later.'

'What about cremation?'

'Even then there are costs – the mortuary-use charges, the government permits, the expensive bronze urn, as well as having to buy into one of those vault places where you inter the urn.'

'You've already investigated?'

'A chat with a very understanding undertaker.'

Horatio thought for a moment. 'There are surely less expensive church-sponsored old folks' homes?'

'We talked about them when we had our family meeting back in Georgia, remember? But they're not that much cheaper.'

'Maybe she should live here with us,' Horatio said, his voice lacking enthusiasm.

'And sleep where?'

'I could build a room off the garage.'

'And pay for it how?'

Horatio held up an index finger. 'Maybe Toledo, now that he's made all that money, can help us pay for taking care of his grandmother.'

'A sad commentary,' Lorraine said. 'I'm the daughter caught in a club sandwich.'

'What do you mean?'

'I'm between three pieces of white bread – Mother Dear's generation, a worthless husband and my son.'

Looking downcast, Horatio said, 'He's multi-grain.'

'Speaking of rich men, where is that son of yours?'

'I'll phone the hotel,' Horatio absently remarked, picking up his operations manual.

'The hotel?'

'Oh, I forgot to tell you. Toledo arrived last night.' Horatio cowered, knowing the wrath of his wife was going to descend on him with the torrent of a summer mountain rain storm. He tried, 'Sorry, sweet, I was so engrossed in my computer I neglected to –'

'He called last night! And I was not told! You miserable. . . .'

Horatio was saved by the the ring.

'I'll answer it,' Lorraine said.

'Hi, Lorraine. Toledo. I spoke to grandmother. Katherine and I are taking Bambi Deer out for a New Mexican dinner this evening at six, a change of scenery for her. Will you and Dad join us at the Borrego Trail Restaurant on Canyon Road?'

'Who the hell is Katherine?' was all Lorraine could say, her face still red with rage at Horatio.

'Horatio knows her. She works for the state, too.'

'You don't say?' Lorraine's colour, like last evening's sunset, grew a fiery burnt orange as she continued to eye her husband.

13

Grace hurried as fast as she could into the Methuselah's Multi-Purpose Room. Already sitting with Carter Calhoun, their chairs pulled close to the round, green felt-covered game table, were two other men.

'Sorry to be late,' she said, 'but after that brisk morning walk and my breakfast, I took a little nap.' As she began to seat herself, she conspicuously set her small, pearl-handled purse on the table. Gesturing towards it, she said, 'My money's in there, boys.'

To greet her formally, the men slowly shoved back their chairs, placed the palms of their hands on their knees and pushed themselves up. The chivalry of polite gentlemen is so gallant, she observed to herself.

Still standing, Carter pointed towards the man on his left. 'Mrs Templeton, may I introduce you to Mr Undergroth? He lives in 320 and is quite a sly poker player.'

'How do you do.'

Carter's other hand went towards the second player as he said, 'And this is Mr Shields – he's from Greenfield, I believe, isn't that right Harry?'

'Indiana?' Grace said, looking directly at Shields, who, with obvious relief, sat down again. 'Greenfield is the home of James Whitcomb Riley, that famous folk poet.'

Shields nodded as if everyone knew, and promptly began shuffling the deck. Several times the cards spewed in disarray across the table, and the other two men had to help restack the deck for him. 'Yes, Mrs Templeton, I used to have a farm on Brandywine Creek,' he finally answered. 'That is, Mrs Shields and I did.'

'He sold the old homestead to move in here,' Mr Undergroth explained in a deep, grating voice that needed lubrication. So Grace would have the entire picture, he added, 'His grand daughter married an Indian from one of the local pueblos. Can you imagine?'

Shields shuffled again; this time the cards neatly melded together with a rapid-fire machine-gun sound, and when there was quiet, he said, 'Yes, Mrs Templeton, Mrs Shields and I used to gather our eggs and milk, drive our old Model "T" into the court-house square in Greenfield on a Saturday evening and sell our produce for pennies. Then we would park our car and, along with all the other farmers, watch the world go by. That was what one did on a Saturday night in Greenfield, Indiana.'

'And Mrs Shields?' Grace asked.

'She's passed on.' Undergroth replied for him. 'He was a Quaker till after she died. Now he's turned into an atheist.' He shook his head in disapproval.

Shields cut the cards a half-dozen times, then shoved the deck across the green felt towards Grace, looked her in the eye and said, 'No, I'm not, I just don't believe in this particular God. Another God, a more sensitive God, would never have taken my love from me. At least He could have offered some explanation, assured me she'd be well taken care of without me around to help, that is. Don't you think?'

Shields was bald except for a horseshoe fringe of straight white hair still lingering round the rim of his shiny head. He hadn't shaved for at least two days, Grace judged, and his shirt was unpressed and spotted. His hands, while obviously weathered from farming the soil over the years, equally as obviously needed washing. She wanted to take charge and shape him up.

But before she could say anything, he announced the rules for his deal. 'Deuces and one-eyed jacks wild, any pair bets, three-card limit to the draw, hundred-dollar limit per hand.'

'Now wait a minute, Harry,' Carter said. 'Mrs Templeton, I am sure, is not accustomed to such enormous stakes.'

Undergroth, the knot of his rumpled tie askew, two of his shirt buttons missing, his bare chest with its curly white hairs showing, croaked, 'He's joking, Carter, trying to impress the lady. He's not got a hundred on him.' His shirt where the buttons were missing pulled further apart as he spoke.

Carter was more neatly dressed, his wardrobe more antique, reflecting the formal Wall Street dress code he had been subject to during his career. While his dress and his polite mannerisms were positive male traits, the way in which he merged self-confidence with the twinkle in his eye attracted her. She found herself taking a fancy to him.

'My grandson Toledo will be visiting me later today,' Grace announced. 'But I shall play until he comes. He will be bringing his friend Katherine along for me to meet. I have a newspaper picture of her taken with Toledo when they were both speakers at an important seminar.' She retrieved the clipping from her purse and passed it around, saying, 'She is quite pretty, isn't she?'

'Is she Indian?' Shields asked, adjusting his glasses and looking at the picture.

'No, but I'll bet she's Mexican,' Undergroth grated.

'I believe I know her,' Carter replied. 'She's the one who manages the state's investment portfolio – a very bright Hispanic. Quite handsome young woman.'

'How do you know her?' Grace asked.

'She comes now and then to ask me about the 1920s and the 1930s,' Carter replied. 'I guess I am sort of a research resource for her about the stock market and its psychology, how investors *en masse* can panic, sell when they should be buying and vice versa. She's very inquisitive – asks questions about the market and international finance and –'

'No, Carter,' Undergroth interrupted, 'us old people are as out of date as the foxtrot. Things have changed so much I can't keep up. I've lost my place in life – like setting down a book you've been reading without marking the page. When you pick it up again, you can't find where you've left off.'

Shields slowly dealt them each five cards.

'The trick, Undergroth, is not to lay the book of life down,' Carter commented. 'You must be like the newspaper editor. To do his job well, he stays up to speed on all the stories going on, ranks them in importance in order to assign each its appropriate headline and select their various placements in the daily paper. That's how the rest of us know what news stories are vital and what are simply interesting feature articles.'

'Where are you from, Mr Undergroth?' Grace asked, steeling herself against his rasping voice, yet wanting to be polite.

81

He ignored her and retorted to Carter, 'You see, you are behind the times. They do it different today. There's television now, you know. They decide what is news based solely on what film they have. Murders, plane crashes, automobile wrecks, rioters being arrested. They can easily get film of those things, so that is what they show on TV. All their cameraman has to do is follow the police around. Gives distorted news, I say. People today are not informed, like they were in our time. That's why I tune out.'

'I bet ten cents,' Grace announced after carefully arranging her cards.

'Ed, here, was with the foreign service,' Carter said, gesturing with a card at Undergroth, in answer to Grace's question. 'So he's not from anywhere, and he's from everywhere at the same time.' Carter laughed as he gingerly plunked fifteen cents in the pot. 'Raise you a nickel,' and he winked at her.

'How did you happen to come to Santa Fe to retire, Mr Undergroth?' she asked.

He studied his cards, grimaced at their apparent collective message, haltingly produced a dime and five pennies and added the change to the growing pile in the centre of the table. Then he looked at her. 'I spent most of my life overseas in the diplomatic corps,' he replied. 'And I got to liking foreign countries, the charm of their old cities and the quaint customs of their people. In fact, I got so I didn't want to come back to this country.' He stopped, pulled a handkerchief out of his hip pocket and blew his nose, which was, Grace noticed, oversize, red and pock-marked. Probably drank a lot in all those diplomatic cocktail parties, she thought to herself.

Shields folded his hand with disgust, turning his head to Grace, signalling it was her bet.

'Yes, but you came to Santa Fe?' Grace asked, adding a nickel to the pile.

'How many cards?' Shields asked the others in the foursome.

'You see,' Undergroth began, 'I was so in love with other places, I wanted to retire in "another place". Santa Fe is the only place within the United States that makes you feel like you are in another country. I came here once years ago, and

82

I knew then I would return. Here I feel like I'm overseas again, back in the diplomatic corps, reliving my life. I even enticed Carter, here, to adopt Santa Fe as his home, told him he would have all the privacy in the world.'

Wondering why privacy was so important to him, Grace nevertheless asked only, 'How did you two meet?'

'When I was on assignment in Italy,' Undergroth said. 'Right after the war.'

'He was dispatched to Albania,' Carter explained to Grace. 'His mission was to set up diplomatic relations with the Communist government.'

'Yes, that's right,' Undergroth managed. 'But while I was there everything went wrong.'

Shields dealt three cards to Grace, retrieved her discards and patiently awaited Carter's decision.

Undergroth drank from his glass, which, judging from its golden colour, likely contained a dash of bourbon. To her great surprise Undergroth suddenly began reciting poetry:

> Land of Albania! Let me bend mine eyes
> On Thee, thou rugged nurse of savage men!
> The cross descends, thy minarets arise,
> And the pale crescent sparkles in the glen. . .

'Lord Bryron,' he quietly advised. Then in a louder voice, he continued, 'Carter and I were both trying to re-establish pre-war contacts in Albania, mine being diplomatic and Carter's financial. Right, old boy?'

Carter nodded.

'But the Communists took over?' Grace asked.

'Yes, but we and our allies supported them,' Undergroth said, shaking his head, still in disbelief at the deal history had dealt, clearly regarding the hand as a major diplomatic mistake. 'I told Washington and our embassy in Rome not to, but there was pressure during the war and afterwards from Churchill to be pro-Russian. That attitude soon changed, of course, but too late to save Albania and Eastern Europe. We wised up to Stalin's agenda much too late.'

He waited while Carter asked for two cards, and then continued, 'By the time I sensed what was really happening, the Western powers were thrown into the middle of a diplomatic crisis.'

'What happened?' she asked, finally picking up her cards and seeing to their proper arrangement.

Undergroth gravelled on. 'Two British destroyers plying the Straits of Corfu struck mines and sank, killing forty-four sailors.'

'Oh, my.'

'While the mines may have well drifted south from Yugoslavia, the British and everyone else in the West blamed Albania, demanding both apologies and reparations.'

Carter collected his two cards. Shields raised his eyebrows for instructions from Undergroth.

The retired foreign service man ignored the Indiana farmer, intent on continuing his story. 'Things went downhill from there on. The Albanians denied responsibility. The British took the matter to the International Court of Justice. Our diplomatic endeavours were bagged, and I had to leave the country – in a hurry, I might add. Like I said, everything went wrong.'

'What happend with the British?' she asked.

While Undergroth examined his cards, Carter spoke up. 'The Brits eventually won a judgment from the International Court. That august body decreed the Albanians to be guilty, ordered them to apologize and pay reparations.' Looking sternly at Undergroth, Carter's hand reached for his cane, lifting it off the back of his chair. 'End of story,' he said emphatically and struck the ivory tip to the floor, punctuating his statement with a period.

Ignoring Carter's demonstration, the diplomat blithely went on. 'The puppet Communist government, under the dictates of the Soviet Union, refused. The British put a hold on the Albanian national gold, which was stowed in a London bank vault for safe-keeping after being retrieved from the Fascists at the end of the war; gold that was mined from the foothills of the Albanian Alps in the 1930s. A lot, too – some eleven hundred kilos, as I recall.'

Grace looked at Carter. 'I think this golden story is still unfolding.'

'You're right, Mrs Templeton,' Undergroth said. 'The ruckus has never been settled.' He exchanged one card for a fresh, unknown one from Shield's ready deck. 'Your bet, Mrs Templeton,' he added.

'How much would eleven hundred kilos of gold be in real money?' Grace asked as she delicately added a dime to the coins in the centre of the table.

Setting the deck down, Shields suggested, 'First, convert kilos to pounds, remembering there are only twelve ounces in a gold pound.'

'I'll call,' Undergroth said as he rolled a nickel towards the pot.

'My turn, Harry,' Carter said softly.

'Uh, sorry, I got carried away with the math problem.'

Carter selected a liberty dime and announced, 'Raise, and you can't have your nickel back, Harry.'

Undergroth put another nickel in. 'Back to you, Mrs Templeton. Raise or fold.' And he chuckled.

'Thirty-one grams to the troy ounce,' Shields blurted out. 'Yes, that's the conversion factor.' He reached in his hip pocket and retrieved a brown envelope which had been folded four ways. 'Anyone a pencil?' he asked as he spread the envelope on the green felt.

Grace carefully laid her cards face down and reached for her purse. Rummaging through, she extracted a yellow number two pencil with red letters spelling *Methuselah Retirement Home*. She handed it to Shields.

'Thirty-one point one and some change,' Undergroth said. 'That's the precise rate.'

Shields looked annoyed, but wrote the number on the back of his envelope. Underneath he marked a large *X* and next to it a *12*, drawing a line below. Laboriously and carefully he multiplied the two numbers, mumbling instructions to himself as he went. Soon he declared in a louder voice, 'Three hundred and seventy-three point two grams in a pound of gold.'

'If we use four hundred dollars as the value of one ounce of gold, then a pound of the precious stuff is worth . . . how much?' Carter asked.

Grace spoke up. 'Wouldn't it be simpler if you all determined the number of ounces in the vault in London and then multiplied that figure by your four hundred dollars?'

Carter beamed. 'You're right, Mrs Templeton. You boys would never qualify as bank tellers.'

'Now, who can tell me how many ounces are in a kilogram?' Grace asked, picking up her poker hand. 'Mr

Shields, if you all had one of those new portable calculators, you'd get the answer much faster. My grandson carries one, but he's not due until later.'

Ignoring her, Shields selected a fresh corner of his envelope and drew a division box, placing a one, followed by three zeros and a decimal point and then two more zeros inside. He entered a 31·1 as the divisor to the left of the symbol. Mumbling louder this time, he set to work on his assignment. Before long, he loudly read his answer for all to hear, 'Thirty-two point one five four three . . . and I'm out of paper.'

'Very good,' Grace proclaimed. 'Now multiply that by eleven hundred, Mr Shields.'

The farmer turned the envelope over. Beneath the address and cancelled stamp he found space to enter his figures. After quite a bit of inaudible talk, during which they caught only the expression, 'carry the. . . .' which he repeated throughout his figuring, he announced, 'Thirty-five thousand, three hundred and sixty-nine point seven seven four nine . . . and I'm off the edge.'

'OK, now all we need do is multiply that amount by four hundred dollars,' Carter concluded.

'I'll call,' Grace announced, entering her five-cent increment to the pot. 'What have you got hidden there, Mr Calhoun?'

'That's barely fourteen million dollars,' Shields announced. He had opened the envelope and was using its insides for his mathematics. 'Why, that's not even enough to replace one of those sunken ships at today's prices.'

'Maybe you dropped a couple of zeros,' Undergroth suggested. 'Easy to do today with the long numbers governments use to account for their finances. Why, one zero dropped will add a hundred million to the deficit. Lose two, and I think you advance matters to the billion column.'

'A far cry from selling eggs for pennies on the square in Greenfield,' Shields said. He added in wonderment, 'Who would have thought in those days. . . ?'

'Yes, but had you leveraged that sum, Harry, borrowed against it, managed the proceeds cleverly, invested the portfolio astutely, you would have a hundred times as much today.' Carter smiled slyly, looked at his cards and announced, 'Three of a kind, Mrs Templeton. Three jacks, as a matter of fact.' He grinned triumphantly as he spread his cards face up on the felt.

Undergroth folded.

Grace beamed. 'Why, Mr Calhoun, this passive green felt table may have been host to many games in its illustrious past, but never has it seen lovelier ladies than these three queens. I do believe I've got you all beat.' She exhibited the three royal women, holding the triptych up several moments for the boys to admire. Then she slowly reached for the pot containing the coinage of the realm.

14

The Country, Albania, 1991

A country moves on through time, advancing from generation to generation, hoping to endure the foibles of each, to
survive and in a positive stance turn its face always towards
the future. In its love-hate relationship with the past, a
country savours the high points while trying to forget abusive
events. From its story a country will choose only memorable
happenings in the same way it selects only certain of its
leaders, whether political or artistic, whether generals or
scientists, to revere, to point to with pride – or, in the case
where history and global public opinion dictates, to lament
in shame.

The Country had endured more than its fair share of
infamy. Battered and abused, left poor and starving by the
brutality of its most recent leaders, The Country now faced
a whole array of problems, hopeful it was due for an entire
body of creative solutions.

Glowing from behind the Albanian Alps, this morning's
dawn hued the sky a sea of crimson. It seemed the devil
himself was over there to the east in Macedonia, decreeing
the coming day's redness – his way of advising The Country
that if it didn't sort out its problems, the hell of anarchy
awaited. Reminding itself so, The Country recited, 'Red skies
in the morning, sailors take warning.'

Only months before, The Country's long dormant soul
had stirred, the soul of free Albania ignited suddenly by divine
or devilish spark. And The Country's revolution had erupted,
rising up, boiling over and raging out of control. Within a
few days five decades of tyranny came to a halt.

This morning in the capital city of Tirana, The Country
watched a large crowd assemble near the fountains and pools

of the ancient Skanderbeg Square. Designed by Communist landscape architects to dramatize their manifesto, these water sculptures were now bone-dry, pleading for water in the same way The Country's new leaders yearned for political and economic solutions.

The crowd confronted a sprawling monument that had stood for forty-seven years commemorating Enver Hoxha. Upon its terracotta frieze, depicted in fantasized glory, was the 1944 Popular Front formed to fight the Nazis, the Monarchists and anyone else who might thwart the Communists from their goal of taking over a war-weary country.

Now, as The Country watched, two men with hammers and chisels scaled the monument and began to hack away at the face of the Communist dictator. Having beheaded Hoxha, they chiselled away at the faces of his lieutenants, turning the frieze into a marching assemblage of faceless flag-wavers, the rubbled clay from their faces falling amidst the crowd. The men then attacked the hated red star of Communism, prying it off as well.

The Country heard no cheers, saw no hoisted placards scrawled with slogans as these men assiduously pursued their destructive purpose. Virtually hushed, The Country's rank and file had assembled as if summoned spontaneously to this special place by a higher trumpet bellowing from three thousand years of Albanian history.

None of The Country's people hoisted a loudspeaker or even a megaphone, no one shouted in a controlling voice, no choreographer directed these players. The Country's struggling television station had no newscasters, so there was no live coverage. Accordingly, none of its people shouted into a camera, trying to broadcast their cause to a viewing audience. For there were no cameras. Clearly this was not a media event.

Weeks before, such an assemblage would have been forcefully dispersed by the secret police. This morning no former authorities who might have fired into the crowd to protect the memorial, to preserve law and order, to support the Communist regime, were in sight. Indeed, the throng likely counted many one-time protectors of the deposed government among its members.

Thinking back to 1944, The Country deplored its brutal

government with the dreaded secret police who had intimidated its people. With numbing threats the iron hand of a cabal of Communists had wantonly administered this beautiful land overlooking the Adriatic Sea.

Here in Skanderbeg Square less than a year after the Berlin Wall was pulled down, blazing the freedom trail for Eastern Europe, The Country's urge for self-determination had churned and then erupted. Barely weeks before in this same Skanderbeg Square, the tall bronze statue of Hoxha had been toppled by the collective effort of Albanian manhood. The Country's imposed government was helpless to suppress the public outcry.

And Albania, the final Communist nation-domino, fell – but not before, in a last-ditch display of gunfire, the police exacted the lives of dozens of The Country's citizens, qualifying them for membership in its exclusive club, the Cemetery of Martyrs, overlooking Tirana. Their memories now lay in that final resting-place across the narrow road from the royal palace of its former monarch, King Zog.

Statues of Lenin and Stalin that had long scrutinized its people as they walked the brick-paved boulevard from the square to Tirana University had followed in sequential surrender to The Country's revolution. Windows everywhere were poked out as if they represented the spying eyes of the secret police. Now the frieze of this last memorial, its Hoxha face pecked away, joined the bone-yard of discarded memorials that lie broken and dismembered in that place in history's hell where oppression must surely roast for ever.

How, The Country pined, could its government have been so bad? How could its leaders, who had the dictatorial power to establish and implement programmes ranging from medical care and education for all to an efficient system of farm-produce distribution, along with the building of the national infrastructure, have been so wrong, and so corrupt, for so many years? The Country felt downcast at the thought of having allowed such a history to have been written. Yet what is a country to do, it asked itself. Does a country choose its leaders?

And how could those leaders in their omnipotent power have instilled a paranoia upon its people that justified the construction of tens of thousands of concrete pillboxes across the country? The Country found itself chuckling as it remembered the bizarre and unbelievable story. 'A defence,' its Communist leaders had said, 'against the threat of an imperialistic American invasion.' As if mutant glands scattered from Mars, these grey concrete blobs appeared across The Country's landscape, ubiquitous breasts with gun-slots for nipples. Worse – The Country's chuckle quickly turned to tears – years of its gross national product had been squandered on useless eyesores.

The Country knew the task of removing these pillboxes would require a spending spree of impossible proportions. Apart from a popular notion of converting them into tiny, vibrating discos, the only sane idea seemed to be to paint them as huge watermelons – the country's national crop – and feature the *faux* fruit on travel brochures as juicy, tasty treats for tourists who might some day be lured to investigate this long-isolated nation.

The threadbare carpet of Communism having been yanked from underneath, The Country wondered what might be in store. The brick pavers in the square stared up in flat reality as plodding but happy pedestrians crossed them, going about their lives, now free, but leaderless like children let go at recess, never to be recalled, their teachers having left.

On this hot and humid August morning, the clock, set in the campanile of its capital city, receiving its first light, showed a few minutes past five. Next to the clock tower, the needle-thin minaret of what had been the Mosque of Etham Bey – before the Communist atheists shut it down – rose as a fraternal twin to an equal height. Perhaps the mosque hoped – if religious sanctuaries are able to do so – now that the Communists had been overthrown, its tiny balcony might again be used by holy men to call the Muslim faithful to prayer. Yes, if The Country could hope, it concluded, so could its mosques, so could its mountains, so could its orchards, and certainly its people.

Indeed, The Country observed, popular energy was reviving the Muslim and Christian faiths throughout the land. No longer was it a declared atheist state. Clergy could wear their sacred garments openly, and the doors of mosques and churches were being opened once again to the faithful. The Communist ban on religions had failed to deliver the intended final knell of death.

In the early-morning shadows cast by the two spires, groups of citizens sat in open-air cafés, sipping weak tea and smoking cigarettes. During the long xenophobic night, the secret police, sipping and surveying from these same tables, had looked out over Skanderbeg Square, spotting and then apprehending any citizen who might dare speak to a foreigner. Now anyone could drink here and converse with foreigners without fear of reprisal.

Gaggles of small children also wattched for the by now not-so--unusual foreign visittor. Spottting a prey, they would swarrm around the tourist, the reporter, the diplomat or occasional businessman as persistentlly as the Albanian flies. The boys would beg for gum, pens, leks, lire, dollars or drachma, even pointing to the T-shirts some touristss wore, asking to receive tthem, as well.

Of the multitude of critical issues soiling the nation, the arguments in the cafés around the square centred on the most immediate: widespread food shortages, undernourished children, reopening the schools in the fall, lack of gold to back the currency in international marrkets, mass unemployment, a high birth rate, the floundering government, deplorably crowded and inadequate housing, or how some day people might afford to buy cars now that the ban on owning them had been lifted. Even the fishing fleet had fled to Italy or Greece, the small boats carrying refugees looking for work had not returned with fish . . . had not returned at all.

Yet The Country felt about as weak as its own tea to resolve any of these problems. As the dawn brightened, The Country's consternations, expressed by its people's arguments in the cafés and elsewhere, grew in intensity.

There were no cars in Skanderbeg Square. Even at this early hour and in the oppressive heat, hundreds of Albanians walked across the square, trouser legs rubbing or full skirts swishing, to what few jobs still existed – mostly in nearby government offices – or to buy produce from vendors who had ridden into town on bicycles or donkeys from their outlying garden patches. Squatting by the streets, these free farmers presented melons, vegetables, straw brooms and meat on whiich the flies rushed to feast. Others sought out the kneeling croupiers, joining them and their spinning arrows as they pointed to numbers or pictures pasted on crude boards – a kindergarten-level game of roulette.

A bedraggled bus, seats long since ripped from their moorings, windows poked out, looking like the morning local from hell, rolled across Skanderbeg Square, Tiranis clinging to its rusty superstructure. Seeing the crowd setting upon the hated memorial, passengers raised their arms, index and middle fingers extended, euphoric 'V' signs reaching skyward. Surely, they thought, all of Earth would take notice and sanction their revolution. Pursuing its own agenda, the bus's horn tooted a warning to pedestrians who gave way, the urgency of the vehicle's passage across the square rivalling that of the rebellious crowd.

Entering from a side-street, a pollution-spewing Chinese lorry weaved through the walkers with a cargo, not of goods, but rather of riders. Its fading thirty-year-old blue bodywork contrasted with the bright new blood-red of a government Albturist Peugeot taxi, the lone car in the square, its interior offering the only air-conditioned space in all of Albania.

Free at last, The Country was euphoric, but its people were hungry – especially families whose fathers had gone off to Greece or Italy to seek work. Those who stayed behind had now been joined by the thousands who had been returned by the other countries – with the result that almost the entire male population remained jobless and idle. The Country despaired in its early morning angst, because the mass unemployment came at a time when the list of work to be done was the longest in memory.

From brick smokestacks in Tirana's periphery, a thick gaseous black belched into the valley confining the capital city, a shroud of pollution from those few factories still operating – testimony to the Communists' disregard for The Country's precious environment. As well, the stately trees lining its rural lanes had been cut for firewood for the coming winter.

The Country knew members of its newly elected parliament pondered how to prepare the nation for the reality of revolution's aftermath. At this moment they were debating how to finance reconstruction, while opening up a free market economy. The farmlands, held so long by the Communist government, must be returned to the farmers if there was to be free enterprise. Should outside opportunists make their fortunes out of this chaos? No, the people wouldn't stand for land-grabbers.

The Country sensed it was momentarily in the calm eye of a storm. Forthcoming events – it dared not predict in what form or force – were likely to engulf it in tempests of unknown strength as the coming winter bora blew in from the Adriatic Sea, bringing hunger and cold.

Did the answer lie in the rumoured proposal by Prince Leka, son of King Zog and Queen Geraldine, to pay one thousand US dollars to anyone who would vote in a referendum to return and restore the monarchy?

Perhaps The Country agreed more with the common people who said the answer lay with America – rich America, officially considered their enemy for generations. That blind hate – along with atheism – was being put aside.

Hadn't *The New York Times* just weeks before on its front page pictured a smiling and waving US Secretary of State visiting Skanderbeg Square? Hadn't his advance people seen to the distribution of thousands of tiny little American flags? Its three hundred thousand curious citizens who gathered in the square had waved the Stars and Stripes in front of the American television cameras and the world press corps. Surely this visit and all those flags were harbingers of American support.

Yes, The Country felt as it contemplated its future, it agreed with the common people whose fledging new leaders fervently expressed the belief that The Country's solutions were 'Made in America'.

15

Greeting an Indian woman from San Ildefonso Pueblo in the portal of the Palace of Governors, Katherine pointed to a particular turquoise and silver piece displayed on her blanket. 'Maria, may I see that one?' she requested.

Maria caressed the bracelet with a polishing cloth. 'You like the traditional design?'

Katherine bent over to look closely at the rest of her jewelry. 'Don't drip green chilli onn Maria's beautiful work,' she warned Toledo.

Admiring the jewelry, Katherine said to Maria, 'I'll take the turquoise bracelet.' Then she turned to Toledo, who was munching a blue corn burrito with Anasazi beans and extra-hot chilli from Hatch. 'Don't you think it'll be perfect for your grandmother?'

'Should my grandmother beware of Greeks bearing gifts?' Toledo asked. 'Or are you planning to twist her arm with the bracelet to induce her to reveal the secret of the gold's location?' He laughed. 'I know, you're planning a Chinese water torture with green-chilli sauce.'

'Be serious.'

'Seriously, she'll love Maria's bracelet. Come on, let's be about picking up my Bambi Deer for our night on the town.' Taking her arm, Toledo escorted Katherine across the plaza. He called her attention to where the heraldic banners were flying. 'Yours is the most impressive,' he told her.

'All our families, along with the priests, ran their own show in this capital city until the Indians revolted in 1680 behind their leader, Popé.'

'I know about this guy Popé. His mistake was he failed to manage the New Mexico territory properly and after a dozen years the Spanish were back.'

'You should have been here to help Pope' forge a powerful Indian nation.'

Past the Cathedral of St Francis, she led him through a wooden gate and along a pathway. They crossed a footbridge over the Santa Fe River, climbed a stone stairway and made their way to the front entrance of the Methuselah.

Along the way, tourists with maps unfurled asked for directions to restaurants and opinions about art galleries and museums. Katherine offered succinct responses and the visitors went off, still confused by Santa Fe's crooked streets.

'You know all the short cuts,' Toledo commented.

'Over the meadow and through the woods to Grand-mother's house we go,' she said.

'Oh, and by the way, Grandmother's going to have a full house tonight.'

'What do you mean?'

'You and I, Lorraine and Horatio and Carter Calhoun. I arranged this dinner for you to study my grandmother, say hello to Carter and meet the telegrapher and the key she's been pounding on all these years.'

'You've dealt too many cards for the hand. Grand-daddy Thatcher's secrets are going to have to wait for a more intimate occasion.'

'How about a Sunday picnic? I promised Bambi Deer I would take her to Glorieta Pass tomorrow.'

'Excellent.'

Outside the Methuselah the tour van was filling with residents. On its door a hand-written sign read, *Evening adventure to Pink Adobe Restaurant.*

The Activities Director, helping residents aboard, saw Toledo, smiled sweetly, and said hopefully, 'Venturing out with us this evening?'

'We're in our own circle tonight, thank you,' Toledo replied.

Inside the Methuselah, Grace was sitting in her favourite South-West chair. From its vantage point she could monitor everyone coming and going.

Seeing her, Toledo stopped, removed his stetson and threw wide his arms.

At his exclamation of 'Bambi Deer', she rose to be engulfed within his gentle bear-hug. Drawing back, he appraised her.

'You're looking very royal,' he observed.

'Oh, I have so much to tell you,' she said. 'And I am so anxious for you to meet my gentleman friend. I am sure you will like him. And this must be Katherine – I feel I know her.'

'Katherine's in charge of the state's investments – stocks and bonds,' Toledo explained.

Grace nodded, accepting Katherine's greeting hand. 'Mr Templeton knew the difference between stocks and bonds.'

'So do you, Bambi Deer,' Toledo said. 'You don't have to play the woman's game of innocence any more – it's out of style.'

Grace chuckled. 'One is equity and one is debt. Isn't that right, Ms Mondragon?'

'Please call me Katherine.'

'Then you must call me Grace.'

'Not "Bambi Deer"?' Katherine asked.

'My daugher and son-in-law insist on calling me "Mother Dear". And Toledo, since he was a dear little boy, has shortened it to "Bambi Deer".'

'Perhaps I should call you Grace, too – especially with your new life,' Toledo suggested.

Katherine presented her with the jewelry. 'Here's a little present for your evening.'

Grace looked at the silver and turquoise bracelet and exclaimed, 'For me? Oh, what a splendid thought!' She slipped the bracelet onto her wrist and looked at Katherine for her approval.

'You see, Toledo, it is perfect for Grace. The turquoise picks up her blue eyes.'

'I'll treasure your gift from this enchanted land and be in harmony with life around me,' Grace said, pleased.

'You are happy here?' Katherine asked.

Grace looked around the lobby and saw Carter Calhoun. She waved at him and whispered to Katherine, 'The people I have met are fun, especially the men.' She chuckled. 'And here he comes now. You know, we're even on first-name terms,' she whispered.

Carter greeted Katherine with a bow, kissing her hand, his practised courtesy well executed. 'So nice to see you again, Ms Mondragon. Our State of New Mexico funds are in such capable hands.'

Grace introduced Toledo and the two men shook hands.

'Yes, Mr Squires, your grandmother has told me about you and your very successful business venture.'

'Please call me Toledo. I like it better.'

Katherine laughed quietly. 'Reminds him of architectural splendour.'

'I've always thought names important. Good ones live on,' Carter said.

'So do some of the bad ones,' Katherine pointed out.

'Ah, right you are, Ms Mondragon. To be written on the dark pages of a country's history. But I believe the good ones endure longer.'

'I cannot endure my hunger any longer,' Grace interrupted. 'Let's go to our restaurant. Oh, and tell me, what does Borrego mean?'

'It is named after the old sheep-herders' trail from Taos,' Katherine replied. 'Vital to the economy here in the last century.'

'The sheep were replaced by tourists,' Carter said. 'Much more profitable for the town.'

'I'll call for a taxi,' Toledo said.

'It's already taken care of.' Carter gestured towards the entrance, where a white limousine waited, its uniformed driver standing at attention.

'Oh, what fun,' said Grace. 'I've never ridden in such a luxurious car. A taxi once when Mr Templeton and I took our vacation trip to New Orleans. And that's been. . . .' She tried briefly to calculate the number of years but was distracted as Carter helped her into the back seat.

'Borrego Trail Restaurant,' Toledo said to the driver.

'Yes, and on the way, loop up the Old Santa Fe Trail so we can catch the sun setting on all the adobe houses,' Carter added.

Toledo turned to Grace. 'There's still enough daylight to see the view.'

'Of one of the seven cities of gold,' Carter said, and winked at Grace.

16

The limousine stopped in front of what at first appeared to be a vernacular adobe house. In the dusk a small spotlight focused on a wrought-iron sign depicting the skull of a sheep. The glistening light from candles seen through the small window-panes hinted at food and conversation awaiting.

Toledo opened the carved wooden door. In the entry room a log fire warmed them, for the mountain evening was already turning cool.

'Cosy fire,' Grace said, gesturing at the burning logs. 'I love its pungent aroma.'

'Piñon,' Carter said.

They were led through several rooms of the restaurant – none was very large – to a private dining-room, its low ceiling supported by wooden *vigas*. A raised *kiva* fireplace in the corner generated prismatic flames. The table was set for six, with as many votive candles, anticipating their arrival. In the centre was a small vase of yellow chrysanthemums, set atop a cutting board in the shape of a howling coyote.

As they sat down, Toledo said, 'Lorraine and Horatio should be along any moment.'

'Katherine, did you choose this charming place for our evening dinner?' Grace asked.

'Yes, I thought you would like our old way station, Grace. Wagonmasters and sheep-herders alike probably drank, ate and engaged in lively discourse here, for this is where the Borrego Trail met the Santa Fe Trail.'

'Then let's have a toast to the meeting of your generation and ours.' Grace looked at Carter and smiled.

Toledo called the waiter.

The water looked closely at Toledo. 'Aren't you Toledo Squires?' he asked. 'Didn't I see you on the TV talk show?'

Toledo smiled. 'Yes, you may have – a few nights ago.'

Eagerly the waiter rushed on, 'I'd sure like to talk to you. I have this great idea for a chain of South-West-style restaurants – "Fanny's Fast Fajitas". . . .'

'The name's a winner,' Toledo said. 'But you really need to talk to a venture capitalist, not me.'

'Right now, my man, we'll have your best champagne,' Carter said.

Returning promptly with the magnum and six glasses, the waiter expertly popped the cork and poured four glasses. 'Two more coming?' he asked.

'That generation may not be represented tonight,' Grace said. Raising her glass, she toasted, 'To Toledo and Katherine. May you travel happily through life.'

Clinking his glass with hers, Toledo responded, 'To Grace and Carter. May our trails be as didactic as yours.'

'Speaking of generations,' Katherine said, 'my generation thought we invented communes. Is your generation copying us? I know the Methuselah doesn't think of itself as being a commune, but nevertheless you have all come from many different places to live together.'

'Carter once lived a Bohemian life,' Grace said. 'I guess you would have called him a hippy.'

Carter laughed robustly.

The waiter brought menus and announced, 'The soup this evening is yellow squash and our special is herb-roasted leg of lamb with a kiss of the chef's special vegetable salsa. I'll be back in a minute to take your orders.'

'I can't imagine you as a Bohemian, Mr Calhoun,' Katherine said.

'Well, that was years ago when I lived in the Village – creative times indeed, writers, poets, artists – but then all times have their own chroniclers.'

'It's a good thing, too,' Grace added, 'because memory can be elusive.'

'There are some memories we just can't erase,' Carter said.

'Well, my first memory is of my christening,' Katherine offered. 'My father was holding me. We were surrounded by my mother, aunts, uncles and a covey of cousins. Bright sunlight streamed through the stained-glass window of the Cathedral of St Francis. This bespectacled man in a snowy-white robe dipped his hand into what I later learned was holy water and touched my forehead. I didn't understand his chant-like voice at the time, of course, but I knew what he said must be important for when he spoke my family fell quiet and listened to every Latin word.'

'The day must have been glorious for your father, one he would always treasure,' Toledo commented.

'Let's not get too sentimental tonight,' Carter said.

'But Carter' – Grace reached over and touched his hand – 'I told you the younger generation feel free to express their feelings – not repressing them as we have been accustomed to doing.'

Carter frowned. 'But this sentimentality is getting a little too ripe for me.'

Grace touched Katherine's hand and announced to the others, 'It's obvious Katherine and her father have been very close.'

'He and I were quite different,' Katherine said, picking up on Grace's surreptitious plea for help in mollifying Carter. 'Yet as I grew up we were able to communicate intuitively. Even when I went away to college I still felt his silent touch.'

'And his love,' Toledo said.

'But, Toledo, how would you know what a father's love would feel like?' Carter objected. 'Seems to me we're delving into more sentimental rot.'

'Maybe so,' Toledo said, 'but if we don't acknowledge our familial ties, we'll sooner or later find ourselves alone in life, perhaps even embittered. I may not feel a close affinity with my parents – we don't have all that much in common – yet I don't exclude them from my life.'

The waiter returned, pad and pencil in hand.

Grace began, 'I think I'll try your special, and the soup sounds good.'

'Me, too,' Katherine echoed.

'Bring me the soup, but instead of the lamb, I'll feast on the vegetable salsa,' Toledo said.

'The special for me,' Carter ordered as he collected their menus and handed them to the waiter. 'Three of us made it easy for you, son.'

Grace broke the silence that followed. 'Toledo, you have more compassion than I do.' She paused. 'If we're learning how to express our true feelings this evening, then I have to say I can't stand your parents.'

Toledo's jaw dropped. 'But, Grace. . . .'

'Lorraine reminds me of my father's attitude toward life – brutal and self-centred.' She laughed. 'But I'm being facetious, aren't I, Toledo Dear.'

Carter chuckled. 'You're certainly not being sentimental about your daughter and son-in-law.'

'You surprise me, Grace,' Katherine said.

'I'm simply expressing my deep-down feelings. Isn't that what your generation does? So why can't I enjoy those same freedoms? All my life I've had to toe the mark, never allowed to say what I truly think. That's what Miss Crawford taught us – observe the social graces to the neglect of speaking your mind. Lives were supposed to be illustrated in a perfectly bound volume. I honoured her credo – as a daughter and then as a wife. But those chapters of my life are written, read and set aside. Now I want to turn the page and hopefully find new heroes and a new story line.'

'But we can learn from the past,' Carter said. 'We can't close it off. It's with us whether we want it to be or not, welcome or unwelcome. I just don't want to gush about it.'

'You're talking about taking an objective look,' Toledo began.

'Like when we study history,' Katherine interrupted. She nodded at Grace and Carter. 'Tell us firsthand how Clio, the Muse of history, has influenced your lives.'

'Yes, good idea,' said Toledo.

'Well, then, I'll ask you Carter: haven't you and I seen a lot of changes in social behaviour down through the years?' Grace queried.

Carter forced a smile and replied, 'Indeed, and we've had a hand in bringing about those changes. You know' – he looked at Katherine – 'you asked me about my so-called Bohemian life . . . well, I've always thought of my generation as riding the second wave of transcendentalism – for we, too, sought our version of ultimate reality. Our actions, believe me, upset the whole apple-cart of what most people at the time subscribed to. For example, the strict Victorian dictates – the remnants of which Grace was taught in her school – were pretty well ignored by us young people in the Roaring Twenties. We regarded ourselves as free-thinkers, but we came to be called by the misnomer "free lovers", because a vocal crusader for women's rights, Margaret Sanger, was concurrently reproving the Victorians by disseminating birth-control information.'

'I have images of women with their new bobbed hair and short skirts dancing the Charleston while the stock market ran amok,' Katherine said. 'Tell us how you felt in the Roaring Twenties – what you did.'

'Well,' Carter began, 'with the advancements in birth control, women and men felt a new freedom of expression – not the promiscuous behaviour predicted by critics. We believed – I certainly did – that the two concepts, marriage and freedom, were compatible and could be pursued together.'

'In my day marriages were thought to be made in heaven,' Grace said. 'And when they were not so blessed, you tried to make the best of it.'

'That was the difference between your life in the South and mine in Greenwich Village. We thought we could have it both ways.'

Grace regarded Carter with curiosity. 'I'd have given anything to have had such an opportunity.' She paused before asking him, 'Did you actually discover such a real freedom?'

Carter smiled, hesitated, and said, more to her than to the others, 'Yes, I did, and you know, I felt no guilt then, and damn it all, I still don't feel any remorse.' He looked again at Katherine. 'And I do not need your bespectacled priest to seek absolution.'

Katherine looked puzzled.

Toledo's eyebrows rose.

Carter returned his attention to Grace. 'My only regret is that I have never seen the son – my only son – who was the expression of my freedom.'

The waiter brought the soup.

17

'My son,' Carter said, speaking out loud to the deserted early morning Methuselah patio, 'how would I recognize him? He would be the same age as Grace's daughter. Would I like him? He and I would be worlds apart – having nothing in common. He grew up with the Communists in a sequestered country. Maybe he would hate me for abandoning his mother. I could explain. . . . But why did I even mention him last night? Why did I make an ass of myself?'

'You didn't, my dear Carter.'

Startled, he turned to see Grace approaching.

'You provided yourself with a genuine reason to become a participant,' she said.

'By playing the fool?'

'Go back to Albania, look up your son, and get directly involved. Therein lies the new challenge you've been searching for.'

'That's impossible. Albania was another time, another place. You can't go back again.'

'But you can go forward to find your son,' Grace said, and started to walk. 'Why else did you mention him last night? And why didn't you then go on to tell us about him?'

'It was 1939. . . .'

'Of course, the war. Why don't you tell me about your son as we walk? There's no point in keeping secrets any longer. I've decided to share mine.'

'Yes, I suppose you're right, Grace.' At the fish-pond Carter paused. 'My son's name is Ardian. It's so hard for me to talk about him. You've got to understand what Albania meant to me during that time.'

'I'll try.'

'As I told you, my association with King Zog began in 1927 after he became king. Those were happy years for The

104

Country. I was his loyal consultant right up through the time of his wedding to Queen Geraldine in 1938, and continued in this business relationship until the king's self-exile following Mussolini's invasion the next year.'

'That was when Queen Geraldine was forced to flee with her newborn son, travelling at night along narrow roads. . . .'

'Through the rugged Acroceraunian Mountains, escaping to Greece,' Carter said. 'Yes, history took a wrong turn, for up until then the future looked so bright for The Country.'

'But you're getting ahead of the story,' Grace pointed out. 'What about your life? You started to tell us last night about pursuing freedom within marriage.'

'Yes, but I didn't realize the consequences. I didn't want to hurt anybody. But I found myself wanting to spend more and more time with this woman. And then one day as she and I were walking through the ancient castle overlooking Gjirokastër, I realized I'd fallen in love with her. Ardian was born the same day as King Zog announced the birth of his son.'

'Two babies born from love,' Grace said as they walked together. At Carter's sand-painting map of Albania, still fresh, she asked, 'Were you with her when she gave birth to your son?'

Carter grasped his cane, his knuckles turning white. His jaw muscles tightened. He looked down and said almost inaudibly, 'No.'

He straightened up, looked at Grace and said, 'Let me explain what happened. King Zog had warned me of the worsening Italian situation and asked me to conduct some financial matters for him while I was in London. I was headed back to Albania when Mussolini invaded on Good Friday morning in 1939.

'Come next Easter your son will be fifty-three years old.'

'Has it been that many years? It seems only yesterday when King Zog and I talked about his dreams for the future of Albania. He drove his own car, you know, actually one of the few cars in the country. So whenever I was in Tirana, he would drive down the hill from his royal palace, and we would enjoy a get-together in our US Embassy. In those meetings we discussed the country's finances. And he also shared with me the knotty problems he was having with the

Italians – they were constantly meddling in The Country's affairs.'

Carter went on with his reminiscing. 'Zog was every bit a king – tall, a commanding presence, cordial, yet firm, in charge but still able to make a visitor feel at ease. How well I remember one particular visit with him late in the summer of 1938 at his resort in Durrës overlooking the Adriatic. On the veranda we discussed Italy's objectives. He knew they were trying to take over The Country, may even have suspected they might act militarily. So by royal decree, he entrusted me with the Albanian gold – its custody and its management.'

'So you were given control over The Country's treasury?'

'Stewardship, I would describe it.'

'Is this the same gold that Mr Undergroth told us about during our little poker game?'

'Yes.'

'The eleven hundred kilos?'

'It's a great deal more than that now. I have used the gold as a nest egg, so to speak, borrowed against it and invested the funds in the stock and bond markets. Down through the decades the portfolio has grown to . . . ah . . . rather enormous proportions.'

'And you're still in charge?'

'Yes. I manage it, with some help from my banker in London. It is a blind account. By that, I mean no one knows whose account it is. Only Archibald McThomson and I know of the Albanian connection.'

'But your more important Albanian connection is your son. I am sure he would understand that under the circumstances there was no way for you to contact him until now.'

'Yes, I couldn't even write. After the war the secret police would arrest anyone talking to or corresponding with a Westerner. Albania became a hermit among nations.'

'Carter,' Grace interrupted, 'since you feel history should have turned out differently, let's compose a new chapter, even if it is only a paragraph, perhaps even only a sentence.' She smiled. 'Carter, use the gold to help King Zog and Queen Geraldine's Albania. They would have liked that, wouldn't they? And your British banker will support you – won't he? How much money are we talking about?'

'Given the success of my investment strategy over the last fifty years, a total of, let me refresh my memory. . . .' He unscrewed his cane's ivory tip and extracted a rolled sheet.

Grace saw it was a computer printout.

'This report from London is a week old,' he said apologetically.

'From now on you . . . we must receive daily reports.'

'I'll arrange it,' he vowed.

18

'Glorieta!' Toledo exclaimed. 'What a day for our picnic on Glorieta Pass!'

'Glorieta, what a night!' Katherine said. 'I still can't get over Carter having a son he's never seen. Up until our dinner conversation I thought our generation gave rise to the sexual revolution.'

'You've been blinded by boomer centrism. Last night Carter gave us an eloquent explanation of romantic egoism and self-liberation – from an historical and personal point of view.'

'You're telling me I must transcend my generation?'

'Yes.'

As Katherine mad a left turn and directed the car along the Alameda towards the Methuselah, her thoughts turned from Carter's bastard son to Toledo's Albanian quest. She asked herself if perhaps his plan wasn't equally illegitimate. And what about her dream? Wasn't it a premonition of dire consequences for Toledo if he continued to pursue his Don Quixote adventure?

Finally she was unable to constrain herself any longer and said, 'Toledo, you must put away these windmills of fantasy for Albania. The people there have been anaesthetized by almost a half-century of Communist Novocaine.'

'A good way of putting it.'

'Now that they have been awakened from their national coma, they'll come alive, they'll be a colony of ants whose quiescent hill has been disrupted. And they'll run frantically in all directions.'

'That's right. And they'll need leadership provided by those who know how to manage and run a country. They'll require fresh points of reference for their lives – lighthouses to show the way out of their dark national night. Just think of the leadership skills of our team. Imagine with me –'

'Talk about my centrist attitude, you're expressing the typical New York–California point of view – the manifesto that says they are way ahead of everybody else, they've got some super-duper deftness, a special ability that only the two coasts possess.' Katherine turned into the street leading to the Methuselah.

'I say we can carry it off,' Toledo persisted. 'I don't delude myself. None of us do. We know it is going to be difficult. If it were easy, everybody would be doing it.'

'But, you see, you wouldn't have the connections. Let's use New Mexico as an example. Here, to be politically successful you'd have to get support from and consensus among groups such as the old Hispanic families up in Rio Arriba County, the scientists from Los Alamos, the pecan farmers in southern New Mexico, the cattle ranchers in the Catron, all the state and federal government employees, the hotel and restaurant industry, not to mention the Indians of our twelve pueblos and the military-industrial interests in Albuquerque.'

'A good list.'

'For you, Albania will be like unwrapping Pandora's box. You'll encounter factions within factions, each with their own agendas. Your team will be so headstrong you won't understand the local mores, the little innuendos, the subleties of people and place. You'll be trying to deal with so many forces, I fear you'll fall flat on your collective faces.'

Katherine wished she hadn't expressed herself in such a tyrannical manner. Was her performance a cover-up for not revealing her dream? Nevertheless, she dismissed her dream as superstitious poppycock.

'*Esprit de corps* is a very powerful force when properly directed,' Toledo argued. 'Our team will be well disciplined by our various individual experiences. We'll be organized as we move in, execute our take-over and put our own people in their proper administrative positions. Given effective symbolism, flags, banners, slogans and the endorsements we'll arrange from spiritual and political leaders, we'll be off and running.'

'And how is it again you're planning to win over these native leaders?'

'With grandmother's gold. The universal persuader.'

'Speaking of which,' Katherine said, 'there she is waiting on the bench at the Methuselah entrance, picnic basket on her lap. And with the wine you brought we're ready to do a little persuading of our own.'

Helping his grandmother into the car, Toledo said, 'How about the rumble seat, Bambi Deer?'

'Glorieta! Wouldn't that be fun?' She smiled at Katherine. 'Good morning, Katherine, you look very pretty for our Confederate bivouac.'

'Good morning, Grace. I'm looking forward to hearing all your grand-daddy Thatcher's Civil War stories.'

Toledo's mouth dropped.

'Once upon a time when I was a little girl sitting on Grand-daddy Thatcher's knee, he gave me a little-known account of what took place at the end of the War Between the States. Toledo, you and Katherine are too big for my knee, but the time has come for me to share this secret of 1865.'

As they drove towards Glorieta, she began, 'The story as told by my grand-daddy Thatcher, who was passionately partisan, goes as follows: in April after news of the courageous General Robert E. Lee's surrender pealed from the bell at Appomattox court-house across the Confederacy, Jefferson Davis, fearing for his life, was compelled to flee Richmond and head for Texas. Grand-daddy Thatcher said he had a plan, a fantasy I suspect, to re-establish the Confederacy there. But I have read where President Davis did have dreams of preserving Southern culture which had been torn asunder by the war. Of course, to pursue his crusade seriously he knew he needed money – not worthless script but real money – gold. Consequently, Grand-daddy Thatcher and a small platoon of soldiers were ordered to guard the Confederate treasury, which consisted of the Southern gold, jewelry that had been contributed to the cause and valuable European banknotes.'

'I remember Ashley's wife donating her wedding ring,' Katherine said.

'And Scarlet O'Hara was obliged to do the same,' Toledo added.

Grace nodded and went on. 'The night he got word from President Davis to cradle up the treasure and load it onto a train and head for Texas, he commandeered an engine and some old coaches and worked his men round the clock in the task of loading so many heavy crates.

'Grand-daddy told me there were two trains that night. His train loaded with dozens of crates pulled out of the station just before the besieging Yankee troops descended on Richmond. And a second train carrying Davis and members of his cabinet escaped with only moments to spare.'

'Didn't they have to pass through Union lines?' Toledo asked.

'Yes, so they travelled by night. Most were weary of war and downcast at defeat. Even Grand-daddy's countenance, he told me, was shaken. Quiet souls who had lost their country and their cause, many of them were utterly lacking in force of character. Even today, remembering Grand-daddy Thatcher's words, I can see soldiers, hungry, dirty, unshaven, sick of war, wanting to be paid, yearning to return home to their little farms, see their families, their wives, their children.'

At Glorieta, they selected a picnic table overlooking the battlefield. From her basket Grace handed Katherine a gingham tablecloth which she unfolded, shook and spread out on the table while Toledo uncorked the wine.

After a toast to those brave men of both sides who had died at Glorieta, Grace continued. 'On the fourth night when the trains paused along the Savannah River, a pack of lawless and crazed soldiers broke into one of the crates. Beholding the spectacle of riches, they became so intoxicated they scooped up handfuls of coins and jewels, so much in fact that in their haste to escape with their bounties, coins and jewelry fell from their pockets as they scattered into the night down dusty cart roads into those endless pine forests of rural Georgia. They dropped small fortunes that present-day treasure hunters continue to seek.'

Toledo's story, Katherine now marvelled to herself, was not a comp'te fantasy. There actually had been, or maybe still was, a Confederate treasure.

'Wasn't Jeff Davis captured in Georgia?' Toledo asked as he sketched the skirmishes of Glorieta on a pad of paper, showing the Union troops in blue and the Confederate in grey.

'Yes. The new Yankee President, Andrew Johnson, issued

a warrant for his arrest. Union troops caught up to Davis and imprisoned him along with Vice President Stephens.'

'But he was released later?' Katherine asked.

'Yes, finally. And spent his last days with his wife Varina at Beauvoir, a country estate on the Gulf Coast,' Grace said. 'He wrote books.

'Well, their situation having grown precarious, President Davis and is cabinet decided to hold one last meeting to rally their cause for the rest of the journey to Texas. Washington, Georgia, a town to the south and west that General Sherman had bypassed, was the logical place for their rendezvous. Grand-daddy Thatcher was supposed to give over the treasure to a bank, but could not find one where he thought the valuables would rest safely. You can imagine the possible treachery. A quarrel arose as to what to do with the treasure. When they reached the Georgia town, Grand-daddy Thatcher chose to entrust the gold to a highly respected general – bidding him vow diligence in keeping it safe for the glorious day of the rebirth of the Confederacy.'

'Which general?' Katherine pressed.

Grace sipped her wine. 'He said I could always remember the general's name by thinking of his home.'

'Why his home?' Katherine asked, her voice gentle, leading.

'Because that's where he lived.'

'Yes, but where was the house?' Toledo said.

'Oh, it continues to exist today. In New Orleans – the French Quarter. I remember. A woman – a writer – bought it.' Grace thought for a moment. 'Her name was Frances Parkinson Keyes. I've read her books – *Dinner at Antoine's* was one.' She raised her finger and said, 'But the gold isn't there.'

'What was this general's name?' Toledo pressed.

'Beauregard. General Pierre Gustave Toutant Beauregard. Miss Crawford made us memorize his full name. And she said because he was an ardent student of the French Emperor, Napoleon, he was called our own "Napoleon in Grey".'

'What became of General Beauregard?' Katherine asked.

Grace finished her wine and took a bite of sandwich. 'Lorraine has photographs of Grand-daddy Thatcher in uniform,' she said proudly. 'They had cameras then. You ask your mother, Toledo, to see his pictures.'

'But Beauregard?' Toledo said. 'If the gold's not in his old house in New Orleans, where is it?'

'West, like I said,' Grace replied.

'But do you remember, Bambi Deer, what became of the gold?' Toledo tried once more.

"Yes, of course I do. Grand-daddy Thatcher told me General Beauregard went to California to . . . Santa something or other.'

'Santa Clara or Santa Barbara?' Toledo asked.

'Barbara, yes Barbara.' Grace hesitated. 'Wasn't she the saint confined to the tower by her pagan father because she disobeyed him?'

'Yes,' Katherine replied. 'She is our saint who defied her father and spread the word of Christianity. I have her *santos* at home. She's depicted in her tower prison seizing a lightning bolt.'

'Yes, Santa Barbara,' Grace said. 'General Beauregard acquired land there and was planning to build a house and grow grapes for wine making.'

'And he took the treasure with him?' Toledo asked.

'Yes, to protect it. Grand-daddy Thatcher finished his story by telling me how Beauregard, thinking no one would ever look out West, buried the gold beneath his vineyard. The general's judgment turned out to be correct, because everyone searched in Washington, Georgia, and even as far east as the banks of the Savannah River.'

On the return to the Methuselah, Grace said, 'Our sojourn to Glorieta has indeed been a fanciful outing.'

'Yes, I've also enjoyed our picnic,' Katherine said.

'And thank you for sharing Grand-daddy Thatcher's secret with us,' Toledo added.

As Katherine drove into Santa Fe, Grace began, 'You know, my new friend, Carter Calhoun. . . .'

'Yes, he's a very interesting man,' Toledo said.

'More than that, he is quite wealthy.'

'He does radiate an air of affluence,' Katherine agreed.

'It is not air. His investments are as solid as gold.'

Toledo's eyebrows rose.

'What do you mean?' Katherine asked.

'Before the war, Carter became a financial advisor to the Albanian king, the husband of my dear friend Queen Geraldine.

My, isn't it a small world? We have Confederate gold in California, and Carter has just told me about what he called the Albanian national gold.'

'Where is it?' Toledo asked, trying to control the eagerness in his voice.

As Toledo helped her from the car at the Methuselah entrance, Grace said, 'Oh, it's in a London bank vault.'

19

The closer to the top of a bank's skyscraper headquarters, the larger and more ostentatious are the executive office suites. In San Francisco, one floor from the top, John Axminster, an executive vice-president, attired in a three-piece Italian suit of Loro Piana fabric, removed his polished leather wingtips and slipped on the latest technology in lightweight running shoes. He examined his official entry for the upcoming Bay to Breakers race and ran his fingers over its number – '85,910'. He considered doing a quick change – donning his California Bear Flag Republic racing shorts and then running laps around his spacious office.

But the head of the international banking section might pop in unannounced. He had the habit of showing up and sitting on the edge of Axminster's desk while interrogating him on European matters ranging from monetary to monarchical. Better, Axminster concluded, to remain properly attired and save his running for after banking hours, when he could zip along the waterfront of San Francisco's Embarcadero. One more evening of logging in eight miles and he'd be ready to race on Sunday.

So instead he sat quietly, employing the latest self-actualization technique learned at the most recent management seminar for senior bank officers. He formed visual images, not of making money for the bank but rather of himself finishing first among the hundred thousand runners. And while at it he also took time to fantasize about becoming personally rich, really rich and powerful. Why not? he thought to himself, 'We are what we think!' those psychologists at the seminar had asserted.

He was interrupted, however, when his secretary transmitted the beeping code – two shorts and one long – to alert him there was a call from an important customer.

'John Axminster,' he said, his formal, icy greeting signifying he was ready to consider but not necessarily grant the forthcoming financial request. Assuming an aloof demeanour allowed him to remain noncommittal no matter how seemingly justified the borrower's plea. This gave him time to consider the customer's supplication, along with its ramifications – for the bank and for how he would look in loan committee as its advocate.

But this particular incoming voice rumpled his poise by asking, 'Is it true, Axy, there are two kinds of men: those with imagination – worthy borrowers with clever and well-thought-out business plans – and those who lack esoteric traits – stingy lenders who hold the purse strings?'

Recognizing his valued customer, Axminster said, 'No, Toledo, there are the dreamers who are so far out with their line that they require the second group to reel them back to reality.'

'Well, if we can't agree on the male population, wouldn't you say there are two kinds of women on our planet – one to love and one to lust for?'

'In banking, these days, when women apply, we have to be equally opportunistic. We male loan officers see our assignment as securing each advance with our extended collateral.'

'Then it follows,' Toledo said, 'that whether one is a borrower or a lender, the overriding purpose of money is sex.'

"Or underlying.'

'But money is only a prop really, showing how those with imagination have prevailed.'

'How is that?'

'They've succeeded in getting everyone else to agree that a piece of paper with no intrinsic value has all the worth in the world.'

'Then by your definition money is a fantasy, like lust, while its opposite, love, is akin to gold which, it follows, must be the real substance of life. And we bankers have the gold.'

'And we borrowers the lust for it.'

'And that is the purpose of your call,' Axminster stated, the tone of his voice promptly on guard.

'Sighted swimming ahead are two schools of these golden fish,' Toledo replied. 'I need your help in reeling them each aboard our ship of state.'

'Two?' Axminster said, betraying surprise. 'That's a one hundred per cent increase. And if netted, I suppose you want not to double, but instead quadruple the dollars available to your team from your line of credit?'

'At least that much,' Toledo said. 'A wise man once said, "With the tool of leverage, mountains may be moved."'

Axminster re-examined his running shoes. 'We'll talk about it Sunday morning, say about seven – down on Howard Street, corner of Speer.'

'The odds of you, or me, winning that race, are as remote as –'

'You and your cohorts taking over and running that Eastern European country.'

Toledo laughed. 'As a matter of fact, our team is meeting secretly tomorrow in Santa Fe.'

'You've progressed quite a ways since we last spoke?'

'Yes, I've a full complement. . .'

'Carter?'

'Yes,' Toledo replied proudly. 'I've reserved the Sangre de Cristo Ski Lodge for the occasion. Appropriate, I think, for our momentous beginnings.'

Axminster chuckled. 'He'll feel right at home in Camp David West even if it is off-season.'

'When I see you in San Francisco I'll fill you in on the other members.'

'Meet you at the race start then?'

'Yes, Sunday morning on Howard Street – you'll find me hoisting an Albanian flag. Look for the double-headed eagle. With your help, the nation it represents will soon be a democratic free-market showcase.'

20

In a ponderosa pine forest high in the Southern Rockies, the mountain lodge in which Toledo's team was about to gather presented a contrast to his Merrill Lynch board of directors meeting in the plasticity of the five-star metropolitan hotel conference room.

In an atmosphere of being up in the clouds and electric with enthusiasm, his team members sensed they were at the point of embarking on a very special mission. Attaché cases clutched, they walked briskly along the pine-needle-covered trail from the gravel car park. As they entered the rustic lodge, a massive stone fireplace with its blazing fire anticipated roaring discussions.

Greeting them, Toledo pinned to their lapels a serrated name badge in the form of a replica of the 1938 Albanian postage stamp depicting King Zog and Queen Geraldine. He turned to Katherine and presented each stamped member.

'Myra Andersen, our economist,' Toledo said.

Katherine smiled. 'Myra and I know each other,' she said.

Myra and Katherine kissed one another as Myra explained to Toledo, 'Katherine and I go way back. She and I were at Stanford together. I admire the smashing job of portfolio management she's doing for New Mexico. I'm going to have our patriotic TV inquirer Hortense Alger invite Katherine for a go at it.'

'As you favoured me,' Toledo said.

Ms Andersen chuckled. 'Sorry I missed your appearance. I hear you stole the show.'

'The best part wasn't on camera.'

'Are we videotaping our discussion today of how we project Albania's monetary policy and her currency exchange rates? Or are we still in a covert mode?'

'The plan to date is strictly confidential. Only those of us

118

here know,' Toledo said, 'plus, of course, John Axminster at the Bank of America.'

'Naturally,' Myra said. 'He's financing us.'

Suddenly a man with a decided military bearing bounded up and reported for duty. Hoping this time to avoid being slapped on the back, Toledo ducked behind Katherine as he introduced General Goforth, his fellow Merrill Lynch board member.

'I am prepared to give the latest report on the political-military situation when called upon,' the general announced. He then moved inside, his eyes darting back and forth, seeming to devise a strategy for taking the conference room.

The woman who followed carried a maroon attaché case embossed in gold letters *Health, Education and Welfare* and was introduced as Ms Hewit. Katherine recalled her stint at HEW in the Carter administration, where she had continually advocated that most problems, whether social or political, global, national or local, could be solved by application of the basic conventions of health, education or welfare. In her post she had repeatedly called out to Congress and the press 'to just HEW it'. She quickly became known as 'Ms Hewit', lovingly by some, with disdain by others. The media nickname had stuck, even after the next President from the other political party replaced her. To Katherine, Ms Hewit's reputation, with her Ph.D., her astronaut husband, and her three children still in nappies, suggested she was really 'Superwoman'.

Next came a grey-haired man with a styled haircut and an impeccably tailored suit. Toledo introduced him as 'Claremont College Professor Emeritus of Political Science, Vasily X. Posin.'

'I thought professors wore dishevelled sweaters with leather elbow patches, smoked an old smelly pipe and wore socks that didn't match,' Katherine said.

'Yes, that's a good stereotype, Ms Mondragon,' he said, and chuckled. 'But when I fled the secret police of Marshall Tito's Yugoslavia, I elected to be a nonconformist in this country as well.'

Arriving behind the professor was a woman whom Toledo introduced as 'Ines Stark'. She shook Katherine's hand vigorously.

'If you ever need a good legal negotiator,' Toledo said, 'I recommend Ms Stark. She was brilliant helping me negotiate the sale of my company to Merrill Lynch.'

Accompanied by two secret service men – obvious, Katherine thought for their eyes searched every person and every object in the room – came former President Jimmy Carter. Impressed, Katherine eagerly shook his hand. She looked at Toledo and whispered, 'You weren't kidding.'

Setting his fly-casting rod inside the entrance, the former President said, 'What a spectacular location. Everyone I know wants a chance to visit Santa Fe.'

Directly off the great room with its chandelier fashioned from elk antlers was the dining-room. The walls were decorated with twenty pairs of rawhide and wooden antique snowshoes. In the other direction was an intimate library with a collection of books on the American South-West, ranging from archaeology to Zozobra. Here they poured themselves cups of coffee, took seats around the centre table, and gave their attention to Toledo.

'Every country looks to its citizens, hoping those individuals who are motivated to become leaders will act for the good of the people,' he began. 'Yet some countries racked by oppression may come up short on human resources and have to reach out to those countries overflowing with talent.

'We adventurous people who are responding to the call and exporting ourselves afar will be following the footsteps of Fulbright scholars, Peace Corps volunteers and Crusaders of all time. We will be called upon in today's free-market world to enhance the process of enterprise. But we will do more. To quell the ill winds of The Country's history and to weave a fabric of mutual respect with dialogue between the generations, we will draw upon The Country's heritage, whether fantasy or reality, and the riches of national gold, whether legend or fact.

'And now to give us an historical perspective, Ms Hewit has asked to go first.'

Ms Hewit opened her case and extracted a sheaf of notes. Sitting beside her, Katherine read the caption *Albanian Meeting – Issues to Stress.* Beneath was her outline:

A) Health:
   1. Medical Clinics
   2. Nutritional education
   3. Parental planning.

B) Education:
   1. Head start for preschoolers
   2. School lunch programme
   3. Adult education for women and men

C) Welfare:
   1. Retraining for new jobs
   2. Child care facilities
   3. Equal job opportunities
      a. Equal pay for equal work
      b. Women's rights
   4. Domestic violence
      a. Battered wives
      b. Child abuse.

Katherine's attention was diverted from the notes by Ms Hewit, who, setting her list of issues aside, began to speak.

'What I am going to tell you is the story of King Zog.' Reciting from memory, she began: 'During the Turkish Empire, tribal chiefs were compelled by the Sultan to send their sons to far-off Constantinople to live and go to school. Under threat of military retaliation, the Sultan's invitations could not be refused, therefore effectively assuring allegiances from the hinterland.

'Picture a darling little seven-year-old dressed in his finest suit and wearing a fez on his head. Ignoring instructions not to make eye contact upon meeting the mighty ruler, our bold one unhesitatingly stared up at the All-Powerful One. He was also told to prostrate himself, but he only bowed, showing deference but not submission, respect but not capitulation. The fire in his eyes impressed the sovereign.

'In a commanding voice the Sultan said, "Tell me your name, boy."

'"Ahmed Bey Zog, son of Xhemal Pasha, descended from four hundred years of virile chieftains, twenty generations of dynastic rule from the castle of Burgayet."

'"You are a young man with a strong will. I like that."

The Sultan bellowed to his court, "I appoint this lad adjutant to my son."

'The young Zog replied, "I will be subservient to no one – others will be adjutant to me!"

'Unfortunately, Zog's behaviour this time stepped over the line and the wrath of the Ottoman Empire came down. Issuing another proclamation, the ruler banned him from court, confined him to a tiny house when not being schooled and limited him to an entourage of only two loyal tribesmen from his Mati Valley home in Albania.

'And thus Ahmed Bey Zog was introduced to his bleak years in Constantinople, longing to return to Albanian soil, where his widowed mother, Sadije, had promised that when he reached manhood, educated and cultured, he would become their tribal chief. At seventeen, he realized this goal.

'Soon thereafter the Turks withdrew from the Balkans and Albania became independent. At nineteen, after Austria-Hungary retaliated for the shooting of its Archduke in Sarajevo, igniting World War I, Zog became an officer in their army. Two years later he was elected president of an Albanian patriot group called the Committee of Initiative.

'And following this event our Zog became Prime Minister of Albania, but not for long in this turbulent Balkan republic. Ousted by a coup, he sought exile in Yugoslavia, where six months later he led a loyal band of supporters back into the country. Communications were meagre and his makeshift army relied upon the sound of their own cannon fire to signal their attack, stretched out as they were along the rugged mountain border. . . .'

'Visual signalling never works, believe me, I know from experience,' General Goforth said, shaking his head.

Ignoring him, Ms Hewit continued. 'His horde advanced on the puppet government of Harvard-educated Albanian Orthodox Church Bishop Fan Stylian Noli.'

'What was a Harvard man doing in Albania in the 1920s?' the general asked, interrupting again.

The smile never left his face as the former President said, 'We even have them in Georgia.'

'Noli was an idealist,' Toledo suggested.

'Aren't we all,' Ms Hewit commented.

'We don't need ideology here,' the general said, 'we need competence.'

Ms Hewit frowned and went on. 'True to his academic training, Noli had set forth a detailed list of reforms. Believing he alone had the answers, he shut down Parliament and, to assure an iron hand in implementing his reforms, instigated martial law. Free elections might have legitimized his regime and encouraged foreign powers to recognize his government.'

'Can't have a real country without diplomatic recognition,' the former President stated. 'The Confederacy proved that. Like Albania, the South needed endorsements from England and France.'

'The Confederacy,' Myra Andersen said, 'should have known better. They hadn't sufficient gross domestic product to compete with the industrialized North.'

'As his retinue marched on to the coastal plain,' Ms Hewit went on, 'our charismatic Zog, a magnet marching through paper-clips, attracted beys and tribesmen to his force. On Christmas Day 1924, Ahmed Zog, aged twenty-nine, and his diverse army entered the tiny new capital city of Tirana. He proclaimed himself President, an act confirmed by the reconstituted Parliament and legitimized by elections. Recognition from the international community duly followed.

'Zog survived several assassination attempts – actually fifty-five – during his life. Once, while entering Parliament, he took three bullets. Wounded and bleeding, he delivered his speech while supporters rounded up the assailant, whom he later pardoned. From that incident, his reputation took on the mystique necessary for royal leadership.

'In 1928, after suppressing another coup, Zog decided the only way to get matters under control was for him to become King Zog I. . . .'

'I can understand that,' General Goforth said, his swagger stick upraised in an exclamation point.

Ms Hewit continued her story. 'Still single at forty-three, Zog announced that he was now ready for marriage, confirming the rumours circulating among the European royal families. Tirana, not an easy place for travel in the 1930s – no trains, and the mountain roads were slow, narrow and treacherous – was abuzz with the hoopla of the social scene.

'On New Year's Eve 1937, Geraldine Stewart, regarding

her chances as remote, wore her simplest dress. She spoke seven languages, but neither of the Albanian dialects. When they met an hour before midnight in the royal palace, she toasted the king in German. She was so enchanted with His Royal Highness she promptly dropped the royal champagne glass. It broke into royal pieces, spilling the royal champagne on the royal carpet. Distraught, she just knew he would dismiss her without another thought.

'Somehow her simple dress and her straightforward manner, even with the royal spill, captivated King Zog. With aplomb he soothed her and asked her to remain into the new year. They conversed daily, with her aunt acting as chaperone. They toured Albania and he pointed out its riches. Following the whirlwind courtship, he proposed to Geraldine and she accepted. Their 1938 wedding ceremony was a momentous event for all of Albania and everyone wept for joy.' Ms Hewit retrieved a hankie from her purse and blew her nose.

General Goforth looked away, his hand rising to cover his face.

The former President's eyes were watery.

Myra Andersen stared into space, trying to deal with emotions that could not be shown on a graph.

Ms Stark appeared impatient.

Katherine looked at Toledo.

'Dark clouds hung over this wedding, however,' a sniffling Ms Hewit resumed, 'as Italy's Fascist dictator, Benito Mussolini, dispatched his son-in-law, Count Galeazzo Ciano, with elaborate wedding gifts. The story has it, that many of these gifts would never be unpacked, for the Italian military aggression followed barely nine months later.'

'On Good Friday, wasn't it?' President Carter said, shaking his head in disbelief. 'Can you imagine that irreverent, evil Mussolini launching an invasion on a sacred Christian day?'

After a respectful pause, Ms Hewit continued. 'The most ostentatious of King Zog's wedding presents was the scarlet 1939 Mercedes convertible with soft white leather interiors and side-mounted chromium-plated exhaust pipes – a gift from Adolf Hitler – and was even more impressive considering there were few cars in Albania in 1938.'

'Hitler!' President Carter exclaimed, his smile vanishing. 'Surely our King Zog wasn't a friend of that Antichrist?'

'Who would refuse a valuable motor car?' Myra Andersen said. 'After all, you could turn around and sell it for real money.'

'Through the next twenty-two sad years of exile during World War II and the beginning of the long Communist rule of Enver Hoxha, the royal family led a nomadic existence, ending with the death in 1961 of our great king, Zog I.' Ms Hewit said, concluding her narration. Then she unexpectedly added, 'You may either believe or not believe any of this story. Your choice. I personally don't put much weight on any of it.'

Astounded, the others stared at her in dismay – except for Professor Posin, who began to smile.

'What on earth do you mean?' Ms Stark demanded to know. 'Have you been misleading us?'

'No, of course not,' Ms Hewit said. 'When I began, I told you mine was a story. And that is exactly what it is – a legend from out of the past, a legend like the one about their fifteenth-century hero, Skanderbeg, who fought the Turks.'

'Yes, separating legends from the discipline of history is an academic necessity,' Professor Posin said. 'Our team needs to know, however, what the uneducated citizens of the land believe in order for us to accomplish our objectives.'

'My point exactly,' Ms Hewit concurred. 'I just didn't want you to believe I was presenting an historical white paper.'

'For us, then, what are you saying?' Ms Andersen asked.

'The truth lies in reality. And reality is the situation that exists in Albania today and tomorrow. For us, the unadulterated facts are going to be awfully hard to get a handle on. I'm simply saying we must involve the local people or we're going to be as removed from reality as is this fanciful legend I've narrated.'

'Exactly, we need the local connections,' Professor Posin agreed.

'Thank you, Ms Hewit, for presenting your impressive message so cleverly,' Toledo said. 'We have our work cut out for us, but we are all up to the task. Now Professor Posin has some remarks from the political science point of view, don't you, Vasily? Perhaps they'll shed some light.'

'Yes, I do have some formal material I've prepared, but first I'd like to comment about legends of the past. The popular axiom that history repeats itself is pure bunk.'

Several gasped.

'You're ignoring the lessons of history,' General Goforth said. 'After all, General Patton always sought the ancient battlefields for guidance.'

'I say life is chaos in the sense there is no order, and I say the same about history,' the professor continued. 'For example, Russian Communist intellectuals were not constrained by history. They didn't think it would repeat, or they would never have taken the actions they did. Instead, they'd have concluded the Czarists would put down their uprising.'

'I take exception, professor,' Ms Stark said. 'We would never have pursued the women's movement of the 1970s if the messages of Elizabeth Cady Stanton and her intimate friend Susan B. Anthony had been ignored.'

'All I'm saying is that now it is our turn to make history, and we must not fail in husbanding the aftermath of revolution in Albania.' The professor paused. 'Now, for the record, I'll give you my prepared material. The country's independence in 1912 was regarded by most observers as a mistake. The little country had no formal written language, was divided by different dialects. The population was almost entirely illiterate. During their centuries-long rule, the Turks promoted feudal-like land holdings. As such, no educated urban class developed from which government officials, teachers, intelligentsia, diplomats, bankers and entrepreneurs could be drawn. And we all know these sorts are essential to a viable country. And so at Versailles when the European powers were redrawing the map, they devised a plan to partition Albania, awarding the north to Yugoslavia, slicing off the south – known as Epirus – to Greece, and giving her coast to the Italians, who longed to annex it, turning the Adriatic Sea into their private lake.

'But President Woodrow Wilson objected. Otherwise, there would be no Albania today. So you can see there is a precedent for Americans becoming involved in the Albanian Question.'

'Exactly, and history will repeat itself,' General Goforth said.

The others laughed.

Toledo rang his spoon against his coffee cup. 'Let's hear

more about how Albania responded to outsiders trying to usurp their autonomy.'

'I'll tell you the story of William of Wied, spelled W-I-E-D,' the professor said. 'After the European powers backed off from partitioning the country in 1919, they cast about for someone to run it, for there was no local leader acceptable to them. They found a German prince by the name of William of Wied, who agreed to serve as titular head of the embryonic government. Well-intentioned and honourable, he was, as they suspected, unable to govern. By then President Wilson was ill, and America had not joined the League of Nations, so the powers reasoned that they could revive their sinister plan of partitioning Albania.

'As an outsider, William soon found himself facing threats to his life from tribal chiefs. He lasted only a few months before fleeing – luckily still in one piece. But the European leaders hadn't counted on Zog and his followers, who took the reins of power.'

'Now there's an idea for you,' General Goforth said. 'We could induce the United Nations to invite us in to establish an orderly government.'

'We couldn't even get an audience with the UN, General Goforth, let alone an invitation,' the professor replied.

'The point is,' Ms Hewit said, 'if we don't follow my advice and seek support from within, we'll end up being ousted from the country as abruptly as the professor's weed from Wied.

'All your points have been noted.' Toledo looked at the attorney and announced, 'Ms Stark will now trace the legal heritage of the country.'

'The legal system was known as *fis*,' Ms Stark began. 'Don't ask me what that means. But it was an unwritten code based on the teachings of a legendary medieval male, Lek. One could simply say "Lek says", as the Chinese quote Confucius, and justify anything. This uncodified doctrine superseded the male-dominated scriptures of the Bible and the Koran. I think they would have been better off had they practised witchcraft.

'In this patriarchal society, blood feuds between men could spring up over the least triviality, to be resolved only with the murder of one or the other. Women did not engage in these blood rivalries because their blood was thought to have no value.

'Marriage was contracted for in childhood and dowries were partly paid, the balance to be given at the ceremony – provided the woman remained a virgin. By custom, a bride's innocent status was investigated and vouched for by a male doctor. Even into the 1930s a husband could shoot his wife for infidelity without anyone questioning his authority to do so. After marriage women were likely to carry guns.

'Though they had no civil or property rights, women really made the important decisions for the family, as well as performing most of the work. When King Zog and his royal retinue were in exile near Ascot, safe from the London Blitz, Queen Geraldine cultivated their large vegetable garden. Zog forbade his male cadre from physical work. So you can see the inbred traditions we will be up against in our desire to transform the country.'

'Thank you for a splendid summary of the role of the sexes,' Toledo said. He nodded to Jimmy Carter. 'Please give us your wisdom, Mr President.'

The Georgian waved his hand in the air, some thought as a call to order, others interpreting his motion as a nervous swat at a south Georgia gnat inadvertently brought along with him.

'Like all of the Balkans,' he began, 'the heritage of Albania has been both colourful and complex since Skanderbeg united Albania in the fifteenth century.

'Now we have peace. And recognition of sacred human rights. Our next step, my fellow Americans, is to forge a modern nation.'

Toledo applauded, and the others stood to give the former President a ceremonious acknowledgment.

21

General Goforth promptly leapt forward. Experienced in war-room presentations, he adeptly tacked up a topographical map of the Balkans, so large it covered several shelves of books. The brass tip of his swagger stick found the former Yugoslav province of Kosovo on the north-east border of Albania. Radiating the contagious fever of manifest destiny, the general began:

'Two million people – almost as many as live in Albania, ninety per cent ethnic Albanians – live here in Kosovo in what is today a province of Serbia. Treated as second-class citizens by their Serb rulers, they are ripe for unification with their Albanian brethren.'

He moved his pointer to the west, towards the Adriatic Sea. 'Still more Albanians live here in Montenegro and' – moving his pointer south – 'also here in Macedonia. So you see, Albania's existing borders are unnatural and illogical, presenting us with an opportunity to enlarge the country to at least twice its present size. We must seize this propitious moment! The removal of Kosovo and these other Albanian ethnic areas from crumbling Yugoslavia can be accomplished before anyone lifts a howitzer to interfere.'

'He's serious about territorial expansion, isn't he?' Katherine whispered to Ms Hewit.

'Very, I'm afraid,' was her worried reply.

The gleam in his eye growing as bright as when a boy manoeuvres toy soldiers, the general marched ahead with his battle plan.

'We'll privatize the collective farms, award everyone a workable parcel, giving incentives for Albanians everywhere – from London, Detroit, Boston and Houston, for instance – to repatriate, while at the same time providing a reservoir of manpower for our army, should circumstances arise.'

'He knows damn well he'll create those circumstances,' Ms Hewit whispered to Katherine.

'As to armament,' General Goforth eagerly continued, 'these days you can't have a country – no matter how small – without several squadrons of modern tanks equipped with the latest in communications equipment and fire-power. That is, if a ruler's going to exert his authority, restrain riots, keep the people in line – present an image of law and order.

'As history tells us, our best defence is offence. We shall, steadfast in our resolve to provide a homeland for all Albanians free from foreign interference, bring about a militarily powerful nation and unilaterally secure our boundaries.'

Perspiring, the military man charged to the coffee-pot and poured a full mug, which spilled over the rim.

'Food for thought, general,' Toledo said. 'Thank you very much for your intriguing plan, which has certainly broadened my perspective. Our first order of business may well be the passage of a Monroe Doctrine for Albania.' Turning to Myra Andersen, Toledo asked, 'Does your economic analysis address the ramifications of emulating the foreign policy of James Monroe?'

'The International Monetary Fund would much rather see a policy of balancing The Country's budget than having us go on a spending spree for new weapons while ignoring recognized borders.' She looked at her notes. 'OK, let's get to the bottom line. History, culture and the military may have their place, but a country must be financed on a solid footing, its currency accepted worldwide.

'In Albania our problems stem from both an outmoded economic practice and a substandard transportation infrastructure. For an example of the latter, a poor road system limits the market for farm produce, confining it to local villages. With farm plots small and distribution limited, farmers are on a treadmill to nowhere.

'Moreover, the country never enjoyed a nineteenth-century railroad boom as did other Western economies. None was built until 1947. Even today, cars and small trucks are a rarity, their ownership having been banned in the past by the Communists.

'Now, when we aquire Toledo's promised gold, we can begin to remedy the transportation problem. The bullion will become the backing for our new national currency, gaining for us international financial recognition and credit. The Bank of America, as John Axminster has committed them to do, will promptly activate our line of credit, giving us dollars to run the country – call it seed money, if you like.

'Providing our governmental budget is in balance and we're not spending money on foolish things, such as those silly concrete pillboxes the Communists built, or expensive tanks and missiles – we'll be off and running, for the IMF will advance us a low-interest-rate long-term loan, enabling us to upgrade our outdated industrial base.

'We'll reactivate our gold and chromium mines, re-equip the offshore and onshore oil wells and refineries. We'll join the European Economic Community, allowing tariff-free trade with Europe.

'Most important perhaps, our supply of competitive labour will attract manufacturing companies. Since our costs will be lower, instead of "Made in Taiwan", the label, "Made in Albania" will become a worldwide norm. New industry will dot the countryside.

'Trucks will ply a network of new superhighways, delivering manufactured goods and farm produce to our refitted port cities of Durrës and Vlores for shipment to international markets. We'll add computerized traffic control to the railroad and acquire new freight cars. We'll lengthen the runways at the Tirana International Airport, allowing for jumbo transports.

'This economic growth and tapping new markets will please the IMF, who will allow us even more credit. With still more money we'll construct high-rise resorts along the Adriatic beaches south of Durrës, replacing the run-down Communist hotels and the abandoned villas of their ousted party leaders. We'll sell time-share penthouses to American yuppies looking for the ultimate in chic foreign travel adventure. We'll build rustic chalets overlooking the well-stocked mountain lakes of northern Albania, attracting fly-fishermen from Western Europe and Japan.'

'Going to get some fishing in, Jimmy?' General Goforth quipped. 'Tell me, do you tie flies differently outside Georgia?'

'There'll be time for hobbies once we've been inaugurated,' the former President replied.

'You haven't seen anything, they tell me,' Ms Andersen

continued, 'until you watch northern Europe drain south to the Mediterranean beaches and cool upland mountain resorts in the summer. And if we legalize gambling – which we'll have the power to do with the stroke of our pen – think of our profits. Move over, Monte Carlo and Las Vegas!

'For you two, Toledo and General Goforth, Merrill Lynch will be eternally grateful that you presented them with this whole new vista for earning underwriting fees. Profits from financing these new ventures wil not be peanuts.'

At the word 'peanuts', President Carter passed around a small burlap bag. 'Boiled . . . ever tried them boiled?' he asked.

Ms Andersen took one, bit into it and made a face. 'And thus our refitting of the Albanian economy will be complete,' she concluded.

Her look seemed to dare anyone to pose a question. 'Have you located the gold?' she asked Toledo. 'You are about to deliver good news, aren't you? An economist can do only so much with mirrors, promises, rhetoric and computer-generated models.'

Toledo nodded and said, his voice reassuring, 'Thank you all for your contributions to our meeting. As promised when you each expressed interest in this great plan of ours, I *will* produce the gold. Strange as it may seem, my grandmother knows where the trove is stashed.'

'Grandmothers are our blessed legends,' the former President said. His smile seemed locked as he added, 'In this constantly changing world, with their grace and purity, they are the Rock of Gibraltar.'

22

Late that night on the second floor of the Methuselah, the repeat of three soft steps could barely be heard along the carpeted hallway. Two were slippered feet and one was the point of an ivory-tipped cane trekking towards the welcoming miniature coach light outside apartment number 215. With his walking-stick Carter Calhoun now tapped out a quiet staccato rhythm on the door.

Grace had just finished lighting the last of two dozen tapered candles, chuckling about how after dinner she had sneaked into the kitchen of the Great Hall and salvaged twenty-four basketed Chianti bottles from the recycling bin for candle-holders. Now every shelf and every table top in her living-room and bedroom glowed with great expectations.

When his cane spoke, she graciously opened her door.

He smiled, perhaps a little nervously and started to speak, but Grace touched her fingers to his lips and embraced him. Their kiss was delicate. No whiskers scratched. And the fragrance of his cologne affirmed his attentiveness to her senses.

They stood together for what seemed like a long time. 'Just being by your side has become what is important to me,' Carter said.

She winked and said, 'You didn't ask me how I managed to drink all this Chianti.'

Carter laughed. 'Must have been quite a picnic with your grandson.'

'Toledo can't hold a candle to you in your silk robe. How handsome you look to me tonight.'

'Why, thank you.' He touched her gown. 'Satin and lace accentuate your endearing qualities.'

Holding hands, they stepped into her living-room and Grace said, 'Please have a seat while I turn on some music and bring you a little glass of brandy.'

'Do you mind if I look about?' Carter asked.

'Please do.'

He read the titles of her books, selecting a small suede-bound volume of Robert Service's *Ballads of a Bohemian*, published in 1921 by Barse & Hopkins, New York. Holding up the book for her to see, he called, 'Is this how you've been checking up on me?'

Grace returned, smiled and handed him the brandy snifter. She switched on a tape deck, and Nelson Eddy and Jeanette MacDonald joined them with *Ah, Sweet Mystery of Life*.

Carter inhaled the brandy bouquet as he peered at the framed oil-painting by Georgia O'Keeffe of a single red lily.

'That's a house-warming present from Toledo,' she said.

Carter sat down beside her on the couch. 'Grace,' he began. His voice was suddenly more serious.

She looked into his blue eyes and searched his face. Her eyebrows rose in a responsive query.

His face moved closer to hers. 'You and I. . . .' He ran his hand through his silvery hair. He hesitated only briefly before whispering, 'What I want to ask you. . . .' He reached into the pocket of his robe and brought forth a small box, which he opened, revealing a diamond ring. Taking her hand, he tenderly asked, 'Will you marry me?'

'Oh, my dear Carter,' Grace said and kissed him. 'Yes, marrying you would make me very happy.'

Carter laughed, 'You've made me feel like a prince.'

'Prince Charming.'

Carter put his arm around her. 'What a night!' He sipped the brandy and stood up. 'Let's pretend we're in the movies.' He began to strut around the living-room. He turned up the volume and began to step in time as Nelson Eddy sang *Stouthearted Men*. His arms gesturing, he lip-synced the chorus:

> *Give me some men who are stouthearted men*
> *Who will fight for the right they adore.*
> *Start me with ten who are stouthearted men and*
> *I'll soon give you ten thousand more.*

Grace swung her arms with the beat, and laughed. 'All you

need is a bright red Mountie uniform and a horse.'

Carter continued with the next verse:

> *You, who have dreams,*
> *If you act, they will come true.*
> *To, turn your dreams*
> *To a fact, it's up to you.*
> *If you have the soul and the spirit*
> *Never fear it, you'll see it through.*
> *Ask, and inspire, their hearts and their fire*
> *For the strong obey when a strong man*
> *Shows them the way.*

Grace applauded.

Carter broke up, roaring with laughter, and they hugged once more.

'The neighbours,' she said, laughing again, 'will be pounding on the ceiling and the walls. Well.' She paused, allowing a conspiracy to develop in her mind. Turning down the music, she said, 'We'll quietly go into our bedroom and give them all something to really talk about.'

She took him by the hand.

In the flickering candlelight his silk robe, which he now removed almost in slow motion told of the gossamer of their dreams.

Gently he took her again into his arms. He slipped off her gown and caressed her as they sat together on the edge of her bed. Large hands, tender hands, sculpted her body. Grace and Carter turned to lie next to each other.

Her momentary worries that the act would not go well were soon dispelled as he applied moisturizer first to himself and then gently to her.

Her climax of their sexual excitement surprised her but her involvement with his orgasm surprised her even more.

★ ★ ★

Grace peeked at the first hint of dawn through her lace curtains, knowing the glow would soon spread across the clear New Mexico sky.

Instantly she was wide awake, not wanting to miss a

moment of her life. Her body tingled, alive with the morning and the touch of Carter Calhoun, absorbing his warmth as he slept by her side. She admired her new ring and held her hand, turning it first one way and then another so the diamond would reflect the early morning light.

Carter's cane lay on top of the down comforter. Grace edged herself over and looked at its ivory tip. The smooth white surface conjured up images of African elephants, lions, giraffes and fabulous wild birds. Maybe Carter's plans called for travel, allowing her to see places until now only visited by studying Pinkerton's travel guides. At last she would have a need for her passport. And maybe, with his promise of shared participation, her life would be so fulfilling she would no longer have to lose herself in fantasies. Certainly, life with Carter would mean glorious sex.

'Yes!' she exclaimed emphatically, adding in a loud voice, 'octogenarian sex!'

Her outburst caused Carter to jump. He sat up, naked as a jay bird, looked at Grace and said, a serious expression on his face, 'Yes, I'll buy ten thousand shares of that!' And he broke into laughter.

She put her arms around his muscular torso.

He looked down, admiring her. 'I'm so happy you've accepted my proposal of marriage,' he said affectionately.

'Say you're not just marrying me for my winnings at poker.'

He laughed again, hesitated and then spoke slowly and deliberately. 'You know, it has been some time, I will confess – and you are not to repeat a word of this to our poker-playing buddies – since I've enjoyed an orgasm quite that fine.'

'Orgasm,' her voice lowered as she struggled with the word that had been so risqué in polite society, 'is a private matter, very personal.'

'No, I must tell you,' he said, 'that as one ages the sexual experience changes, from the pure ecstasy of a young man to the intense, almost stinging build-up that takes place within the organs of an older man. The music of the muscular chords leading up to the climax and the ejaculation itself are quite a different melody, sometimes strained, often out of tune like an idle piano. But mine last night was as warm and symphonic as a full orchestra.' He hesitated before asking, 'But tell me how is it for you? Does your . . . ah . . . expression come differently?'

She blushed. 'I never really knew sexual intercourse could be so enjoyable. I'm looking forward to our next time and every time after that.'

Carter stood up, and she watched him slowly pull on his shorts and finish dressing.

'Now it is time for our morning walk,' she announced. 'We must not allow ourselves to become a sedentary couple. We need our exercise.'

23

'Higher and higher,' Toledo exclaimed as his private jet rose from the runway of the Santa Fe airport.

'Yes, you were great!' Katherine said.

'There's nothing like the exhilaration that follows a successful meeting,' Toledo said, radiating a smile of contentment. 'Especially when the result moves you closer to your goal.'

'I admire you, Toledo. In your life you reach for the pinnacles. You merge with the largest brokerage company in the world. You gather a prestigious assemblage of people on a mountain top. And now you're flying across the roof of the American West. I expect you've booked us into the penthouse of a San Francisco hotel atop Nob Hill.'

'But of course.' Toledo said. 'Clearly there are many ways of getting high. And tomorrow I'm going to do another of them.'

'The race with John Axminster?'

'Yes, and then it's on to the gold.'

The pilot announced their course – the south of Utah, north of Las Vegas and then into California. When they crossed over the peaks of the Sierra Nevada Mountains where a century and a half earlier the forty-niners dug for gold, Katherine gestured downward. 'Those prospectors left their homes and families and rushed to California for gold, just like we're doing now. I hope we find our grandmother lode.'

Toledo laughed. 'Yes, and I hope without too much digging.'

'But how are we going to know where to insert the shovel? Santa Barbara's a big place.'

'For openers, we know General Beauregard owned land there. Tomorrow when I run with John while you're soaking in the Jacuzzi, I'll ask for his help in identifying the specific parcel.'

'Public records?'

'Should be. Axy will find us someone down there who

knows where and how to look up property, providing the official records weren't destroyed by the 1925 earthquake.'

'That's right, we're back in earthquake country. I forgot to ask if the land shakes in Albania,' Katherine said.

'I think we have enough to worry about without adding natural disasters to our list.' Toledo changed the subject. 'So, how do you assess our team and our meeting at the Sangre de Cristo Lodge?'

'Well, Mr Spanish Town, what I see are a lot of hidden agendas.'

'Then let's address them. Talk to me about what you perceive to be their special interests.'

Katherine laughed. 'I am supposed to tell *you*, when you are the one who based your entire company on diagnosing motivations of security analysts? I remember what you said on the TV talk show – it's the hidden agenda people have, not what's readily apparent on the surface, that determines their performance. And you got ten million dollars for being so innovatively perspicacious.'

'You exaggerate my talents. In my company the staff was required to give their input. In fact, I'll tell you our secret.'

'Every company, like every person, has at least one. So what was yours?'

'It was not simply one person looking into the minds and biases of thousands of security analysts. That'd be impossible. The secret of my company's success was its software, which was programmed so that the staff – after they had examined the statistics of each mutual fund – had to input their own professional opinions about the self-seeking priorities of the fund's management before they could print out their report.'

'So you want my report?'

Toledo nodded.

'Well then, so long as you're asking, I'll share my reactions to your team members and also add the dividend of my idea as to what I think the team should do with that little country in Eastern Europe.'

'Your assessment of the people, then, for openers. You have time while we cross the great central valley.'

'I know my geography. Next we pass over the coastal range and arrive at the city by the bay. And thanks to the general and his huge map, I am now quite familiar with

Balkan geography.'

'What did you think of the general?' Toledo asked.

'Type A personality. I think we're going to be laying him to rest before very long.'

Toledo looked at her in surprise.

'Yes, he's hyper. And overweight, as well. These obvious visual signs are a health warning.'

'He said visual signalling doesn't work.'

'For his sake I hope he's right,' Katherine said. 'But if I were you, I wouldn't totally rely on him. Besides, if you allow him to pursue his plan, he'll get you and me and the others into World War III. One bomb dropped on Tirana will do us all in.'

'We'd never let that happen. The general really means for Albanians to reunite in their expanded and rightful territory, and I am sure only peacefully.'

'An army invades another country in the spirit of brotherly love?'

'Well, no, there'll be no invasion.' Toledo assured her. 'They'll invite us in. Like neighbours having a block party. And what'd you think of the others?'

'A very impressive lot.'

'Your individual reactions?'

'Well, the President is, well, the President. He's your frontispiece, your eye-catcher, your logo, your . . . well, what else can I say?'

'And the professor?'

'Professor Posin is pretty academic,' Katherine replied. 'I guess that's to be expected. I suspect he's not too practical.'

'He's a recognized expert on the Balkans, with all its different languages, religions and cultures. He's lived there, as well. He was in Belgrade and understands the Serbs, how their minds function. Talk about knowing where the bodies are buried. . . . He's our local connection everyone was harping about. He has promised to introduce me to members of the new Albanian Parliament.'

'Promises, promises.'

'Believe me, he's got the contacts,' Toledo said. 'He didn't say much about it at the meeting, but he's privately assured me of the channels he's going to open up for us as soon as we have the gold and the time is ripe.'

'Did you see how ripe he was for Ms Hewit, ogling her?'

'You've got a vivid imagination. I think Ms Hewit made her arguments quite splendidly for the immediate need to get health, education and welfare systems in place.'

'No doubt she is the Superadvocate,' Katherine said. 'She's got a one-track mind with three trains running on it – health, education and welfare. But turn her loose with a supply of blank cheques and you'll see the biggest budget deficit in history – she'll spend ten times the country's national income on social programmes.'

Toledo laughed. 'Yes, there's no limit to her agenda. She'll have to be contained. That's why we have a team. They'll serve as checks and balances to each other. That's what's wrong with the dictator system of government: no one dares ask questions, let alone criticize. Besides,' Toledo added, 'we had to get her to get the former President.'

'They came as a package?'

Toledo nodded. 'And Ines Stark?'

'Our resident lesbian?' Katherine asked. 'Her agenda for gay rights is limitless, even fuller than Ms Hewit's three sub-headings.'

'But Katherine, she was on the short list for a federal judgeship in the last administration. With her party back in power and given her record for fairness and impartiality, she'll undoubtedly be nominated for a prestigious appointment. Besides, she's a skilled arbitrator. I know from personal experience.'

Katherine nodded.

'And what did you think of our eminent economist, Ms Andersen?'

'My friend Myra has an excellent grasp on Albania's economy, or rather lack of it, and what she thinks should be done to solve the country's problems.'

'Yes, she is brilliant. But you don't agree with her far-reaching plans?'

'Not with what should be done, although I'll acknowledge her solutions would receive laudatory grades as being what I would label "economically correct".'

'But not politically correct?'

'No. But I believe there is a solution that is both.'

'If you had been asked for a presentation in the lodge, what would you have said?'

Katherine looked startled. 'Me?'

'Yes, ours is an equal-time team. Compose and deliver. You're on.'

'Did you say there was some wine in the plane's galley?'

Toledo unbuckled, stepped to the tiny galley, decanted a red wine from Greece and poured two glasses, handing one to her. 'This is the closest I could get – the Albanians have no export mechanism for their wine or their brandy, as yet.'

Katherine took a sip. 'Thank you. There are times any wine will do.'

Toledo laughed. 'Yes I like the New Mexico better.' He toasted her and said, 'You're on.'

'The cabin's too low to stand, so I'll sit here with my seat-belt fastened,' she said.

'In case, as the captain might say, "we encounter turbulence".'

'I'm probably going to encounter turbulence with my report. . .'

'Do what you must – and that is to fly through it. . . .'

'I've been thinking a lot about it – for days actually, and especially during and after the team's meeting,' Katherine began.

Toledo seemed impressed.

'Why convert Albania – sweet, innocent, lovely little Albania – into another cookie-cutter industrialized, auto-mobilized and polluted country? We have a country with few cars and no traffic lights. And I am sure there are no shopping malls with endless paved parking lots, no used-car lots, new car showrooms, instant lube places, ubiquitous stores selling auto parts, or junkyards brimming with abandoned automobiles. Cars and highways are socially expensive, economically inefficient. That same money could be better spent on some of Ms Hewit's projects.

'Albania is the most underdeveloped country in Europe. Let's capitalize on that – retain one unspoiled, innocent country, make it into a pristine place, a museum nation, a Williamsburg of Eastern Europe. Simple innocence is her most saleable natural resource. The quaint antique towns like Berat and Gjirokastër – from the pictures I've seen – will attract tourists. Her bucolic valleys, mountains and sea coast

142

will lure Japanese, Germans, French, even Americans to see, to feel, to touch, but not to spoil.

'Our responsibility is to save this bite-sized piece of Europe from the blight of industrialization, superhighways and smokestacks, from truck exhaust floating endlessly through pure air, from toxic discharge flowing into clear streams. With preservation of the old houses, the farms, the castles, the narrow cobblestone streets, Albania's tourist economy will prosper more than with trying to bring it belatedly into the world of industrialization. And the reason is it will be the only museum country in the world. She'll have no competition.

'We have the power, the skill, the money and knowledge to do it right. Generations from now, we'll each be regarded as visionaries who dreamed a different dream. Instead of birthing yet another environmental nightmare, we'll be remembered as having brought forth a happy, natural, and beautiful scenario to one little corner of the world.'

Katherine drained her glass of wine as the jet touched down at San Francisco International Airport. She hinted at a smile while wondering if she had overstepped her bounds. Who was she to rock the boat of the powerful? But to her, theirs was a ship of state plying towards an armada of icebergs. She looked at him through her clear wineglass to see his reaction.

To her surprise and delight Toledo embraced her, their passionate kiss transporting them both into new heights.

24

During the night, the fog snuggled around San Francisco, a blanket pulled up high, concealing the tops of the city's skyscrapers and the pylons of its bridges. In this early morning a hundred thousand runners made their way through the mist to the start. And twice as many spectators began to line the seven-mile course from San Francisco Bay across town to the Pacific Ocean breakers. Gathering impatiently behind the starting-line, the runners knew they would soon be freed to break loose and chase the fog ahead of them back towards the ocean from whence it had come.

Toledo sensed the drama of the contestants, their weeks of disciplined training preparing for the event, their eagerness to begin. He was impatient, too, not so much for this race as he was for resuming the endurance test he and the members of his team must run.

Carrying his Albanian flag, he effected his rendezvous with John Axminster. 'I've given up a beautiful woman in a marble Jacuzzi to be here in the cold fog with my banker. Now, there's real loyalty for you.'

'Pales in comparison with mine. You will recall I stuck with you through thick and thin in your first crazy business endeavour. I say that's a better example of loyalty. But today I'm not going to remain by your side, because I'm going to outrun you.'

'You'll be lucky to keep up with me,' Toledo said.

The mayor fired the starting-gun, and the crowd of runners was off. Toledo and Axminster worked their way around slower runners, runners with infant pushchairs, runners dressed in costume and runners attached to one another forming human centipedes, the throng endless.

'You've gotten the members of your team firmed up?' Axminster asked.

'Yes.'

'The same ones you told me about originally?'

'Yes.'

Spectators waved from the second and third storeys of old buildings fronted with fire-escapes. One held high a tape deck blaring forth theme music from the soundtrack of *Chariots of Fire*.

'Very impressive. In fact, your whole mission of taking over and running a country is a little mind-boggling. I've never asked you before – how'd you come up with it?'

'While running,' Toledo replied. 'Running and creativity are right brain activities – where imagination is nurtured.' He dodged a little boy and laughed. 'Bankers are born without that bent. That's why they make slow runners.'

'Give me some running room and I'll be in Golden Gate Park before you can struggle up the Hayes Street hill.'

Axminster eyed the women runners making up the centipede now running alongside them. The shape of the canopy was that of a condom, and its message read *Run for Safe Sex*. Two dozen legs and feet protruded from beneath the canvas. Axminster ducked under, inserting his head through an opening already occupied by a blonde head, his pace in rhythm with hers. 'My friend over there thinks I haven't any imagination,' he said.

'I'd say you have too much,' she answered. 'Now get out of here, you'll disqualify us from the Women's Centipede Category. We're an official entry.'

'Oops,' Axminster said, ducking back out as they ran. 'But I need your advice about safe sex,' he said to her, and laughed. He turned to Toledo. 'Meet Melissa Rogers, one of our international banking officers. She, too, likes to champion causes.'

Recognizing Toledo, Melissa said, 'I saw you on the Hortense Alger show the other night. I liked your bit about it being your turn to pay dues to society.'

Toledo smiled. At the mention of his mission, he looked at Axminster. 'Speaking of causes, I need your help again.'

The runners crossed Market Street. Up ahead loomed the awesome Hayes street hill. A little girl stepped out from the crowd lining the road. She held a crayoned banner: *Go, Dad!* She spotted her father. He waved.

'Then it's back to business. You said on the phone there

was a second source of gold?'

Between gasps for breath on the uphill course, Toledo managed, 'Yes, the Albanian national gold. I understand it's in a London bank vault.'

'Rather unbelievable,' Axminster commented. 'I've never heard anything about it, but if you are officially asking me, I'll make a discreet inquiry of our branch manager in England. See what he knows.'

'Don't reveal who is asking or why.'

'Don't worry. But I'll need to know whose name the gold is held under – a corporation or a person – and which bank it's supposed to be in.'

'I don't have any answers. That's why I flew in here – to ask you for help. The gold's exact location and size must be common knowledge among London bankers.'

'If it's of any size at all, I should think someone would know. The trick will be to find the right person and see if they will share confidences with me. You know, bankers over there have a less open approach to revealing information about depositors.'

Music from a band playing up ahead floated back to meet them before they reached the third uphill block. Feeling the strain, Toledo lagged. Axminster slowed to run with him. Looking back, he saw tens of thousands still struggling. Ahead towards Divisadero, thousands more were jogging towards Golden Gate Park.

'And our other stash of gold?' Axminster asked.

'I have confirmation that the Confederate gold is in Santa Barbara. I need your help with it, too. General Beauregard carried it there.'

'On his back?' Axminster said, laughing. 'If that's the case, it can't have amounted to much . . . you told me it took an entire train to transport it out of Richmond in 1865.'

'The treasure was partially depleted along the way . . . even so, the residual is quite significant, and that's what we're looking for. I need your assistance in pinpointing its precise location.' Toledo gasped for air. 'And I think I need assistance in getting up this hill.' He stopped to walk, and looked at his banker. 'Say, why don't you come with us to Santa Barbara, help us?'

'You and the beautiful woman in the marble Jacuzzi?'

'Yes, Katherine and I are flying down after the race.'

Axminster turned around and ran backwards, his pace still faster than Toledo's resumed pace. 'You should train for these races,' he said. 'Yes, OK, I'll join you. That is, as long as Katherine doesn't object to a *ménage à trois*.'

'I've told Katherine all about you.'

'Uh oh.' He stopped and covered his head with both arms.

'Don't worry about Katherine, she can take care of herself. I find her a real challenge.'

'You're attracted to challenges, aren't you?'

Toledo looked over at his banker. 'You bet. What would any of us be without them?'

Axminster jogged on. 'Santa Barbara's a big place. So where'll we look first? Do you think it's buried in one of those caves up in the Santa Ynez Mountains?'

'No, it's most likely somewhere in the old part of town.' Toledo got his second wind. 'Because Beauregard purchased property there after the War Between the States, planted grapes and started a winery.'

'I'll call my real-estate expert, tell her we're coming. She's the one who can find the parcel he owned.'

'Good, I'm impatient for answers.' Toledo accelerated his pace on the downhill. 'It's great you're coming with us because I'll also need an introduction to your branch manager there.'

'Why?'

'We'll need a place to stow the treasure.'

'Banks always have huge vaults.'

As they ran on, Toledo asked, 'Speaking of banks, how are things going for you at your bank? Personally, I mean.'

'Well, you know banks,' Axminster said. 'I've hit a dead end. My superiors are only slightly older – nowhere near retirement – and the bank has taken aboard a lot of talented people through recent acquisitions. So there are a lot of us clamouring for promotion, and very few openings.'

'My experience with Microsoft,' Toledo sympathized.

They had room to pick up their pace as the other runners dispersed onto the park's wider boulevard. 'I've a limo waiting for us at the finish – if we can locate it in the crush of fans along the Great Highway,' Axminster said. 'I'll use its cellular telephone and call my friend in Santa Barbara. On a Sunday morning she's probably surfing or running or biking, but at least I can leave a message on her machine.'

'She's into fitness, too?'

'The only way to be today, with all the stress.'

'Yes, helps, doesn't it,' Toledo said.

The fog retreating ahead of them, they ran on amidst the cheering spectators lining the roadway. The tops of the pine-trees contorted inland, their branches bent by coastal winds. The fragrance of the great Pacific Ocean filled their nostrils as their pace increased.

'And also phone London?' Toledo asked.

Axminster inhaled the crisp sea breeze. 'Yes, I'll be happy – even if it is the Sabbath – to call our manager over there,' he replied, his voice eager. 'He should be back from his country weekend and nestled into his West End flat by now. Evening over there. Get him at dinner.'

Turning the corner onto the Great Highway, they saw the finishing banner and redoubled their efforts towards it. A digital clock read seconds under one hour.

'You must know by now, I'm really enamoured with your plan,' Axminster said.

'I needed your support in the past and I'm glad I have it now.'

'I'd like to continue to be part of your team. I mean, I feel as if I am now, of course. But once you're all over there, I mean, you'll be a long way away.'

'Yes, a long way.'

Axminster hesitated. 'I've been wondering . . . what are my chances of being awarded the McDonald's franchise for Albania? Your group's going to control matters of this sort, aren't you?' His laugh was nervous. 'I mean, in case things don't work out for me at my bank.'

'As far as I'm concerned, if you want it you got it,' Toledo said.

'Glad to hear you say that.'

Toledo raised the Albanian flag, holding it high for the television cameras as they charged through and then beyond the finishing-line, where they accepted their rewards – colourful designer T-shirts commemorating the Bay to Breakers race.

Downing a bottle of mineral water, Axminster said, 'This

is a race I'll never forget.'

Toledo laughed. 'We'll schedule one in Albania.'

'I'll come in costume as the Golden Arches.'

25

Beneath the bustling world financial centre that is the City of London, troves of treasure are tucked away in bank vaults. Great pains are taken to protect this hidden wealth. Special timers are needed to open the complex locks on the thick, drill-proof doors. And when open, security officers stand guard, protecting their valuable contents. Vaults also have officials who log each authorized opening and closing, monitoring additions and removals of the currency, bearer bonds, and bars of silver and gold bullion stowed within. A far cry from burying canisters of cash in one's backyard.

Sometimes those valuables can be stashed away for so long they're practically forgotten. As are the officials assigned to watch over them. Both the bank vault and the custodians to the Albanian national gold fit this portrait.

Those officials who had initially monitored the treasure had long since retired. The audit ledgers they once diligently maintained were now yellowed with inactivity, their pages' own acid eating away at the entries. In fact, the vault in which this particular treasure was housed had not been opened for years. The official bank seal remained unbroken and un-tampered with, its fading words whispering *Pledged to Trans-European Bank as collateral for loan to National Cause, Inc.*

There was no clue as to the identity of 'National Cause, Inc.' It could refer to a company long since merged into another, re-merged or possibly even eliminated in a corporate down-sizing, having faded from memory like another passing train in the London Underground. That its name was shown, not in the European 'Ltd' or 'PLC' company style but rather in the American manner of 'Inc.' was the only indication of its corporate nationality.

Were anyone to ask, the reply would likely have been, 'Oh, that loan's probably been paid off.' Not that anyone was nosing around, for virtually no one knew either the vault or its contents existed, let alone that the treasure held inside was pledged as security for a loan still on the books, well secured and current in its regular payments of interest, all these years rendering a tidy profit for the Trans-European Bank.

Virtually no one, that is, except for Archibald McThomson, an old man in a wheelchair. He was housed up on the bank's fifth floor, down a remote corridor, where over the years he had held forth in his tiny garret. For some reason the bank had never presented Archibald with the gold watch of mandatory retirement. He simply continued with his responsibility of watching over this one particular loan, secured by the contents of this one particular vault. Probably when the time had come for his retirement, someone realized he was the only official left who knew the bank's customer and the nature of the collateral securing the loan. Personnel must have allowed him to remain on staff in case some auditor or examiner made inquiry. Or in case the customer came out of the London fog one day, paid off the loan and demanded return of the collateral.

McThomson had decorated his little office with Albanian memorabilia. A flag with a double-headed eagle stood beside the Union Jack. A photograph of King Zog, Queen Geraldine and their baby, Prince Leka, taken the day of Mussolini's invasion, was framed behind his desk. Hand-coloured turn-of-the-century etchings of men and women dressed in their native folk costumes adorned two of the other walls. On the fourth was a huge 'Wanted' poster on which were pictured the cabal of Communists who had run the country as a private club for some forty-five years. Underneath each mug shot was a hand-lettered word, either *Apprehended* or *Dead*.

This late afternoon, as he was completing his weekly report on the status of the investment portfolio for Carter Calhoun, the phone rang, cutting into the silence of his cubicle-size office.

'Are you there?' Archibald said, posing his usual greeting.

'Yes I am,' Carter said.

'Carter!' he exclaimed, recognizing the voice from Santa Fe. 'Good to hear from you! It's been a while.'

'Oh, I'm so glad you're still there.'

'Of course I am. I've no plans to leave. They'll have to carry me out. But tell me, have you given up the ghost – or become one yourself – living in that retirement home?'

Carter laughed. 'On the contrary, I've met all these wonderful people. I'm feeling younger every day. And I want you to be the first to hear my splendid news. I'm going to get married again.'

'You're kidding?'

'No, it's true. And Grace has this terrific idea. . . .'

'But ideas are for the young,' Archibald interrupted.

'You'll change your attitude when you meet Grace.'

Archibald's voice grew sullen as he lamented, 'I once had an idea, but then came the war, and I was wounded.' Cupping the telephone under his chin, he wheeled his chair a few feet across his tiny office and looked at a photograph of himself and Carter. They were each in uniform, one American, one British, standing outside Buckingham Palace. 'Circumstances change,' Archibald said. 'Ideas don't always work out.'

As his man in London fell silent, Carter thought their connection was broken. Clearing his throat, he tried, 'Hello?'

'Oh, I'm here all right,' Archibald assured him. 'But I'm not believing what I'm hearing you say, Carter. You think you can go on forever? Only Methuselah did that.'

'I live in the Methuselah,' Carter said.

'But that doesn't mean you are going to live as long as he did.'

'Did? Why, aren't you aware, he's still alive and well, sometimes joins us at dinner here in the Great Hall.' Carter laughed once again. 'But you know, it is quite apparent – although I of course never say anything to him personally – but just between us, he *is* showing his age.'

'They say age does not really begin to show until you enter your second millennium,' Archibald said, and laughed.

'Listen, if you and I can hang on long enough, they'll perfect this technique of cloning, and we'll each be able to become a Methuselah, replicating ourselves in some test-tube once each century.'

'Perhaps, but I'm not certain I can deal with the changes in society, they're coming so fast these days,' Archibald said. 'But we must be serious, my friend. Accept the fact or not, science or not, the time has come to indeed turn your affairs over to someone younger.'

'I don't agree with you.'

'But you do see that younger people are better equipped to deal with today's world,' Archibald continued. 'Life has become so complex it is no longer possible to simply rely on business and social connections. The world is populated with so many people that no one – except perhaps a president or a prime minister – can possibly develop enough meaningful connections. So, that's what I mean about the merits of passing authority along.'

'But still, it is not right for any man to be idle, especially one whose mind is alert and whose bride-to-be is encouraging him to make a difference in the world.'

'She's really influencing you, isn't she? Carter, you and I go back a long way. I'm here to do whatever you say, and so is the bank. After all, you're the one Zog entrusted with the gold – the bank recognizes that, and so do I. But you must be realistic.'

'I've never been more keenly aware of my responsibilities,' Carter said.

'Giving up the reins is never easy.'

'In some cultures that's a moot point. The Chinese feel that the older you get, the wiser you are.'

Archibald tried another tack. 'Well then, have you ever thought about the possibility of teaming up with someone younger who might eventually step into your position?'

'Who'd you have in mind?'

'What about Ardian? I know you don't like to be sentimental . . . and I realize you haven't been receptive to information I've tried to pass along to you about your son, but. . . .'

'Archibald, that's the other reason I called you. I want to find Ardian.'

'It is good you can at last say his name. You know, I've hesitated to give you any news about him because I dreaded your brooding silence.'

'It's my turn to apologize to you about my past depression.'

'No need to apologize. I understood,' Archibald said. 'How well I remember his mother – that time when I was in Tirana and you introduced me to her. She was such a striking woman. Ardianna.' Archibald spoke her name softly, almost reverently.

'I've told Grace all about my affair,' Carter said.

'I'm dumbfounded you would do that. But surely not about Ardianna's death?'

'No, I didn't get into wartime atrocities.'

'Carter, do you still blame yourself for her death?'

'Yes, I still wrestle with the guilt. But Grace has shown me I cannot deny the existence of my son in seeking a solution to that dilemma.'

'You must convince yourself you couldn't have saved her, even if you'd parachuted into Albania in 1944 with David Smiley and his commandos. Had you done so, you'd have been lucky to get out alive.'

Carter swallowed. 'I wanted to go in with them. I thought I could rescue her from the Fascists, bring her out, along with my son.'

'But you weren't properly trained.'

"I could have been if I'd insisted.'

'You had different orders . . . Carter, for God's sake, you were in your army's finance corps. . . .'

'Finance men can fight, too.'

'Only with dollars,' Archibald argued.

'You fought. . . .'

'I was in the bloody infantry, Carter.'

'That's all behind us. Now you must tell me the news of my son.'

Archibald paused. 'Well, I don't know where to begin. I must confess so much has happened since I marked off the last Communist.' He looked at his wall poster and smiled. 'I remember once a year Enver Hoxha used to send his regular nasty letter demanding we return the gold to him, or really to his personal numbered Swiss bank account in Zurich.'

'A letter which you promptly shredded,' Carter reminded him.

Archibald chuckled. 'But the letters stopped coming after the tyrant's death.'

'And nothing from his successors?'

'No, we've had five years of silence.'

'And now I'm breaking my silence and asking you about Ardian.'

'Well, the latest news from Tirana is that your son has been elected to the new Albanian Parliament. And the prime minister has appointed him to head the National Finance Committee.'

'That's exciting news indeed.'

'He's probably got his acumen in finance from you.' Archibald hesitated before going on. Finally he said, 'In fact, his first order of business was to contact me about the gold.'

'But Archibald, I see these developments as a dream come true. Don't you see, my son is now in a position to assist us with our plan?' Before Archibald could reply, Carter went on. 'Grace and I want to support Albania's fledgling democracy by using the gold to financially back its government in their efforts to rebuild The Country.'

'Why don't you allow Ardian to help implement your plan?' Archibald asked.

Carter thought for a moment. 'I am certain if Zog were still alive he might decree that Ardian and I work together for the good of The Country. You know, the portfolio is worth a billion US dollars. That's real financial clout for a small country.'

'Yes, Ardian understands, and. . . .' Archibald was silent for a moment.

'Yes?'

'Well, I must tell you Ardian has already placed an advertisement to fill the position for the head of the Albanian Central Bank. Setting a national monetary policy and solving the currency problem are top priorities for the young government, so he is in a hurry to give the name of the nominee to Parliament for their ratification. He has been funnelling the replies through me – he asked me to screen the applicants – and now he's coming to London for the final interviews.'

Carter gulped. 'I'm not sure I can deal with these fast-moving developments, Archibald, but I realize I must do so. All these years I've blocked him out just as the world has blocked out The Country of Albania.'

'One change in today's world I do welcome is that isolationism is no longer in style.'

'All your news of his importance in the new Parliament and now his coming to London – well, it's all really quite momentous for me. You'll actually be seeing Ardian? And you could give him a belated message of my love?' Carter asked.

'Why don't you and Grace deliver it personally?'

'That's a splendid suggestion,' Carter said. 'Yes, we shall fly to London and have our reunion with Ardian. I know Grace will applaud your idea.'

26

The Santa Barbara mission enjoyed a commanding view out across red tile roofs, palm trees, the Moorish-style 1920s county court-house and beyond to the ocean and its distant offshore Channel Islands. From the gardens in the mission's foreground, wide steps led up to a broad stage area in front of the sanctuary's entrance. There in the bright afternoon sunlight, a woman waited beside her bicycle, taking in the clear view.

'There's Peggy,' Axminster announced. 'She's cycled up here to meet us.'

'But you didn't tell us why we're meeting here,' Katherine said. 'Records are usually kept in the court-house, aren't they?'

'Peggy said that as part of the salvage work after the 1925 earthquake, the old property archives were relocated here to the mission,' Axminster replied. 'She says we'll find them bound in ledger books and locked away in an archival vault. Father Eric will open up these catacombs for us after mass.'

Axminster jumped out of the taxi, kissed Peggy on her cheek and introduced Katherine and Toledo.

'How do you two know each other?' Toledo asked.

'From college. Peggy and I took a course in the history of architecture together.'

Peggy gestured towards the mission. 'It's the only Spanish mission in California with a Greek revival façade.' She made a triangle with her hands, forming a pediment. 'See the columns with their Ionic capitals? How they stand out from its pinkish-coloured stucco? The priest who designed it, they say, found a book on Greek architecture and became enamoured with the style.' She looked sheepish and smiled. 'Just thought you'd like to know.'

Peggy was in her biking clothes, black knee-length latex shorts, biking gloves, helmet and a T-shirt commemorating the recent Santa Barbara century bike race. 'It's my business, you see – historic preservation. I'm a consultant. An important skill here in Santa Barbara. Everyone wants to preserve the past, especially our Spanish heritage.' She laughed and took off her helmet. Red hair tumbled down across her shoulders.

'Santa Barbara is the quintessential mecca for all Hispanics,' Katherine said.

'Yes, and this mission is the queen of all the Spanish missions along El Camino Real,' Peggy said. 'In the 1780s Father Junipero Serra, with a lot of help from the local Chumash Indians, persevered here with his grand plan. His rosary of religious settlements eventually stretched to the north of San Francisco, all the way to Sonoma.'

'Up in the wine country,' Toledo said, licking his lips.

'Yes, the Spanish had to have their wine for sacramental rites, and of course for drinking.' Peggy laughed quietly. 'Come on, we'll go in the side entrance at the end of this portal. Father Eric said he'd meet us there.'

They had to duck their heads under the weathered wooden header of the opening, which was cut through three-foot thick adobe walls.

'Cool in here. Musty,' Katherine said. 'It feels like we're going back in time. And here comes Father Junipero Serra now.'

Peggy chuckled and whispered, 'Reincarnated into our Father Eric. He is accommodating us today because I tweaked his interest with the mention of General Beauregard. Father Eric is a fanatical Civil War buff.'

The padre was short, mostly bald and attired in a rust-coloured robe with a belt sash tied in front. 'Ah, Ms O'Neill, been riding your bicycle again,' the priest said.

'Yes, father, you should try it. Lose a little weight as well as commune with the saints on those downhill speed bursts,' Peggy said.

'The saints and I are getting along just fine as it is,' he said, his chuckle raspy, his smile broad. 'Come with me,' he added, leading them across creaking wooden floors through a series of rooms. 'In fact, their manifestations in these antique wood carvings adorning my walls are blessing you as we pass.'

'Do they work miracles in locating real estate?' Katherine asked.

'Let's find out,' Father Eric said, with another rusty laugh. He retrieved a huge key from under his tunic and unlocked an ancient wooden door. 'Here we are,' he announced as he pulled a cord that turned on a single light bulb dangling from the ceiling. The cord danced around and the light bounced off leather ledger books stowed on dusty shelves.

'These record books go back into the mid 1800s,' Father Eric said. 'Many of the early documents are written in Spanish, of course. Some signatures are merely *Xs*, witnessed by someone who could read and write.'

'I can read Spanish,' Katherine said. 'Are we going to look at each land deed from 1865 on?'

'With so many books, that could take years,' Axminster said, surveying the walls. 'There must be some sort of index.'

Father Eric went to one wall and pointed at a top shelf. 'Can you reach that book on the left there?' he said to Toledo.

Toledo stretched, pulled the ledger book down and spread it on a rickety wooden table beneath the hanging light bulb. Father Eric blew the dust from the leather. Producing gold-rimmed glasses from under his robe, he turned one large page after another, stopping in the *Bs*.

'Yes, we have an index,' he said, and rasped out another laugh. He looked at Peggy. 'You asked me on the phone if I knew anything about General Beauregard coming to Santa Barbara. I've placed the Confederate general in New Orleans, where after the war he helped establish the Louisiana lottery. Oh yes, and I also remember reading he was offered the position as head of the Romanian army, which he turned down. But then, these are only scattered fragments of his very colourful life. And I'm simply a Civil War buff, not a biographical authority.'

He returned his attention to the ledger and soon exclaimed, 'Holy *Santos*, here it is.'

They crowded around and followed his finger across a line in the ledger. Sure enough, under the column headed *Grantee* was the general's full name, handwritten in ink. In front of the grantor's name was the date of the property's transfer of ownership, followed by a code.

'What do these letters mean?' Toledo asked.

'They refer us to another book,' Father Eric said. He turned to the wall behind him, searching. Soon he pointed up. 'Can you reach the top shelf again, Mr Squires? I believe the ledger we're looking for is over there on the right.'

Toledo stood on his tip toes and pulled down another, larger volume and laid it on the table. It was as dusty as the first. Father Eric opened it and hunted for a particular page as the others pressed close to watch.

'Ah, here is the deed page,' he announced.

'Where is the property?' Toledo asked, unable to conceal his impatience.

'Of course,' Father Eric said.

Looking over his shoulder, Katherine echoed his statement, 'Of course.'

'I'm missing the point,' Peggy said.

'The property is on De La Vina Street,' Katherine explained.

'Vines,' Toledo said, almost jumping up and down.

Father Eric nodded, and read on. 'And wine. We're in luck today. It must have been my second litany of prayers this morning.'

'Why do you say we're in luck?' Axminster asked.

'There's supposed to be a map as an exhibit to the deed,' Father Eric said. 'That's rare.'

'Yes, we're really in luck,' Peggy agreed. 'Few of the early plat maps remain. But it means another book.' She looked at Toledo. 'The top shelf over there, but it's probably going to be a big one, right, Father?'

He nodded.

'You'd better stand on the chair,' Peggy said.

Toledo retrieved the third book.

Father Eric opened it, more dust billowing. He coughed and finally unfolded a large map. 'Yes, here is the parcel in question.'

They leaned so close, their heads blocked the light. They backed up. The bulb's light shone down on the map.

'It's a large parcel,' Peggy announced. She pointed to the dimensions. 'It's measured in chains, but I'll convert it for you.' She figured quickly, mumbling numbers. 'Yes, it's a little more than four hectares,' she concluded.

'What's a hectare?' Toledo asked.

'A Spanish measurement of land size equal to 2·471 acres,' Katherine said. 'My family owns one hectare in Chimayo.'

'Yes, that's right. Beauregard's parcel size converts to ten acres,' Peggy confirmed.

'Wow,' Axminster said, 'if all that land is still intact, that's a lot of valuable real estate in the old part of town.'

Father Eric pointed to the map. 'What do you suppose this X signifies here – near De La Vina Street?' he asked.

All their heads converged, blocking the light, then retreated again so the bulb illuminated a large X scrawled in ink. It was obvious the mark was added after the surveyor had drawn the map, for it was a slightly different colour.

'Eureka!' Axminster exclaimed.

'Bambi Deer . . . Grace . . . my grandmother . . . was right.' Toledo looked at Katherine and said, almost with disbelief, 'Her story is actually true.'

Toledo and Axminster, then Katherine, exchanged high fives. With a questioning look, Peggy joined in, as did Father Eric, not wanting to be left out of the spirit of the moment.

'What's happening?' Peggy asked.

Scrutinizing them, Father Eric said inquisitively, 'You are behaving as if you've identified the site of an important lost treasure.'

'We have,' Axminster said, the tremor of excitement in his voice so contagious Katherine clapped her hands and hugged Peggy.

Toledo pulled Katherine loose and kissed her. He shook the priest's hand vigorously. 'Your mission here is due a token of our appreciation, padre.'

Father Eric smiled. 'It sounds as if we should have a sip of the sacramental wine.' He reached into his robe for another key, and left.

'You didn't tell me on the phone what this was all about,' Peggy said to Axminster, the hint of a reprove in the tone of her voice.

'Well, I wasn't sure myself. In fact, I will confess I had my doubts.' The banker looked at his watch. 'Speaking of phones, I do have to make a call to London.'

'Don't go into the wrong booth,' Toledo said.

Axminster laughed. 'I doubt the priests take plastic in the confessional.'

'Use your credit card on my cellular,' Peggy offered. 'It's locked onto my bike. Here's the key.' She tossed it to

160

Axminster as he left.

She turned to Toledo and Katherine. 'There's one important matter you need to know about this property.'

Toledo raised his eyebrows.

'There are houses on this particular piece of land. I know this part of town well.'

'So? We'll bulldoze them, recover our trove. That's simple enough, isn't it?'

'But we don't own the property,' Katherine said.

'We'll buy it. That's simple enough, too.'

'But we don't know if the owner wants to sell.'

'Don't worry,' Toledo said. 'Everything's for sale. It's just a matter of price.'

Peggy shook her head, her red hair swishing from side to side. 'But you can't bulldoze even if you are the owner unless you want to go promptly to jail,' she said emphatically. 'You daren't touch even a hinge on the front door. This property is within the El Pueblo Viejo Historic District. Nobody does anything there without approval from the Historic Design Review Board. Not even choose a different paint colour. And, most assuredly, you can't demolish anything without having your replacement plans pre-approved.'

'We'll test the law in court.'

'Forget it,' Peggy advised. 'It's been tested all the way to the Supremes, state and federal. I'll call an architect friend of mine. He'll help you though the maze of red tape at city hall.'

Father Eric returned, holding five glasses and carrying a wine bottle. He poured and proposed a toast to the hallowed souls of the Civil War.

'We better make a copy of this map to show the architect,' Katherine suggested.

'Good idea,' Toledo said. 'Father, do you have a photocopy machine?'

'Yes, in the mission office. But with the size of this map, it'll take two sheets, That'll cost you twenty-five cents.'

Toledo looked at Katherine. 'You got any money on you?'

'I do,' Peggy said. 'I always carry money with me on the bike in case I need an orange or a muffin. My coin purse is on the bike, too.' She handed Toledo another key. She laughed. 'I'll tack it onto the bill I'll be sending you for my services.'

161

Outside, Toledo saw Axminster walking around the little fishpond in the garden, talking on Peggy's cellular. A fountain bubbled, the noise of the water drowning out Axminster's conversation. Looking into the water, Toledo saw little goldfish swimming about. He watched Axminster's reflection. There was a look of surprise on his banker's face.

Seeing Toledo, Axminster quickly ended his cellular conversation. 'I've got to go to London right away,' he announced.

'Now?'

'Now.'

Toledo looked askance at his banker. 'Didn't you get the answers to your inquiry on the phone?'

'If I'm to get the straight scoop I must appear in person,' Axminster replied slowly. 'The banker my manager said to call won't give me the details over the phone. Like I said, they go about things a little differently over there.'

'Then I'll have my pilot fly you down to LAX. They must have non-stops every hour on the hour.'

Axminster smiled and put his arm around Toledo. 'Yes, that would be very kind of you. I'll stop on the way to the airport and buy a toothbrush.'

'Good thing you changed clothes after the race.'

'Yes, that would be funny, wouldn't it? Showing up in the City of London in running clothes and wearing my Bay to Breakers T-shirt.'

Axminster whistled for the parked taxi. 'Good luck with General Beauregard's land,' he said. 'Are you going to dig up the treasure? Wish I could be with you, but. . . . By the way, I'll be at the London Hilton. And our Santa Barbara branch manager will be expecting your visit tomorrow morning.'

'You're going to miss out on all the fun,' Toledo told him.

27

Katherine and Peggy bounded out of the mission, following right behind Father Eric, who chased after Toledo, waving the photocopy he had made of the map. They saw Axminster leave in the taxi.

'He's off to London,' Toledo explained, 'on another treasure hunt.'

'I'm off, too,' Peggy said as she bid them each goodbye and pedalled away.

The priest thrust the map at Toledo, holding out his other hand. Toledo handed him a quarter and asked politely, 'Do you have a car Katherine and I might borrow for a quick trip down the street?'

'Of course, seeing as how you are a cash-paying customer.' He rasped again while reaching inside his robe and fishing out a set of keys. 'Keep my car for a day or so, you'll need it to get around town. It's parked over there in front of the entrance to the mission in the slot marked *Reserved*. You can't miss it.'

As Katherine slipped behind the wheel of Father Eric's late-model Lincoln Town Car, she said, 'Our banker bounces around as much as you and I.'

A string of prayer-beads dangled from the rear-view mirror and swung to and fro as they shut their doors.

'Did you see the bumper sticker?' Toledo asked.

'No, what does it say?'

'*My boss is a Jewish carpenter.*'

Katherine ran her fingers across the leather upholstery. 'Their shop must be prosperous.' She looked over at Toledo and asked, 'Are we off to the Beauregard property?'

'Yes, it's on to the treasure spot. I'm anxious to phone the members of our team and tell them we have the gold.'

'Grace will be elated we've found the precise location of

Grand-daddy Thatcher's Confederate trove. But first, which way do I drive?' she asked.

Toledo studied the Santa Barbara map given him by Peggy, found the street and gave directions. 'Turn onto Mission Street, cross State Street and then turn left. It's as simple as one-two-three.'

They were soon driving through a transitional area where many of the original houses had been divided into rentals. Some of the old houses had been torn down to make way for newer housing. 'A few of these nineteenth-century houses are being restored.' Katherine observed. 'Our generation, you know, invented gentrification.'

'Grace and Carter might beg to differ with you,' he said. As they approached the next cross street, Toledo leaned forward and pressed his head against the windscreen. 'I see it! There it is! Beauregard's land!'

'You mean that house on the corner?' Katherine asked. 'It appears to be abandoned, lonely, lost in time.'

'Apparently, with all their powers, this Historic Design Review Board to which Peggy refers is unable to require owners to maintain their property.' Toledo examined the photocopy of the map Father Eric had sold them. 'Yes, for sure that's the property. Drive down to the next cross street. We'll park around the corner, walk back and explore the general's grand estate.' Suddenly he exclaimed, 'Hey, wait a minute, it's for sale.'

By the side of the house, nailed to a palm-tree whose fronds almost obscured it, was a hand-lettered weathered sign. Katherine read its message out loud, '*For sail by owner.*'

Toledo laughed. 'How many knots do you suppose they want for it?'

Katherine stopped the car and extracted a pen and notebook from her purse. 'There's a phone number, *CR-7 9503* – dates back before the phone company changed to an all-number system, which means it's been on the market for a long time.'

'Yes, so we've probably got a motivated seller,' Toledo said excitedly. He jumped out of the car and scooped up a handful of sun-warmed soil and held it up to his nose. Breathing deeply, he said, 'Let's visualize for a moment. Beauregard's land a century ago must have been in quite bucolic countryside: the château with its *cuvier*, grapevines in neat, cultivated rows stretching alongside a narrow dirt roadway; oak vats and storage tanks, the trademarks of wine and wine-making, their exteriors gleaming with varnish, their interiors swelling with fermenting juices from the fall harvest; pungent aroma sweetening the air.'

'A very poetic picture,' Katherine said as she looked out over the land. She turned to Toledo. 'And now let's use your imagination to locate General Beauregard's buried Confederate treasure.'

'OK, follow me.' They passed an old barn and walked towards the house. Behind the dilapidated outbuilding stretched an open but weedy field. 'There's a lot of vacant land here. And I see a grapevine or two poking up through the weeds.'

'Do you think the treasure is underneath the house, or maybe beneath that old barn?'

Toledo re-examined their parcel map. 'Let's locate exactly where our *X* lies.'

'We could pace off the distance from the property line.'

'Yes, good idea. I'll do it. I have a three-foot stride.'

'But you said the street may have been narrower then. How will you know where to begin your measurement?'

'Back in the days before cars, property lines ran from the centre of the street. I remember reading that once. So I'll pace off from the middle of De La Vina.' Looking up and down, Toledo waited for a break in traffic.

'Be careful,' Katherine yelled as he hurried out towards the yellow centre stripe.

'Look at the map and tell me how far it is to the *X*,' Toledo called out.

'Fifty feet,' she shouted back from the pavement.

Stepping off the distance, Toledo crossed the street, the kerb and the pavement, counting each of his long steps as he went. He parted a row of bushes that were in his way and continued. At thirteen paces he was abruptly stopped by the wall of an old garage, its small size only able to accommodate vehicles of its own vintage. The narrow door, one hinge off, leaned open, exposing rusty appliances, dusty boxes, old newspapers and debris. The refuse heap openly defied the Historic Design Review Board members.

The residence behind the garage also thumbed its nose at

those authoritarian directors. Not only did the house and veranda need paint, but some of the ornate Victorian columns had been replaced with rough four-by-fours. A broken window, bits of jagged glass remaining in its frame, confirmed Katherine's description; the house was indeed abandoned, lonely and lost in time. In the front door a stained-glass window featuring a Paris goblet with jewelled grapes, fearing a similar fate, cringed as Toledo came closer.

A pit bull, roped to a porch column, watched his measured approach, the hair on its back rising higher with each of Toledo's strides. The dog began to snarl, pulled its leash to the absolute limit and then launched into a barking tirade.

'Watch out for the dog,' Katherine exclaimed.

Adeptly Toledo skirted the animal. 'The owner must have posted a vicious guard dog here to deter people from entering his abandoned house,' he surmised.

Endeavouring to maintain his measurement, Toledo moved right, stepping away from the growling animal, and resumed his pacing. Looking forward, he counted three more paces. 'Yes, for sure fifty feet places our X squarely beneath this old house.'

'Marks the spot,' Katherine said.

'Yes, this old garage and house are clearly in our way – in fact, they're outa here.' He gestured as an umpire might in throwing an arguing player out of the game.

'Now wait a minute,' Katherine said. 'I bet the interior has some features – ceiling mouldings, plate rails, wide plank floors, built-in bookcases, a butler's pantry – the craftwork we try to duplicate in our new houses today. It would be fun to fix it up, wouldn't it? We should at least save the stained-glass window. What's our next step?'

'Let's go buy the property.'

'Haven't you got the cart before the horse? Shouldn't we be talking to Peggy's architect friend before we try to buy it? Remember, she said we'd need help at city hall in getting a demolition permit?'

'Which comes first? The owner or the architect?'

'Well, if we spend money on the architect and the owner won't sell, then we've wasted time and money.'

'Right.'

'So let's telephone the owner.' She hesitated. 'But it's

Sunday evening.'

'If he wants to sell, he'll talk any time.'

Down the street they found a pay phone on the wall of a laundromat. Toledo telephoned. Noise from the washers and driers as well as the passing traffic made it difficult for him to hear the answering voice. He made out only the words *casa* and *uno*. He said, '*Momento*,' and then handed the phone to Katherine. 'He's speaking Spanish,' he explained.

Katherine took the phone and said, '*Si*,' into the mouthpiece.

Toledo watched her.

'*Si*.'

Toledo raised his eyebrows.

'*Si*.'

Toledo fidgeted.

Katherine turned to him. 'Mr "*Si*" wants one million dollars . . . in cash . . . no cheques . . . cash.'

'Ask him if his wife or mother or cousin or anyone else holds title along with him, or is he the sole owner?'

Katherine conveyed the question and then said to Toledo, '*Si*, he's the sole owner.'

'One other thing – ask him if he still owns the full ten acres,' Toledo said.

Katherine questioned the owner again and said, '*Si*' to Toledo.

'Tell him to meet us first thing in the morning at the Bank of America on Upper State Street.'

'*Si*.'

'Will he?'

'*Si*,' she said as she hung up. 'You know, a million dollars cash for a dilapidated house and a large weed patch is too much money. Even in Santa Barbara. Aren't you going to try to negotiate a lower price?'

'*Si*. Between now and tomorrow morning we'll come up with a strategy,' Toledo said as they walked back down the street towards Father Eric's car.

28

John Axminster smiled at the stewardess as she served him complimentary sherry and shrimp canapés on the flight from Los Angeles to London. In his banker's disciplined mind-set, he reviewed the essence of what had turned out to be quite an unexpected telephone conversation. He had intended his call to be simply a formal banking inquiry, but to his surprise the conversation quickly shifted to a job interview for himself.

He was pleased he had been so quick to pick up on the turn of events. On the other hand, taking a sip of the amontillado, he tasted his reticence at not being open with his friend Toledo about the real purpose of his hurry-up trip to London. He fretted that his rapid-fire explanation as he and Toledo were standing outside the Santa Barbara mission was a cop-out.

As he saw Toledo come out of the mission, he realized he knew more about what was happening in Albania than Toledo did. So why hadn't he conveyed his news immediately? Why did he hesitate to explain his telephone conversation? His first reaction, not wanting Toledo to overhear, was to quickly bid Archibald McThomson a long-distance goodbye, promising the Scotsman he would board the next possible non-stop to London. And then he had faced Toledo.

Wrestling with his dilemma as he stood by the little fishpond in front of the mission, he had debated in his mind how much of his conversation to relate. In the end he had elected to say simply that a trip to London was necessary to learn the complete story of the Albanian national gold. And that was true. After all, Toledo was in a hurry. And, Axminster had learned from his banking career, people who are in a hurry not only bounce around themselves but also expect everyone else to do so. So announcing his sudden trip meshed with Toledo's display of impatience for answers. And Toledo had bought the explanation, Axminster felt certain – yet that raising of an eyebrow had hinted at a shred of doubt.

As the flight wore on, Axminster continued to worry about his behaviour towards his friend. He didn't need to remind himself he must be honest in his relationship with Toledo. Perhaps, living in those hallowed halls at Brasenose, Oxford, as a Rhodes Scholar, if he hadn't learned anything else, he had learned to value friends. He knew he must tell Toledo the whole story. But when and how? And, he asked himself, what was the entire story?

Yes, he must determine the whole picture first, and not transmit misleading bits and pieces to his friend. After all, the job might be awarded to someone else. And what if it paid in worthless Albanian leks, not in real money? It could also be a temporary job, lasting a few weeks or months until some local politician or banker thought he had learned enough to take over.

There was also the possibility that his appointment would mean he and Toledo could work in tandem. Axminster concluded that as yet he really didn't know enough facts to explain anything to Toledo.

It had all started with the telephone number given to him earlier by his London branch manager. When Axminster placed the call from Peggy's cellular, he was prepared to launch into his query about the Albanian national gold, and so he announced his name.

Instead of a routine reply such as, 'What can I do for you?' the man with the very Scottish name had said, 'So good of you to call, laddie. I've been anxious to talk to you. I was planning to call you first thing in the morning. You're at the top of our short list.'

Axminster didn't know what the man was talking about.

McThomson, first making certain his caller understood his name was spelled devoid of the more traditional 'p' – as if that were a matter of some importance – had then said, 'You must drop everything and fly over here. The head of the Albanian Parliament's National Finance Committee is making a special trip to London – arrives tomorrow, in fact –

169

and I'm arranging interviews during his stay. You understand, he is quite prepared to come to his decision on the spot. And he stresses time is of the essence. One of your fellow Yanks will also be here,' he added.

'Who is that?' Axminster inquired.

'Ah, that is confidential. You must meet him in person, but I can tell you he's quite enamoured with your Oxford paper.'

'He's read it?'

'Oh, yes, we all have. So, shall we say my office at the Trans-European Bank, promptly at fourteen hundred hours tomorrow? You do know where we're located?' McThomson asked.

After Axminster said he didn't know, McThomson followed with some rather detailed instructions, which Axminster had tried to note down on his planning calendar. It was awkward holding the cellular while trying to write, and with McThomson's accent he wasn't sure of the directions, nor did he recognize some of the landmarks, other than St Paul's. But then, getting around London was the least of his worries. After all, he'd been at Oxford, had often come to London and certainly knew how to hail a taxi and use the Underground, so he was sure he could reach any destination.

Still trying to figure out what short list McThomson without the 'p' was referring to, Axminster decided to stall for time. So he went back to his orginal purpose in making the call. 'My London manager says you are the one to talk to about the Albanian national gold. I understand you are the officer who knows about the Corfu Incident, the reparations, and who is now in control of the gold. Can you give me a snapshot of its status?'

'Oh, yes,' McThomson said, 'The Country's national gold is, of course, part of the package. I just assumed you knew. Goes with the territory, as you say in America. That is what you say, isn't it? Never been to America myself. Difficult to travel in a wheelchair, you know. I've booked you into the Hilton Hotel – at Hyde Park Corner,' McThomson added. 'You can jog in the park. You are the one who jogs, aren't you? Have I given you enough time to shower and shave?'

Axminster used his banker's laugh, allowing as how he could shower without dillying.

Then McThomson said, 'Oh, and one other thing.'

'Yes?' Axminster managed, a picture beginning to take shape in this conversational fog of what the Scotsman was really talking about.

'We're going to want your answers to a number of questions. You will be prepared? Of course you will, a man with your track record. Silly of me to ask.'

'Which questions are foremost in your mind, Mr McThomson?' he asked.

'For example, we'll want to ask you, do you feel you can divorce The Country's politics from the task of properly performing your duties? After all, you would be functioning as the principal controller of the money supply and therefore exerting a dominant influence on The Country's economic condition.'

'Yes, avoiding contact with the general public would be the key,' Axminster answered.

'Good. And we shall also want to know your scheme for introducing The Country's new currency. Have to pull in the old leks, you know.'

'Leks?'

'Is it that you think a new name, a fresh label, would give things a boost? Get rid of the past? Issue new currency? Yes, very commendable idea, I should think. A new name and a new look. Yes, perhaps you do have a novel idea there, laddie.'

Axminster then commented about the importance of the coin of the realm while still wondering as to the identity and the role of the other Yank McThomson had mentioned.

'Gold? You think gold coins might do it? You will expand on that idea for us, won't you? The matter is dealt with in some detail in your paper as I recall – currency, its proper backing and gaining the public's confidence – that sort of thing.'

'Yes, public confidence is the critical issue,' Axminster replied, 'as well as, of course, that of the international banking community.'

'Yes, your paper is well written. Those Oxford dons are indeed tough taskmasters. Anyway, the more precise and clear you can make your remarks, the better for all of us. Isn't that right? We need your input. And we shall have a few questions for you when you appear before us,' McThomson had concluded.

Finally, after finishing off yet another glass of sherry, as the short summer night eventually darkened the sky outside, still speculating as to what actually lay ahead of him in London and still troubled about accounting to Toledo, John Axminster fell asleep. Yet even with the hum of the jet engines and soothed by the sherry, he slept only fitfully as his big plane droned east at thirty-five thousand feet above the Atlantic Ocean through the night and into the morning that was quick, too quick, in following.

29

Katherine parked the Lincoln Town Car parallel to the Brinks armoured truck. Watching the uniformed courier hoist two satchels, one in each hand, balancing their weight equally as he carried them into the branch bank, Katherine said, 'Looks like they're delivering your cash.'

Toledo smiled. 'Yes, but before we go in let's review a few basic principles of negotiation I learned from Ines Stark.'

'Oh?'

'First, it's important to identify the seller's needs and then to address them.'

'He said he wants cash.'

'And to express our proposal in terms that serve his needs.'

'He wants the cash this morning.'

'And then not to demean the seller,' Toledo went on, 'and especially not to become embroiled in any argument or dispute which allows the seller to adopt what could quickly become an intractable position.'

'We'll simply pay him.'

'But you said we should try for a lower price.'

'Yes, that's addressing *our* needs.'

Toledo tapped loudly on the glass door of the bank, still locked to the public on this early Monday morning. Responding, a staff person with only a hint of a smile peered questioningly at them.

'Tell your manager it's Toledo Squires and Katherine Mondragon,' he shouted through the glass. 'John Axminster arranged an introduction for us.'

The staff person's smile broadened as she unlocked the door and welcomed them into the deserted lobby. 'Right this way, folks. Our manager is expecting you.'

The manager rose from his seat. 'Any friends of John Axminster are friends of ours. How can we help you?'

'I need one million dollars in cash and right now,' Toledo told him.

The manager laughed. 'Axminster does have some strange friends.'

The staff person returned. 'There's a gentleman to see Mr Squires and Ms Mondragon,' she announced, smirking. 'And he's carrying a gunny sack that I think must be full of empty cans.'

'Please show him in,' Toledo said.

The seller's cans clanked together as he crossed the lobby concourse.

'Your job's going to be more difficult than mine,' Toledo said, addressing the branch manager. 'You've got to convince our seller the cash he's about to receive from the sale of his land will be safer deposited in your bank vault than buried in his backyard. All I have to do is to negotiate a bargain price.'

The property owner came into the office, saw Katherine, and grinned. 'It is indeed my pleasure to make your acquaintance. You are as pretty as your lovely voice. Your smile is radiant. You have brought sunshine to my day.'

'You speak English?' Toledo said, surprised.

'Si.'

'Flattery will not get you a million dollars,' Katherine said. 'You've neglected your property. You've blighted your lovely neighbourhood. You've committed cruelty to animals by tying your dog to a post and leaving him there. You ought to be ashamed. Your land is worth not a penny more than five hundred thousand.'

'Humiliating me won't get you the property. My wife's been ill. I've devoted all my time to her care. I have all these medical bills to pay, and she needs another operation. Seven hundred and fifty thousand – all cash, and nothing larger than twenty-dollar bills. And that savage dog isn't mine.'

'Sympathy won't enhance the price,' Katherine told him. 'But it might get you an extra ten thousand provided you donate it to Father Eric at the Santa Barbara mission for your wife's speedy recovery. Whose dog is it?'

'Extortion just drove the price up. Eight hundred thousand plus your ten for Father Eric. Look, I'm prepared to deliver a clear title. As I told you on the telephone, I'm the sole owner. And there are no taxes, assessments or liens owing on my property. Now that's full disclosure.'

Toledo finally spoke up. 'You haven't enough cans in that gunny sack of yours to hold that much money.'

'Well, full disclosure on the seller's part is deserving of our adjustment, isn't it?' Katherine said to Toledo. Before he could answer, she turned back to the seller. 'That's worth six hundred thousand and forget Father Eric.'

'You got yourself a deal.' He grinned. 'But that crazy pit-bull belongs to a homeless squatter. Good luck in getting them off the property. They go with the old house.'

'We need someone to type a new warranty deed,' Toledo said to the branch manager.

'No, you don't,' the seller said, handing the banker an old tattered deed with an elaborate seal and ribbon affixed to the signature line. 'Use this one, it shows the original legal description of the property. And it's made out to me. The seller's signature when he sold it to me years ago is notarized and witnessed.' He pointed to the back of the legal-size paper. 'See here, Mr Beauregard signed it – right here.'

'Beauregard!' Katherine exclaimed.

'Yes, his great-grandfather was some Civil War general. See here's the general's signature on the front, and here' – he pointed to the back – 'the county clerk has attested to the transfer of the property from the general's last will and testament to his sons, Henri and René. They passed it on to this Beauregard, who sold it to me. All properly signed.'

Toledo asked to see the deed. Caressing the antique legal parchment, he tried desperately to contain his exuberance. 'OK, I'll write in my name here as the new owner and you sign below,' he directed the seller.

'Ah,' the bank manager interrupted, 'if you allow us to open an acount for you in one of the world's largest banks, you will earn interest, and your money will be insured by an agency of the federal government. . . .'

'I don't trust banks. I want my cash. In twenties, too.'

Shaking his head in disappointment and disbelief, the manager buzzed for the staff person. 'Bring up six hundred thousand in currency – twenty-dollar bills – from those satchels the Brinks man just brought in,' he told her.

Toledo wrote a cheque and handed it to the manager, who said, 'Let me just verify your balance.' He made another call and quickly nodded his approval.

The staff person returned, carrying her notarial book, official stamp and seal. Without a smile she said to the seller and Toledo, 'For proper identification, may I please see your drivers' licences, gentlemen?'

30

Outside, treasuring the signed deed, Toledo exclaimed, 'Beauregard's land! We've made the direct connection with Grand-daddy Thatcher and the Civil War general. Do you feel their presence, Katherine?' He looked at the document and smiled. 'I do.'

Katherine matched Toledo's fervour. 'Yes, it is splendid! After all these years Grace's secret has manifest itself in this glorious discovery.'

'Do you realize what that means?' Toledo went on.

Standing by the car door, Katherine said, 'I'm beginning to.'

'Now historians will have to rewrite American history. We've just supplied them with new and vital information on the aftermath of the War Between the States.'

'The whole Reconstruction period.'

'Yes, we – you, Grace and I – have identified a new state of affairs for scholars to discuss.'

'They'll be thrilled as long as our discovery doesn't turn out to be another Piltdown Man,' Katherine said.

'Nonsense.' Toledo climbed into the car. 'Just think, if only the South had been allowed to finance its Reconstruction based on the Confederate gold, most of which rests under what is now my land –' he pointed to his deed – 'and they could have done so if General Lee had incorporated the gold into the terms of the surrender at Appomattox. Why then, Reconstruction would have been a different story. And it might not have taken them a hundred years to enact civil rights legislation.'

'But if the Yankees could have gotten their hands on the gold they would have confiscated it as war reparations, wouldn't they?' Katherine pointed out.

'Not if Lee had insisted the treasure remain intact – set

177

aside in a special fund, such as with our social security system. General Grant would have gone along with that provision, I am certain, for the terms he did set for Lee's surrender were pretty lenient. Grant was motivated to stop all the bloodshed and hoped to convince the remaining Confederate armies in Texas and the West to lay down their arms peacefully. He didn't want guerilla warfare breaking out across the South. But when generals are the only ones determining the order of the day, important financial matters are often overlooked.'

Katherine turned the ignition, and the car's powerful engine fired. 'But if General Lee had done what you are suggesting, we wouldn't have a treasure to dig up.'

'You're right,' Toledo said. His eyes lit up as he added, 'You know, there are obvious parallels with Albania. Now with the gold we will be able to make the right decisions for the economic and political benefit of The Country – determine its history, its course of events. Pretty heady stuff, if you ask me.'

'So it's on to the architect's office to obtain our demolition permit?'

As Katherine drove off, Toledo said, 'According to our street map, his office is supposed to be . . . let me see . . . toward the municipal wharf.'

The office was in a building overlooking the marina. Displayed on the walls of his reception area were framed photographs of the architect at various social events. Some pictures showed him shaking hands with the mayor and city councillors, other snapshots were of him arm-in-arm with members of the Historic Design Review Board, while another glossy caught the same smiling face during a presentation before the Planning Commission. Each image was labelled with its date and the particular function. Here was a detailed portrayal of self-importance.

'This guy's really connected,' Toledo said. 'We shouldn't have any problem getting a demolition permit.'

'Be diplomatic, he may have a bit of an ego problem,' Katherine warned.

'Go right in, Ms Mondragon and Mr Squires,' the receptionist announced. She directed them through a large room where men and women were working at computer stations, their monitors showing façades of various buildings and houses.

Katherine watched as, with sequential touching of keys, a woman switched the style of a house from English Tudor to Spanish Colonial. 'She has in less than a second redesigned a project that would have taken months to do in the era before computers,' she commented.

'Computers accelerate our lives,' Toledo said.

'Any friends of Peggy O'Neill are friends of mine,' the architect greeted them. 'How can we help you?'

'We want to tear down an old abandoned house, a real eyesore,' Toledo explained.

'I can help you with that. We'll schedule the preparation of the application.' The architect exhibited the same smile Toledo saw in the photographs. 'We should be ready to file our preliminary forms in about two weeks.'

'Two weeks!' Toledo exclaimed. 'We need to tear it down today.'

'No, no, no,' he said. 'This is Santa Barbara, not Bakersfield. You can't move that quickly here.'

'But two weeks!'

'No, no, no, you don't understand. That's just for our filing your application for demolition. But the city won't issue you a permit on the spot. They have to meet in chambers and consider whether or not they're going to accept your request. Be assured you'll need our help, because those people who have tried to go it alone without the services of a professional architect haven't met with much success.'

'I'm sure with you crossing every "t" and dotting every "i" our application will be approved immediately.'

'No, no, no,' the architect said. 'Your application is then passed on to the Pueblo Viejo Historic Design Review Board. But before they'll consider it, you'll need my architect's drawings of whatever it is you plan to build there – that is, the replacement structure for the existing house.'

'Well, punch out a generic design on one of your computers.' Toledo gestured to the outer room.

'No, no, no. For you to win approval of any design, your plan must be compatible with the streetscape within this particular historic district,' the architect went on. 'We'll need to study the neighbourhood and sketch the existing character of buildings already there.'

'Well, send out an artist with an easel and start drawing.'

'No, no, no,' the architect said, 'it doesn't work that way. We'll need to meet with city staff – get their input on our proposed design. And then they'll want us to conduct meetings with local neighbourhood associations, get their ideas on what they want for their neighbourhood. And we're required to give proper notice – thirty days – by sending invitations to the meeting to all property owners within one mile. You'll need to compile the list from official records at the court-house and pay a fee to the city staff to send out the mailings.'

'Hey, wait a minute!'

'No, no, no, nothing falls between the cracks any more. Our is a democracy, and people are entitled to express opinions about their own neighbourhoods. I mean, America is made up of lots of good neighbourhoods – the backbone of our great nation.'

'You've got to be kidding,' Toledo said, his impatience obvious.

'Then it's on to a hearing before the full Historic Design Review Board, assuming the staff hasn't forced us into a redesign or we've met with opposition from neighbours or, heaven forbid, the media.'

'But all these procedures will require months,' Toledo exclaimed. 'We'll be for ever getting our demolition permit.'

'No, no, no, not more than nine or ten months, I should think,' the architect said. 'That is, unless the board turns down our first design.'

'In that case?'

'We'll design what they want to see built there. They really have some good ideas, you know.'

'That means we'd be back to square one,' Toledo said in dismay.

The architect's phone rang. He spoke into the instrument. 'No, no, no, tell him he'll have to be patient – wait until next month, because we missed the filing deadline for this month's hearing.'

The architect looked at Toledo and Katherine. 'Everyone's in a hurry. By the way, what's your big rush? These days real-estate projects take time and money, a lot of each. Why do you think housing is so expensive?'

Growing even more impatient, Toledo said, 'OK, let's get

to the bottom line. Peggy says you're a member of this board, so you ought to accordion this whole approval procedure into a shorter time frame, like maybe days.'

'No, no, no,' the architect said again. 'My being a board member only assures proper procedures will be followed. I've prepared the standard contract.' The architect produced a thick stack of papers and said, 'It calls for payment of one-third of our estimated fee of ninety thousand dollars up front.'

Katherine watched Toledo's fists clench and unclench. His face was ruby red. 'Before you even begin work?'

'Professional standards,' the architect replied, leaving no room for doubt that the matter was indisputable. 'We'll of course do our best,' he added.

Toledo struggled to control his temper. 'Damn it, we've simply got to move faster than that!'

'No, no, no, there is no way,' the architect said, losing patience. 'You do it my way – the city's way – or you don't do it at all.' As Toledo rose to leave, he added, 'Let me know when you're ready to play ball.'

Outside, Katherine said, 'He wants to take you for a ride, right?'

Fuming, Toledo said, 'No, we're going to take our own ride, on our own big yellow bulldozer – if I have to buy one and drive it up De La Vina Street myself.'

31

Casa de las Pulgas was a neighbourhood bar set in a nineteenth-century adobe on Salispuedes Street, somehow having survived Santa Barbara's invasion by Hollywood stars, celebrity golfers and the maritime crowd. Known simply as 'The Flea', it served as the last bastion for the town's blue-collar workers. It had even once survived a skirmish with incendiary long-haired students from the nearby Isla Vista university campus out on a Saturday night rabble-rousing expedition.

Standing at the bar, a beefy man, unshaven, his dark hair askew, identified by the crowd of construction workers as 'the bulldozer operator', offered to buy yet another round.

Responding, the bartender retrieved bottle after frosty bottle of Corona from the cooler, stuck a wedge of lime into the lip of each and handed a fruited brew to the eagerly waiting recipients of the bulldozer operator's generosity.

'What's the occasion?' one asked. 'You strike gold with that blade of yours?'

'He's got himself a big bulldozing job for that yellow toy of his,' another said. He turned to the bulldozer operator. '*Salud*! You're lucky, man, there are so few jobs for us any more, what with water shortages and all them building regulations. We shoulda all moved to Bakersfield long ago. That's where the action is today, man.'

The bulldozer operator smiled a big smile. 'At midnight, man. It's on the q.t. and the Anglo paid me a lot more to hire a couple of extra hands. I'll be able to make my payments for the rest of this year.'

'If you don't spend it all on beer or lose your operator's licence for performing an illegal demolition,' the architect's receptionist shouted from the pay phone. Then she punched out a special number that would get her a little bonus for passing on a titbit of hot information.

Listening at the end of the bar, the Brinks driver downed his Corona.

His companion, the staff assistant from the bank, picked up her cellular and dialled a number.

Next to her, a young novitiate from the Santa Barbara mission got up and stood in the long line now forming, to wait his turn at the pay phone.

The bartender locked the cash register and retreated inside his cluttered private office. Amid the crates of bottles he located his private phone and punched out his own set of numbers connecting him with an intimate accomplice.

'Madam Mayor,' he said, 'your friendly bartender here. How's my horseback-riding centrefold? I thought you might like to know there's to be a bulldozing tonight – at midnight. Somewhere between Upper State Street and the 101 Freeway. I think he said De La Vina. You may want to meet me there – official business, you know, and then we could slip off into the bushes. . . .'

32

The Methuselah had opened its doors to elderly residents a mere three years earlier. During its first year a number of social events were established as family traditions of this Santa Fe retirement home. In addition to the customary holiday dinners, each month had its 'How Many Candles?' celebration for everyone whose birthday fell within that month. There were the now-we're-going-to-have-fun Friday night 'Happy Hours'. Thursday mornings offered 'Two-Card Limit Bingo'. And on Wednesday afternoons the cook, who was also a pianist, played for the 'Sing-along'. In adhering to her regular party routine, the Activities Director would recite the prosaic refrain, 'This is how we do it at the Methuselah.'

But there was nothing in her rule book to cover a *bon voyage* party. In fact, there was a total void of ceremonies of departure, merely the whispers among residents that so-and-so had either 'left us', or 'gone on', to be followed by a relative retrieving personal items and a crew refurbishing the apartment for some new move-in.

So when Grace Templeton and Carter Calhoun announced their engagement and travel plans, spontaneity took charge. Residents gathered in the Great Hall in happy pandemonium.

Harry Shields blew up snow-white balloons and passed them out to the self-invited guests, some of whom tied their balloons to their walkers. Rising from the comfort of the lobby couch she always shared with her look-alike, Mrs Jensen, Mrs Symington busily twisted crêpe-paper ribbon through the backs of the folding chairs. Her now-active bookend, Mrs Jensen, serious about her task, punctuated Mrs Symington's ribbon with big white bows. And, pushing her glasses up on her nose, a petite Mrs Winestein arranged the floral decorations.

A tumultuous ovation greeted Grace and Carter as they entered the room.

Ed Undergroth, wearing a starched and pressed shirt, popped the champagne cork and poured for everyone. 'Here's to Methuselah's first romance,' he said. 'Let it not be the last.' Glasses clinked their agreement throughout the Great Hall.

The cook, in his white chef's apron and hat, brought in a three-tiered cake topped with a bride-and-groom ornament. 'Get over here and cut this cake for all the folks,' he said lovingly to Grace.

'Wait, I want to take a picture,' Mrs Jensen said. 'Carter, you get in this picture, too.'

Carter stepped up and placed his hand over Grace's, and together they cut the cake, meting out large slices to their friends.

'Play us some waltzes on the piano, Cookie, I feel like dancing,' Harry Shields sang out.

The Steinway came alive with Al Jolson's nostalgic song, *Oh, how we danced. . .*

Harry bowed. 'May I have the pleasure of this dance?' he said to Grace.

Grace extended her hand to Harry. 'It is my pleasure.'

Round and round in three-quarter time, accentuating the first beat with coordinated arm movements, following a step-step-close pattern, they circled the room while the others sang the lyrics to that familiar melody. As they breezed past him, Carter tapped Harry on the shoulder and said, 'My turn, Harry.'

Grace smiled at the other dancing couples as she and Carter completed the waltz.

'Something old, something new, something borrowed, something blue,' Mrs Symington called out.

'Grace, you don't need anything old, you got Carter,' Harry Shields called back.

Tom the Painter, his hands shaking with two small gift-wrapped packages, presented one to Carter, a sly smile on his face, and the other to Grace. 'Here's a couple of new things for you.'

Grace opened hers to discover a fresh deck of Ace poker cards. She looked at them closely and shook her head. 'Now I'll have to mark these like I did the old ones.' She looked at Carter. 'What do you have, dear?'

Apprehensively Carter undid his bow and paper, revealing

a box of Trojan condoms. His face turned red as Tom and the other men laughed uproariously and slapped him on his back. 'Just more balloons for Harry to blow up,' he said to Grace.

'Here is my Ouija board for you to borrow,' Mrs Jensen said to Grace and Carter. 'It was touted as the latest and most scientific method of fortune-telling when it was copyrighted in 1919. You simply place the alphabet board upon your knees as you sit and face one another. Your fingers rest lightly on the little heart-shaped trivet so as to allow its mystifying movement to spell out answers to all your intimate questions.'

'You mean it would tell me all the secret ingredients Sara Lee uses?' the cook asked.

Mrs Winestein held out her hand to Grace. 'Here's something blue for you, my dear, a beautiful cobalt-blue bottle of Evening in Paris perfume. I found it in the bottom drawer of my dresser and didn't have time to wrap it.'

Grace held the bottle up to the light and noticed the liquid inside had completely evaporated. 'The perfume of my past has vanished. But I shall fill it with today's aromatic fortune.'

Ed Undergroth handed Grace a bouquet of flowers. She gave him a kiss on the cheek, and then in a grand gesture she tossed her bouquet high in the air. The bouquet sailed across the piano, missing the cook, who ducked just in time. At that moment the Activities Director came running into the Great Hall to see what all the commotion was about. She and the bouquet collided.

Everyone applauded.

As Grace and Carter hugged their goodbyes, Tom threw a shaking handful of rice at the happy couple.

33

'My son!' Carter exclaimed proudly in response to the British passport official's query as to the purpose of their visit. 'That's the reason we've come to London – to see my son at long last. And,' Carter said as he put his arm around Grace, 'for him to meet my lovely bride-to-be.' Wound up, Carter nervously added, 'And also we're here to retrieve the Albanian gold.'

'Is that business or pleasure?' the official asked, uncertain which box to tick off on his form.

Grace smiled. 'Our pleasure.'

Carter signalled a porter, who collected their luggage and escorted them through Customs to the taxi queue.

'Now I know I'm in London,' Grace said as she saw the line of boxy black London cabs. She laughed. 'Where the English drive on the wrong side of the road.'

Yet as their taxi sped along the A4 and into the congested streets of London, Grace became more and more overwhelmed by this counter-flow of traffic. Nevertheless she felt if she were to voice her anxiety she would be intruding on Carter's thoughts and his expectations of their impending meeting with Ardian.

The taxi soon pulled up in front of a canopied entrance. The hotel doorman, in morning coat and top hat, opened her door, his gloved hand outstretched, ready to assist. At Reception, the desk clerk welcomed them, accepting their passports for identification, and handed Carter a message.

His hand shaking, Carter took the envelope. 'A message from Ardian,' he said.

'Let me help,' Grace said. She opened the envelope and unfolded the note.

'It's written on the stationery of the Albanian Parliament,' Carter said, pointing to the embossed letterhead.

Grace read out loud:

My dear father and Grace,
I am so looking forward to seeing you both. Have a
little rest – recuperate from your long trip and the time
change. Tomorrow we have a full day with the other
members of Parliament who are anxious to meet you.
This evening I shall come by for you as planned at seven
p.m., and we shall go to dinner and enjoy our private
reunion.

Love, Ardian

Carter smiled and said, 'But how am I supposed to nap if
I am racked with anticipation?'

'Now, don't worry, we'll just unpack, lie down on the
bed, turn on the BBC, and soon we'll fall fast asleep.'

★ ★ ★

At ten minutes to seven, holding Grace's hand, Carter
positioned himself at the hotel entrance. Anxiously waiting,
he shifted his weight and fidgeted, anticipating.

At seven sharp a taxi drove up. A man emerged, saw
them, waved and rapidly approached, stretching out his
arms in welcome.

'That's him,' Carter cried out, his voice quavering.
'There's Ardian, Grace!' He turned to her. 'You've done
it. You've brought us together!'

Grace squeezed his hand.

For a moment Ardian and Carter looked at each other.
They smiled. Then, coming together, they embraced, arms
around each other, slapping one another on the back. Their
emotions were expressed with their laughter.

Carter said, 'My son, my son . . . we are together . . .
at last.'

Tears ran down Grace's cheeks.

Carter turned to Grace, put his arm around her, drawing
her close into the intimate circle.

'I never thought the day would come when we would
stand side by side,' Ardian said to Carter. 'Tell me, Grace,
do I look like a chip off the old block?'

Carter laughed, and then in a gallant gesture he introduced

Grace. 'Ardian, may I present my bride-to-be.'

Grace stood on her tiptoes. Reaching upward, she kissed Ardian's cheek.

Ardian put an arm around her and his other around his father. 'We've got a lot of catching up to do.'

Ardian was as handsome as her groom-to-be, Grace observed, a younger image of Carter, taller by an inch or so, his wavy hair only tinged with grey. Ardian's clothes were a different cut – probably, Grace thought, an Eastern European style and likely not expensive. But with his stature, his broad shoulders, he appeared fastidiously dressed. He was certainly a strong man, not only physically but in countenance, yet he acted in a gentle manner and was certainly considerate of Carter and herself.

As she watched the two men, she felt certain their reunion was working wonders for Carter, allowing him to express his love for his son, and she presumed Ardian, judging from his display of affection and laughter, had also found a release for his feelings. Grace was thrilled how splendidly Carter and Ardian were connecting.

She looked more closely at Ardian and saw deep facial lines, caused, she suspected, by the constant stress of having lived under a Communist regime. And she wondered, with his election to Parliament, would new lines appear?

'I survived ten years in political prison,' Ardian was saying. 'I'm fortunate, more fortunate than some. But those dark years are behind us. Now we must address the present.' Ardian smiled at Grace. 'Let's continue our conversation at dinner. I've made reservations at a French restaurant in Shepherd Market.

The September evening was warm. The narrow cobblestone streets leading off the square were crowded with lively pavement cafés. The head waiter directed them to a table with an umbrella displaying the Perrier logo. He struck a match to the candle wick and signalled for the waiter.

The waiter, a white towel folded over his arm, brought a bottle of Bordeaux Blanc, allowing Carter to taste, and then filled their glasses. Ardian promptly raised his glass. 'I would be honoured if you would permit me to be your best man,' he said.

Instead of a quick perfunctory clink, they touched their

glasses almost silently, and held them together for an extra moment.

'Ardian, you make me very happy,' Carter said. 'I must confess, however, Grace and I haven't set the date or place for our wedding. But, of course, you must be my best man.'

Grace tingled with happiness. She extended her left hand so Ardian could see her engagement ring.

'Let's talk about the plans for your wedding,' Ardian said, admiring the ring.

The waiter returned, bringing a basket of French bread and little crocks of whipped butter, filled their wineglasses and took their dinner orders.

Ardian quickly resumed. 'Speaking on behalf of The Country, other members of Parliament, and certainly myself, we want very much for you to be married in Tirana. And my assignment this evening is to extend the invitation officially. Now, before you say yes or no, allow me to explain the reasons.'

'On behalf of The Country,' Carter said slowly, repeating his son's words.

'Yes,' Ardian said. 'As you know, all the peoples of Eastern Europe appear euphoric with their overthrow of Communism. But this exuberance is only momentary, I'm afraid. Their lives have an emotional emptiness, a quiet sadness. We have a void of truly charismatic leaders. For all the years since World War II we've had nothing but demagogues – their faces appeared everywhere simultaneously with marching military, their idolatry forced upon us by the secret police.

'Some people remember how, going back before World War II, we had kings and queens, not so much to rule, because each country had its Parliament, but to honour, to revere, to admire. In America you have your corporate heroes, your movie stars, your first ladies. You create your own Camelot.

'Today Albania has no one. So, my idea – what I am offering – is for you two to become our someones, the titular heads of The Country. Your wedding will be a royal one, capturing our national values – family, stability, timeless love – ideals our people treasure.'

Carter looked at Grace. 'A little bit of romance has done wonders for me.'

'Exactly,' Ardian replied. 'Our people need to be reassured

that happiness is their birthright.'

'That's a lovely thought,' Grace said.

'But couldn't you do that by resurrecting the monarchy?' Carter asked.

'No,' Ardian replied. 'A true monarchy is out of the question. No one wants to revert to the past. The people, The Country, our newly elected Parliament – we all want to go forward, address the future with new ideas, new faces.' Ardian hesitated only momentarily before saying, 'We want to introduce you to the people as our inspirational leaders – emissaries for those ideals your friends King Zog and Queen Geraldine once envisioned for Albania.'

Grace smiled. 'I've dreamed of such a role all my life. The social fabric could be re-woven in bright, new colours,' she added.

Ardian nodded.

The waiter served their dinners. Ardian didn't begin to eat. Instead he continued, 'So, here is what we have in mind.' He looked at Carter. 'King Zog's royal residence overlooking Tirana is being opened up again after all these years.'

'A beautiful palace in a glorious setting,' Carter said to Grace. 'I remember the fragrance of the pine forest surrounding it, the commanding views from its balconies across the city, and especially my conversations with the king and, later, his queen as well.'

'And do you also remember the lovely Italianate villa in Tirana which housed the US Embassy?' Ardian asked.

'Yes, of course,' Carter replied wistfully. 'Brings fond memories. King Zog frequently extolled these same ideals you're now talking about.'

'Well, your State Department people are restoring the embassy to its original grandeur – actually making it even more magnificent. So, we shall celebrate your wedding vows in the royal palace and hold a festive reception afterwards in the US Embassy – a fitting culmination of your story-book romance. The people of Albania will love the pomp and ceremony, and they will love you two, as well.'

'Did you know Grace was a childhood friend of Queen Geraldine?' Carter asked.

Ardian looked surprised.

Grace nodded.

Ardian picked up on the news with enthusiasm. 'Even more appropriate. We'll arrange for the women of Albania to fashion a copy of Queen Geraldine's wedding dress for you, Grace. We found bolts of satin and lace stored away in the palace.'

Grace smiled. 'I couldn't be more honoured.'

'You will become our royal family,' Ardian said. 'Not in the legal sense, of course, but more importantly in the hearts of the people. And you, Grace,' Ardian said as he took her hand and held it in his, 'will be for all of us the queen mother.'

Grace retrieved her hankie and touched her eyes.

'And you, Carter,' Ardian went on, 'will wear The Country's Medal of Freedom, the one I understand King Zog bestowed upon you years ago.'

'Yes, I've treasured it.'

'And we'll have a splendid tuxedo tailored for you, Carter. And you will both wear jewelled crowns designed especially for the occasion by the silversmiths' guild. It will be an opportunity for us to bring back craft guilds, to re-establish the artisans in their trades. Those contributing wares for your wedding will receive the official seal of *Provider to the Kingdom by the Sea.*

'People will voluntarily form clean-up committees, sweeping the streets of revolutionary debris, replacing the broken windows across the capital city, and planting flower-beds once again. We'll stage a stately procession through the streets of Tirana and across Skanderbeg Square, where the water fountains will flow once more.

'You will serve as our link to America,' Ardian went on. 'You'll answer our people's questions about American consumer products. Everyone dreams of buying "Made in the USA". And as Archibald McThomson may have told you, we're going to change our currency – base it on our gold, the gold you've been looking after. So, we're planning to feature your portraits – each of you – on this new paper money, symbolizing its stability.

'You see, your wedding is the first step in putting The Country back together – re-weaving the social fabric, Grace. Why, part of the ceremony will be Islamic and part Christian, part recited in the Tosk dialect and part in Gheg.'

Carter chuckled. 'It will be a long ceremony.'

192

'All the better,' Ardian said. 'More opportunity for television coverage from our new station and its fledgling crew of reporters.'

'But, Ardian, what you are proposing is for us to remain in Albania – the rest of our lives,' Carter said slowly.

'Oh, Carter, that would be thrilling,' Grace exclaimed. 'I would like that very much.'

Carter looked at her. He was silent only for a moment before replying emphatically, 'Well then, you shall have it! We'll leave the Methuselah behind and usher in Albania, welcoming our new destiny.' He laughed heartily and winked at her. 'There is, my love, life after a retirement home, after all.'

Grace squeezed Carter's hand and turned to his son. 'Thank you, Ardian,' she said softly.

34

The red, white and blue Stars and Stripes billowed from the adjacent US Embassy in the late afternoon September breeze as Grace and Carter emerged from their hotel. They walked along the edge of Grosvenor Square and soon passed a plaque *Headquarters of General of the Armies, Dwight D. Eisenhower.* Carter gestured at the building, telling Grace about his own military duties and how he often reported there during World War II.

Looking across the square, Carter nodded towards a house on the corner of Duke Street. 'Number nine over there,' he said, 'was John Adams's home while he served his country in London as our first US ambassador in 1785.'

'Yes, I remember from my history. He was Abigail's husband. She admonished him when he was attending the Constitutional Convention in Philadelphia to "remember the ladies".'

Together they crossed the street, entering the lush green gardens in the centre of Grosvenor Square. Hand in hand they stood by the memorial to Franklin D. Roosevelt. 'Another American dealing with problems abroad,' Grace commented.

'They've set fine examples.'

Grace turned to Carter. 'Now we'll be following in their tradition as we lend a helping hand to our adopted Albania.'

'But are we up to the task?' Carter asked, worried. 'Do we really want to be become expatriates?'

'Moving overseas doesn't mean we'll turn into different people. Let's not allow relocation to trouble us. We will simply have another stage on which to perform. These Americans' – she gestured around Grosvenor Square – 'stood steadfast in their beliefs. And so shall we.'

Grace and Carter resumed their walk through the gardens.

'Our meeting this morning was fruitful ... all the business you decided and agreed upon with those men,' Grace said, putting her arm around his. 'You were really quite splendid.'

Carter twirled his cane. 'Once our role was ratified by the others, the meeting gathered its own momentum and we readily resolved the remaining issues. All the players agreed on the main course of events. From here on the details will be easily worked out.'

'Ardian was really in charge, wasn't he? Your son knows where he is going.'

'And The Country with him.'

'Yes, and that young man from San Francisco,' Grace said, 'the American banker, John Axminster, is going to be an eminent spokesman as head of the Central Bank.'

'I'm pleased he and Ardian got on so well. My friend Archibald was astute in selecting him for the post. And, as Ardian says, they will appreciate me throwing in my two cents' worth from time to time.'

'And as John Axminster said, your judgment, after making decisions over many decades, is a deep reservoir of data that no computer can ever be programmed to display.'

'Yes, a fine young man. What a coincidence it is that he knows your grandson.'

Grace laughed. 'Small world, isn't it?'

'But it's rapidly expanding for us.'

'You're right,' Grace said, and beamed. 'You and I shall be the ones hosting a great many of The Country's ceremonial events.' She thought for a moment. 'Carter, do you realize the many official duties we'll be performing in our new regal capacity?'

'We'll be cutting hundreds of ribbons at the ground-breaking ceremonies for those new roads and bridges, and the airport runway extension, too,' Carter said. 'In fact, all the projects that were talked about in our meeting this morning will require us to be present at their dedication.'

'And there'll be the openings of new medical facilities and schools, as well.'

'And the new hotels and department stores.'

'Those could be charitable events,' Grace said, 'at which we could raise money for worthy causes.'

Carter nodded. 'We'll have to greet officially the representatives from international aid organizations who want to support the new democracy. And, of course, we'll be asked to entertain royally the visiting diplomats.'

'Yes, Carter, you and I will always be there – the two of us. We are to be, as Ardian put it, symbols of The Country's stability.'

They walked on further through Grosvenor Square. Suddenly Grace stopped and looked at Carter. 'But will we still be able to take our daily walks?'

'Of course we will,' Carter said. 'That routine won't change. And we'll have lots of people who will be curious to meet us, wanting to ask us questions. They will join us, walk along with us, talk with us as we stroll around Skanderbeg Square.'

'Our days will be exhilarating, won't they?' Grace squeezed his hand. 'And, Carter, you and I are going to be enriched with five million new friendships.'

35

Toledo parked the heavy-duty Ryder truck across the street from General Beauregard's land and away from the neighbourhood's sole street light. He looked about. 'This place is eerie in the middle of the night.'

'Are you still feeling the ghostly presence of General Beauregard?' Katherine asked.

'Yes, and we're about to wake the dead.'

'We'd better wake your homeless tenant and his dog,' Katherine said. 'Remember, the seller warned us the pair would be difficult to evict. And we can't simply bulldoze them! Aren't we going to allow the man time to collect his belongings?'

'That's why we're a few minutes early.'

'Suppose he refuses to leave?'

'With a behemoth bulldozer bearing down, he'll move in a hurry.'

Toledo ran across the street towards the corner house, being careful to skirt the pit bull, who was growling at his approach. Toledo knocked on the front door. The dog stretched its rope to the limit and burst into a barking tirade.

As Katherine drew closer she saw candlelight flicker in a kaleidoscope of colours through the jewels in the stained-glass window. 'The window . . . try to save the window in the door,' she called out to Toledo.

Toledo acknowledged with a wave of his hand.

Katherine watched as a bearded man, naked and muscular, opened the door, confronting Toledo. He made no effort to quiet the growling dog. Seeing Katherine, the man withdrew, only to return quickly, wearing blue jeans.

The animal continued to protest Toledo's presence, straining its rope and standing on its hind legs, its lips curling, its teeth gnashing, its mouth frothing, its bark menacing.

Katherine was now close enough to hear the man's words as they filtered through his beard. In spite of the barking dog, she heard him say in a French accent, 'But, *monsieur*, I've been here for months, and I don't want to move down to that big fig tree by the railroad station where all the other homeless hang out.'

'But this house is about to be bulldozed. . .' Toledo said.

The man went on as though he hadn't heard Toledo. 'The police harass them, and being among them is demeaning. I'm not like most of them – I've a recent college degree. I've come to love this old place – it's intoxicating. I'll find a job soon and then I can afford to pay rent. That's what I told the owner several months ago when he was here. Now you leave me alone.'

'I'm the owner now,' Toledo said. 'And will you shut that dog up?'

'He's not my dog. He won't leave. I feed him from time to time when I have any scraps.' He glared at Toledo. 'He keeps away other squatters and anyone else trying to bother me.'

'What's your name?' Toledo asked.

'Léon,' he replied, 'the acute is over the *e*.'

'What's your degree in, Léon?'

'Wine-making.'

'Viticulture?'

'*Oui*,' Léon said, becoming more friendly. 'You know the craft?'

'Yes, a little. So why aren't you up in the Napa Valley?'

'With all those vines dying up there, there's no work. Nobody's hiring. Prospects for employment have changed completely since I came to this country to attend college.'

'Why not go back to France?' Toledo suggested.

'They still want to make wine the old way – have no use for UC Davis graduates – so there's nothing there, either. Santa Barbara is where I want to live and work.'

Toledo introduced Katherine.

Léon bowed.

'Maybe you could stay in the barn for the time being,' she said. 'The house is the only building targeted for tonight.'

'But why are you pulling down this fine old house?' Léon protested.

198

'It's a matter of utmost urgency – I'll explain later,' Toledo told him. 'Say, before the bulldozer goes to work, will you help me take out the window?' Toledo asked.

'I've a tool or two in my pack.'

Léon returned, and together the two men went to work removing the front door, salvaging the one remaining bright spot in the old house.

'These antique stained-glass windows can buckle, so be sure the frame stays intact,' Katherine instructed as they removed the pins from the door hinges.

Her words were drowned out by the rumble of an arriving flatbed truck transporting a giant yellow bulldozer.

Toledo and Léon carried the door with its stained-glass window to the rental truck. Léon ran back inside the house to retrieve his backpack and bedroll.

Toledo greeted the bulldozer operator, who, together with his two helpers, decanted the giant machine. 'It's the one on the corner,' Toledo said, gesturing towards the house, adding, 'without a front door.'

Toledo, Léon and Katherine retreated to the safety of the weedy lot that was once a vineyard and watched the weapon of destruction thrust forward as an invading armoured vehicle might. Bent on conquest, its treads climbed the kerb, crossed the pavement and rolled up the driveway as it surged towards the garage and vacant house.

With its diesel engine roaring loudly, the giant yellow monster struck the garage with all the force modern destructive technology could muster.

'The dog!' Katherine screamed suddenly.

Toledo turned quickly and ran to liberate the animal.

Without waiting, the bulldozer rolled over the garage, crushing it along with its decades of harboured debris. Caught crazily by the bulldozer's blade and pried loose, a narrow board ripped from the garage door and sailed through the air.

'Watch out!' Léon yelled.

Toledo looked up just in time to see the airborne missile coming towards him. He ducked. The spear whistled over his head. Its sharp point penetrated the pit bull's unprotected breast and a gush of blood erupted. The last raging bark was silenced permanently as the dog slumped to the ground. Its lifeless body was scooped aside and buried by the big yellow machine as it accumulated rubble and dirt into a neat mound.

Recovering from his near miss, Toledo embraced an hysterical Katherine, who had come running to his side.

Léon rushed up. 'That's one way to silence that ugly dog.'

Almost instantaneously, from out of the dark, from a distance not far away, from many mouths, came murmurs and then someone said, 'That spear was meant for Squires.'

Alarmed, Toledo looked over his shoulder, 'That's a familiar voice,' he said to Katherine.

Startled, too, Katherine looked behind her. 'It's the architect,' she said with surprise.

'Here comes a woman on a horse,' Léon said, pointing. 'See, she's passing under the street light. It's the mayor. We homeless know her. She's always riding up and rousting us.'

Through the dust billowing in the air around them, they saw more white faces reflecting the dim light. And they heard a voice shout, 'It's going to hit the house next!'

They turned to see the yellow monster, without hesitation and exercising no mercy, strike the old house. For a brief moment the structure resisted. Groaning, the house was slowly moved from its foundation. Sparks flew from broken electrical connections. The bulldozer operator adeptly manipulated the machine's levers. Back and forth the giant thrust, pursuing its relentless mission of demolition.

The bulldozer operator stopped his machine for a moment and mopped his brow. Seeing his friends from The Flea, he waved proudly at them, then resumed his assignment. And soon another neat pile of rubble accumulated as the house was rapidly erased from the De La Vina streetscape.

The old house out of the picture, the way was now clear for the dirt bully to dip his blade into the earth, which he did as he began to slice away at the tender and now exposed sandy soil underneath.

Through the dust and in the dim light the crowd pressed closer. The Brinks guard was there, still in uniform, and Katherine saw his armoured truck parked behind him. 'He's waiting to help with the treasure,' she said to Toledo.

'But I didn't order an armoured truck,' Toledo said. 'And look at all these people,' he added in surprise. 'Why, there's my pilot.'

'Yes, and there's the bank manager,' Katherine said.

'And his assistant, too. How are we going to slip away with the treasure with so many people watching?'

The bulldozer operator, expertly lowering his blade into the ground, raising it, moving it to the side and then dumping its contents, moved load after load of dirt. After a dozen or so scoops, the rough stone walls of the foundation were uncovered from where, for a century, they had loyally supported the old house.

Toledo ran right up next to the yellow machine, monitoring its every move. It was Christmas Eve, and surely the next scoop into the pile of presents would uncover the really big one.

Toledo was joined by the crowd of pressing people, all looking down into the enlarging hole. Katherine saw five people on the right side of the mayor, each shaking their heads in dismay; members of the Historic Design Review Board, she surmised. To the mayor's left, holding the reins of her horse with one hand, his other arm around her narrow waist, was a burly man with a beer.

Katherine looked around and recognized Father Eric from the Santa Barbara mission. Beside him stood a line of priests and choirboys, each holding a lighted candle.

A postman walked up to Léon. 'Did you put a fowarding address in? Your mailbox is gone so I won't be able to deliver your mail any more.'

Katherine came up beside Toledo and whispered, 'There's the property seller. He's brought along some gunny sacks. And do you suppose that's his wife next to him?'

'Yes it is,' Léon answered. 'She often rides her bike past the house, checking up on me, I guess. . . .'

'But I thought she was in the hospital,' Toledo said.

'Her?' Léon asked. 'Heavens no, she's a bike racer – in excellent health. See, she's even brought her bike with her tonight.'

By the wife's side, also holding a bicycle, its headlight on, was Peggy O'Neill. 'When you have a minute I'd like you to meet my friend and biking companion,' she called to Toledo. 'We're registered for the upcoming cross-country trip down the Baja to Cabo San Lucas.'

Toledo smiled and waved to Peggy. 'Looks like the whole town is here,' he said to Katherine.

'Yes, you really know how to recruit a team.'

Suddenly the bulldozer blade scraped against an object buried deep in the dirt. Over the huff and puff of the engine they heard the sound of metal against metal. Toledo, Katherine and Léon watched, transfixed, along with the spectators, who by now, Katherine estimated, numbered in excess of forty people.

Peering into the abyss impatiently, Toledo waved for the bulldozer operator to stop the mechanical monster. Eager to examine what its blade had struck, he jumped with alacrity in front of the machine and into the basement hole.

The bulldozer operator beamed his headlight down. Kneeling in front of the sharp edge, Toledo – with his bare hands – eagerly brushed the dirt off first one crate and then another, revealing that each was fortified with metal straps.

'Buried treasure!' the crowd murmured.

'See, I told you what they were up to,' another said loudly so as to be heard over the noise of the engine.

The onlookers pressed even closer.

'How many crates are there?' Katherine yelled down at Toledo.

'A lot,' he shouted back. 'Time to back up the truck. You and your men give me a hand down here,' he yelled to the bulldozer operator.

The trio of burlies hopped off the bulldozer. They were reeling. Tipsy, Katherine observed in horror. They eyed her but staggerd to Toledo's side and began prising the crates loose from what had been their century-old subterranean resting-place. By the time Katherine backed up the truck to the edge of the chasm, the men had stacked at ground level two dozen dirt-covered grey crates.

Toledo shouted at them to transfer the cargo into the truck, and Katherine swung open the rear doors. 'This is it!' Toledo hollered from deep in the hole. 'We've unearthed Beauregard's stash!'

Spontaneously a cheer went up from the crowd.

A loud neigh from a horse at the edge of the hole distracted Toledo. 'You are in violation of Santa Barbara Municipal Code, Resolution Number 4125, adopted 10 May 1960, requiring you to pay for and have in your possession a valid demolition permit.' As the woman rider clutched the reins, she added, 'And I know you don't have one because I would have had to sign it personally.'

No one paid any attention to the mayor. Instead they focused on the stacked crates.

'Toledo, I'm dying to look inside one of the crates, aren't you?' Katherine said. 'Let's prise just one open. Please. I mean, one doesn't dig up treasure every day.'

She beamed a flashlight for Toledo as he used Léon's tool to prise open the first case. Dust flew and the rusty nails squeaked with protest as Toledo slowly removed the lid from the old crate.

Holding the light, Katherine peered inside. Nested in the yellowed packing straw was a glistening object. 'Glass,' she said, her voice flat. She pulled away more straw. 'More glass.'

'Bottles,' Toledo said in dismay.

'Wine bottles,' Léon added.

Toledo lifted one out. 'And there's another underneath.' He brushed more straw aside. 'Old wine bottles – this crate if full of wine bottles,' he said falteringly.

Frantically they prised open the second crate and then the third. Soon they had the lid off every one.

'It's all wine,' Katherine said.

'I can't believe it. What did the X mean on our map?' Dejected, Toledo fell into a stupor-like trance. He began to walk around the crates. He looked into one a second time and then another, not believing his eyes. His brow furrowed as perplexity etched across his face.

Suddenly Toledo reached inside one crate and extracted a magnum, raising it high above his head, ready, so it seemed to Katherine, to hurl it at a big rock.

'No, don't!' Léon called out. 'It may be valuable old wine! I can tell from the bubbles in the glass and the shape of the bottle – this wine must be more than a hundred years old.'

Coming out of the dark and restraining Toledo, Father Eric said, 'Yes, this may be the lost stash of sacramental wine. There is a story – I always hoped it was true – that a local winery once made wine for the mission, but none of us could ever find the cellar. As legend has it, it's very good wine.'

'Let's taste a bottle,' the bank manager called out as he stepped into the light from the bulldozer's spot. In his hand he held a stack of plastic glasses.

'Yes, why not?' Peggy O'Neill agreed. 'See if we have real treasure here.'

Several now standing by Peggy's side, including the mayor and the bartender, murmured their approval. Members of the Historic Design Review Board announced their consent, voting five to nothing in favour.

Toledo seemed not to hear. But, dissuaded from his destructive deed, he did lower the bottle, placing it in Léon's waiting arms. Peggy reached into her bum-bag and handed Léon her Swiss Army knife with its corkscrew extended. The bearded Frenchman began to work the antique cork out of the big bottle's neck.

'But where is the Confederate treasure?' Toledo said quietly to Katherine, who now stood by his side. Still disbelieving, he inspected another crate with the hope of finding the real treasure, but it, too, held only bottles of red wine.

'I'm dumbfounded,' Katherine said. She held Toledo's hand.

'How will I explain to the members of our Albanian team?' His head lowered, he spoke almost in a whisper. 'They were counting on me.'

36

'Why don't you two go back to your hotel?' Léon suggested. 'I'll pitch my bedroll in the barn and watch over the wine for you.'

Toledo nodded. 'Yes, that would be very good of you.'

Katherine drove the Ryder truck to the Biltmore Hotel.

'Park it down the street,' Toledo said, 'I don't think they'll want to see a big rental truck in their guest parking lot next to all the Mercedes.'

'Don't be silly, those Mercedes are rented too.'

Toledo perked up his spirits. 'I know what we'll do. We'll call Grace. She'll clear up this mystery for us. She'll have an explanation. There's probably some simple little thing about her story . . . Grand-daddy Thatcher's story, we didn't quite get right.'

'Remember, she told us it *was* a story.' She hesitated. 'But surely you're not going to disturb her at this hour of the night . . . or morning?'

'It's OK. Grace told me to call her anytime day or night.'

From their suite, Toledo telephoned Grace at the Methuselah Retirement Home. There was no answer.

'I don't understand,' Toledo said, 'she can't be out on the town at four a.m.' He attempted a chuckle.

'Maybe Grace is at a late-night poker party,' Katherine said. She also tried to laugh but couldn't.

Toledo let the phone ring. Finally he hung up and called the Methuselah office. He explained to the night guard the difficulty he was having in contacting his grandmother.

Soon the Activities Director came on the line, identifying herself in a sleepy voice. Once she realized Toledo was calling, she grew more alert and asked hopefully, 'Are you in Santa Fe?'

'No, I'm trying to reach my grandmother.'

The Activities Director waited a moment before saying, 'I'm sorry to have to be the one to tell you, Mr Squires, but your grandmother has . . . ah . . . left us.'

'She's left. . . .' Toledo repeated. 'Oh, my God, Grace has died. . . .'

Katherine's hand went to her mouth.

'No, no,' the Activities Director said. 'She hasn't . . . ah . . . departed us in the usual manner. . . .'

'What are you trying to tell me?'

'She's left on a trip.'

'With my mother and father?'

'Oh, no,' the Activities Director stammered, 'She's . . . ah . . . actually run off with Mr Calhoun . . . ah . . . they've eloped.'

'Eloped?' Toledo exclaimed.

Katherine broke into a broad smile.

'Yes, and all the residents – it was so sweet – threw a *bon voyage* party for them. We've never had that type of farewell party at the Methuselah before. . . .'

'But old people don't elope.'

'Maybe not, but they have.'

'Where to?'

'I believe they flew away to London,' the Activities Director said.

'London!' Toledo exclaimed. 'But. . . .'

'If you have no further questions, I think I'll go back to sleep.'

Toledo thanked her and hung up. 'Can you imagine that?' he said to Katherine. 'Grace and Carter!'

'They are a lovely couple,' Katherine said simply, 'so much in love.'

The phone rang. It was the desk clerk with a message. 'A doctor called earlier for you from Los Angeles,' he told Toledo.

'A doctor?'

'I apologize, the clerk on the previous shift neglected to put the message in your box. I just now found it. Some general – I can't make out the name – has had a heart attack.'

'What is it?' Katherine asked.

'Oh, my God,' Toledo said as he wrote down the Los Angeles telephone number, 'it's General Goforth.' Toledo hung up the phone and told Katherine, 'I've got to answer this call right away.'

'Toledo, you're calling everyone in the middle of the night.'

'Doctors never sleep.'

After three misdials, Toledo finally connected with the doctor. Speaking from the Los Angeles General Hospital, Dr Haig enunciated his words carefully. 'Yes, Mr Squires, I called you a few hours ago. But it's too late now.'

'Too late?' Toledo asked, his voice weak.

'Yes, your name was on General Goforth's dog tags, along with instructions to notify you in case of anything untoward.'

'Untoward?'

"Yes, but I'm afraid the brave general died a few hours ago.'

'Died?' Toledo's voice was incredulous. 'But we both attended a meeting just a few days ago.'

'Yes, as I recall, his last words were a mention of that meeting. General Goforth said he was a member of a team whose mission was to resuscitate Albania.' The doctor paused. 'Say, do you have some really attractive investment opportunities going over there in Eastern Europe? I hear they don't pay any income taxes in some of those countries. Is that right? I'd appreciate getting in on –'

Toledo ignored the doctor's question, thanked him and hung up, then related the conversation to Katherine. 'You could see this coming, couldn't you?' he said to her. 'You said he was hyper, a Type A personality.'

'Yes.'

Toledo asked, 'Am I Type A?'

'We all have to learn to relax once in a while and smell the flowers.'

'I smell food.' Toledo said. 'Let's get some breakfast. I'll never be able to sleep.'

They walked down the thick-carpeted corridor and onto the large red hexagon tiles of the lobby, covered here and there with Persian carpets. On the walls were oil-paintings of the Santa Barbara mission, the annual fiesta celebration, the restored Presidio and other historic buildings. 'This lobby makes me feel as if I'm in a museum,' Katherine remarked.

'A bit of local colour,' Toledo said, admiring an oil-painting depicting flowering gardens among the old buildings surrounding the Paseo de Mercado.

Routinely Katherine bought a morning *Los Angeles Times*. Scanning the headlines, she exclaimed, 'Toledo, look here, Myra Andersen's been awarded the Nobel prize for economics.'

'*Our* Myra Andersen?'

'There's only one. Yes, my friend, our friend. Isn't that a splendid development for her career?' Katherine went on to read the article out loud while Toledo listened intently. 'I'm so very happy for her. But you realize what this means?'

'She may not want to stay on our team and go with us to Albania,' Toledo said softly.

'I think you're right, for the article goes on. . . .'

'Yes?'

'It says there are rumours, which have it, and I quote, 'Ms Andersen specifically did not deny. . . .'

'What rumours?'

'She's on the President's short list for appointment to be Chairman . . . no it actually says here "Chairwoman" of the Federal Reserve Board.'

'In Washington, DC?'

'That's the only Federal Reserve System I know of in this country.'

'A woman?'

'A Nobel prizewinner,' Katherine said. 'You do know how to pick a team. I'm very impressed.'

'But I'm losing my players.'

'Yes, but think of our new connection.'

'Federal Reserve members are sworn to secrecy about revealing the economy, interest rates, their monetary intentions. . . .'

Katherine smiled. 'Myra and I have always been close friends.'

As they passed the desk clerk, he said, 'I have another message for you, Mr Squires. It's from your pilot. He just this moment called. Must have been while you were walking down the hall from your room, because I buzzed. . . .' He handed Toledo an envelope. 'The message is confidential, but it says you are to return a phone call from Washington.'

'Washington?'

'Yes,' the desk clerk said. 'It seems a friend of yours is being considered for a federal appointment and she wants to alert you she's given your name as a reference, and the FBI will likely be contacting you.'

'Myra Andersen?'

'Who? No. that's not the name he gave me, not the name at all. I don't know that person.'

'Who, then,' Toledo asked, 'is the caller in this confidential message of mine?' He was growing a little annoyed.

'Ines Stark,' the desk clerk replied.

'Ines Stark?' Katherine said.

'And this federal appointment?' Toledo asked.

'To the Supreme Court! the clerk exclaimed, clapping his hands. 'Yes, she's lesbian. Gay. One of us. I know her from my work on the National Committee for Gay Rights. Now she's out of the closet. And onto the Supreme Court.' He danced a jig. 'And the rest of us with her!' Suddenly more sedate, he added, 'Well, not yet. But the White House is pulling out all the stops and promoting her as the best candidate. She'll get the appointment, I just know it! Isn't our new President simply marvellous?'

'My pilot told you all that information? From Ms Stark's one phone call?'

'Yes,' the clerk replied, his expression suggesting there was no need for doubt. 'Of course,' he added, 'your pilot's tickled pink, too.'

'Two women in high places,' Katherine said.

Toledo chuckled. 'What's the world coming to?'

'To the twenty-first century,' Katherine told him. 'But right now I'm headed for a twentieth-century breakfast. Coming with me?'

Toledo nodded and put his arm around her. They chose a table by a large arched window overlooking the Pacific Ocean and sat side by side.

'Look,' Katherine exclaimed, 'they have blue corn pancakes on the menu.'

'But I'll bet they're sold out.'

'I can understand your discouragement, but listen to me. We can't let all this news get us down. First, it's not all bad news. . . .'

'Bad for our team – its roster isn't fully subscribed any more, and bad for my plan.'

'Rich men can't be shaken by developments that adversely affect their plans. They have deep pockets – deep reservoirs of strength – to buffer untoward happenings. Isn't that right?'

Katherine ordered for both of them, specifying pure maple syrup.

The desk clerk was back, holding a telephone. He plugged it into the jack. 'A call for you, Mr Squires.'

Riled, Toledo asked, 'Who now?'

Katherine held his hand.

He took the phone, waited and then nodded. 'Yes, Ms Hewit? Thank you, Katherine's well, she's here with me now. . . .' Toledo listened intently, his gaze staring out across the ocean as Ms Hewit talked.

'What is it?' Katherine asked, impatient, unable to hear her words.

Toledo waited, continuing to stare. The nod he finally gave was almost imperceptible. 'I guess congratulations are in order, Ms Hewit,' he said, without any strength to his voice.

Katherine heard a laugh from the other end of the line, followed by more conversation from Ms Hewit.

After a moment Toledo said, 'Yes, three heartbeats is a bit much to contemplate. Triplets in addition to the three you have now. . .'

Katherine's hand went to her mouth.

'Let's see,' he said, 'that'll make six babies under the age of four. . . .' He listened again. 'Yes, I can see why you can't go to Albania just now. Yes, I understand fully. Yes, I will keep you informed of our progress. Yes, and we do have the benefit of your research and your position paper on the country's social n
eds. Yes, we will keep health, education and welfare heading up our agenda. . .'

Toledo was about to hang up when he returned the instrument to his ear and a deeper frown formed on his face.

Katherine watched him closely.

'Thank you very much for passing on that message.' He bid Ms Hewit goodbye.

'Professor Posin is having a December–May affair in Paris,' he said to Katherine.

'With one of his students?' Katherine asked.

'Yes, Ms Hewit says Vasily called her, told her he's taking a few weeks off, travelling with one of his graduate students who needed his help with her research paper on the French Revolution.'

'And he's passionately dedicated to his work?' Katherine said, and laughed. 'Good for him,' she added.

Toledo smiled a little. 'So we must add him to our list of defectors.'

'Well, as to Ms Hewit, do you suppose their failure at family planning could be attributed to her astronaut husband? Maybe there's some sort of special gamma rays or cosmic dust up there. . . .'

'Acting like an aphrodisiac?'

Katherine laughed. 'Or fertility booster. I mean, she's having so many babies in so few years. . . .'

'Yes, some sort of a record, I should think.'

Their blue corn pancakes arrived, served on Spanish ceramic plates, adorned with a slice of orange and a sprig of parsley.

'If I weren't so hungry maybe I'd have the energy to deal with all these developments,' Toledo said after several bites.

Katherine held her fork poised above her plate. 'Well, let's try to sort it all out.'

Toledo poured more maple syrup. 'It's obvious our entire team and our entire gold supply have floated away with the tide.'

'But there's been no news from President Jimmy Carter.'

'He'll call next.' Toledo chuckled. 'He's probably flown off to some trouble spot in Asia or Africa to try to arrange a cease-fire or oversee some election. Don't read any more of this morning's newspaper.'

'Well, let's look at it in a positive way: you've bought some very valuable land in Santa Barbara – good grape-growing land. And it appears you're about to gain a grandfather-in-law, if there is such a thing, and a cosmopolitan one, too.'

'Don't forget I've probably broken the local law regarding demolition without a permit.' He looked at Katherine and smiled. 'But you and I are still together.'

'Yes, me and what is apparently a cache of very fine wine.'

'Beauregard had an awfully good year back then,' Toledo said. 'Maybe the soil is rich in minerals and every year can be a good one.' He finished his pancakes. 'Yes, I like your positive attitude. You and I shall revisit the scene of last night's circus and check in with Léon, our French wine friend.'

She nodded. 'Let's take a long walk back to the land. But first I must go to our room to brush my teeth and take my vitamins.'

As they entered the room, the telephone by their king-size bed rang.

'Toledo, it's John . . . calling from London. . . .'

Toledo sparked. 'Ah, good. With news?'

'Yes, quite a bit, as a matter of fact.'

'Axminster's on the phone,' Toledo said to Katherine. 'Here, you take this one and I'll jump over to the other phone.'

'Good morning, John,' Katherine said.

'It's early afternoon here. I thought you'd be up by now.'

'We were out a little late last night,' she said.

'Well, I don't know where to begin. There is so much good news to report.'

'John, my news from Santa Barbara isn't so good,' Toledo said. 'I was about to call, but I've waited . . . don't really know quite how to put it.'

'You first, John,' Katherine invited.

Axminster began with his own question. 'Did you dig up the Confederate gold?'

'Have you found out who has the vice grip on the London gold?' Toledo asked.

'John, you start with the good news,' Katherine repeated.

'Well, OK, here's the developments from this side of the Atlantic. Ah . . . first, I'll answer your question. The London gold is controlled by a retired Wall Street banker who was a confidant of King Zog back in the 1930s. He has a lock on the bullion . . . a hold the London bank continues to honour.'

'Who is he?' Toledo asked.

'The bank is sworn to conceal his identity. King Zog was apparently afraid of assassination attempts. In those days in the Balkans, people did away with whomever got in their way. Zog must have feared such a fate might befall his trusted friend, so in his decree he stated nobody was to know his identity.'

'But you found out who he is, didn't you?' Toledo said impatiently.

'He's been quite clever with his investments,' Axminster continued, 'leveraged the original gold, built a portfolio up to what they say is at least a billion dollars. That's not

212

counting the gold behind it, which by now, given the price in world markets, is worth many times its value back in the late 1940s when the British confiscated it from the Communists.'

Toledo whistled.

'They say he can remember every trade, every investment ever made,' Axminster went on. 'His mind is like a high-capacity hard disk on a state-of-the-art computer. And they say he gets better with age – like good red wine.'

'We know a bit about wine,' Katherine said.

'More all the time,' Toledo added.

'You'll be pleased to know that this remarkable man is Carter Calhoun, the fiancé of your dear grandmother.'

'Well, I'll be. . .' Toledo began.

'Grace is having a real adventure,' Katherine observed. 'I'm so happy for her.'

'There's more. The newly elected Parliament has invited your grandmother and Mr Calhoun to be married in the royal palace in Tirana, and then to stay on in Albania as if they were the actual king and queen of The Country. It's all a bit of play-acting, of course, but still serious and quite splendid.'

'Grace will be so happy,' Toledo said. 'Her fantasy is finally going to come true.'

'Well, I'm reluctant to tell you the rest of the news. . .' the banker said slowly.

'There's more?' Toledo asked.

'Yes, I've been asked to take over . . . actually to become head of the Albanian Central Bank.'

Toledo looked stunned.

'Congratulations, John,' Katherine said.

Toledo recovered. 'Hey, that is great news . . . for you . . . and for The Country. Yes, my congratulations, as well. But when?'

'Actually right away. I'm tendering my resignation at the Bank of America effective immediately and staying on in Albania,' Axminster replied quickly.

'Wow!' Katherine exclaimed.

Axminster spoke rapidly now, his enthusiasm carrying him on. 'Yes, and I'm to be in charge of The Country's finances, its new monetary policy. Mr Calhoun's turning it over to me, the gold and all. It's an opportunity to put into practice the concepts I set forth in the paper I wrote when I was a

Rhodes Scholar at Oxford.'

'John, this is a great opportunity for you,' Katherine said.

'Yes,' he replied. 'All is right with Albania. But I want to tell you, Toledo, it is your inspirational genius that has set these events into motion,' he was quick to add.

'Thank you for the compliment, John. It's apparent the baton has now been passed along to you.'

'Tonight has been a newsy one indeed. But the news from here is that we didn't retrieve the Confederate gold,' Katherine explained.

'We found grey crates, but they were loaded with magnums of vintage wine,' Toledo said.

'That's gold of a sort,' Axminster offered.

Toledo laughed loudly, dropped the phone and charged back to the bed, where he embraced Katherine. He picked up her phone and said to Axminster, 'John, let's save our telephone calls for when we have some real news to report to each other.'

Axminster chuckled. 'Yes, I'll call you back when I've organized the Tirana to the Sea race.'

'Send me an official entry form and be sure to put on enough postage.'

37

Holding each other's hands, Toledo and Katherine walked along the footpath leading towards the old wooden municipal wharf. The Pacific surf surged against the sandy beach on their left. Cabrillo Boulevard, engulfed by towering palm-trees, lay on their right. Beyond to the north the Santa Ynez Mountains soared high, their multiple peaks greeting the now-rising sun.

Katherine pointed towards the moutains. 'Santa Barbara does have a beautiful setting.' She looked south. 'And I love the ocean. We're so far from water in New Mexico.' She pointed. 'See the puffs of clouds out there on the horizon? They seem to be floating like an armada of ships sailing toward the Channel Islands.'

'Those islands can be reached only by crossing a rough sea,' Toledo said, holding his stomach and feigning sea-sickness.

They laughed together. Toledo put his arm around Katherine's waist. 'Far-away places with new-sounding challenges.'

He kissed her tenderly. Drawing back, he looked at her and said softly, 'You and I can meet any new challenge, whether across the waters or right here in Santa Barbara.'

'Yes, we don't have to sail off to the horizon for our adventures.'

Walking on, they reached the point where State Street ended and the wharf began. There tourist services, bike rentals, T-shirt stores, and ice-cream parlours were opening for the day ahead. Further on at the West Beach, they turned right and walked inland up De La Vina Street.

The street was quiet, still too early for morning traffic. The sunlight filtered through centuries-old California live oak-trees. People's yards displayed the orange and blue colours of birds of paradise, which complimented the spiky hot poker reds. The air was warming. A fragrance of tiny white stars of jasmine filled the air. The events of the past few days, the morning's news and telephone conversations, slowly began to fade from their minds.

'How beautiful it all is,' she said. 'The white stucco houses with their red tile roofs and the lush flowers. . . .'

Toledo sniffed the air and smiled. 'Fragrant, too,' he added.

'See the bougainvillaea vines,' she said. 'Their flowers look like trumpets summoning us to regroup on this beautiful September morning.'

They soon arrived at the land where General Beauregard had years ago nurtured his vineyard. Side by side, hand in hand, they stood beside the quiet gaping hole where only hours before it seemed the entire world had gathered.

The freshly exposed dirt was dark, soft, inviting. Bending over, Toledo scooped up a handful of the cool soil, held it up to the sunlight, examined it and then allowed the loam to sift through his fingers, returning – seemingly in slow motion – down to Earth.

Looking out over his ten acres, Toledo began to laugh.

'What are you so amused about?'

'All those people last night. Had there been gold in those crates instead of wine bottles, what would they have done?'

'Enrich themselves, I believe is the expression.'

'Judging from the crowd at our show last night, never before have so few people told so many the wrong information,' Toledo said, and chuckled. 'I guess we'll never know how the word got around Santa Barbara.'

'Does it matter?'

'No.'

From behind they heard a voice. 'Good morning, you two are returning to the scene of the crime in a hurry.' Léon laughed, and then they heard a dog bark.

Apprehensive, Toledo and Katherine both turned around.

'It's OK,' Léon assured them, 'she's friendly.'

Tugging at a rope was a full-grown Weimaraner dog, its short grey hair contrasting with Léon's beard and his tattered and loose clothing.

'Where'd she come from?' Toledo asked, petting the animal, whose tail began to wag excitedly.

'Her name's Mariah, and according to her dog-tag she

belongs to the mayor of Santa Barbara. Must have followed her here last night. The mayor will surely be beholden to us when we return her dog.'

'Yes, we'll need every ounce of influence we can muster to get back in the good graces of city hall,' Toledo said. 'We'll have to demonstrate we can be model citizens.'

'Perhaps with Father Eric's help, we can rebuild the house and assure the city fathers and mothers of our good intentions,' Katherine suggested.

'To pay our due to the local culture?'

'Yes,' she said, 'and culture some wine, as well. I'll bet they'd like to have a winery inside the city limits, a replication of General Beauregard's endeavour. What could be more historic for this piece of land?'

'Exactly what I'm thinking. But we'll need some professional assistance.' Toledo turned to the Frenchman. 'How about it, Léon? Will you help us establish a vineyard and build a microwinery here?'

'You mean, like the family-owned *domaines* of Western Europe?' Léon said.

'A boutique winery,' Katherine added. 'We have a beautiful stained-glass window for our new beginning.'

'A new château shall rise from the ruins,' Léon said.

'Yes,' Toledo agreed. 'I can paint a perfect picture of halcyon life right here in the middle of Santa Barbara.' Toledo put his arm around Katherine, pulled her close and pointed out across his property. 'See how the land slopes towards the ocean? Good drainage is necessary for growing grapes. Cultivate the land. . . . Yes, and graft French Bordeaux and Chardonnay vines onto a selected American rootstock, train and trellis them, and you'd have a bona fide vineyard. Add a stainless-steel storage tank or two and a computer-controlled grape crusher and you'd turn Beauregard's old estate into a modern winery.'

'Let's not forget Beauregard is a respected French name,' Léon pointed out.

'We could name our winery in his honour,' Katherine suggested.

'I believe with this much land we could produce forty thousand cases a year,' Léon said.

'Starting off,' Toledo said spiritedly, 'I'd like to devise a marketing plan that would bypass the normal distribution channels and sell directly to connoisseurs through mailing lists and by filling orders via modems connected to computer networks – all those mailboxes in the sky. We'll hand-deliver the rest of our production – a few cases at a time – to specialty retailers and prestige restaurants.'

'We'll design special personalized labels for each of the vintages,' Katherine said, 'allowing the wine buffs to lay away our distinctive wines in their temperature-controlled cellars.'

'You know, it all comes down to an art of making fine wine from little grapes. Kind of like raising children,' Léon observed.

Toledo and Katherine joined hands and twirled around and around.

Mariah barked.

'We'll get started today,' Toledo said. 'We'll clear the land, buy the rootstock, hire a tractor with a plough. . . .'

38

That evening The Country looked west past the Greek island of Corfu lying off its shore and watched the sun set across the Adriatic Sea. The sky radiated a brilliant crimson. 'Red skies at night, sailors' delight,' The Country recited as it contemplated what vessel might sail into its harbours on the morrow, what events might take place and what people might arrive, writing for it the next chapter of its history.

Well, The Country mused, it was still in one piece more than eighty years after its birth and several millennia since its ancient ancestors first settled its lands. But this evening what The Country sensed was more than a simple satisfaction of having endured a long life, actually much more. The Country enjoyed an optimism as, along with a bevy of new leaders, both domestic and from overseas, it peered into the future.

What was the name of the young American whom the newly elected Parliament had selected to be in charge of its monetary policies? The man who was going to insist on a free market for its farmers, its industries and its businessmen. The man who extolled the economic system that had won out in the now almost past twentieth-century scramble among ideologies.

No longer would there be troublesome experiments with Fascism, Communism, Socialism or any of the other splinter schemes once advocated by theorists and implemented by hoodlums. In the months and years ahead, The Country would no longer be constrained by a centrally dictated Communist system of bureaucracy in which the motivation of those in charge was to skim away the wealth personally. Now The Country was to ride the mainstream of world thinking, benefiting from an economic system in which people, expounding free enterprise ideals and encouraged to advocate new ideas, would flourish in an open society.

What was this man's name? Was it Toledo Squires? No, The Country now recalled being advised by its Parliament, the man was John Axminster, a rather British name. Fitting, for he was bringing with him The Country's gold, housed for so many decades in London.

Yes, hope did abound for the century ahead. Especially now, with the approaching royal wedding. With pride The Country read again its engraved invitation:

Grace Templeton and Carter Calhoun
cordially invite all of Albania
to Skanderbeg Square
to celebrate with them a marriage made in heaven
1st October at three p.m. Albanian Standard Time

What a devoted couple. And what a romantic ceremony of dreams. A royal palace. A king and his queen. And her portrait would soon appear on the new Albanian postage stamps.

The little kingdom by the sea, happy at last, could now enjoy each day of its new-found freedom.